HITS
NEIL COSS

Dedication

This book is for my wife and kids, who put up with me when I was writing and (more importantly) when I wasn't. And for my family and friends, who always had more faith in me than I did. All of whom knew I could do this before I did.

PROLOGUE

"Billy, could we run it again, just once more?" Jeanette asked, cringing as she awaited his response.

"Jesus, Jen. We've been at this for four hours. My fingers are practically bleeding."

"Please. Just once more," Jeanette begged "I promise, this is the last time. Terry has a great idea for the break just before the solo."

"Yeah, Billy, come on," Terry Dean urged. "I'd like to try it with the clapping like we talked about, today. I think it will set up the solo and make it stand out on its own. Just once, and if you don't like it we'll scrap it. Whaddaya say kid?"

"Alright, alright," Billy agreed. "But I don't like the single clap. I think it should be syncopated. Like - Clap, clap clap. Clap, clap clap. And four times, not two."

"You're the artiste, buddy, whatever you want."

"Get out there and help out, Jeanette."

"Me? I don't know…"

"Yeah, you. You *do* know how to clap don't you?"

"Go!" Terry insisted pointing toward the door to the sound booth.

Hesitantly, she got to her feet and made her way into the studio and took up a spot alongside the studio musicians that awaited their cue.

"Ok, let's take it from four bars into the refrain, and then hit the break crisp. Then everyone clap, clap clap, you know the drill. All in time, please. In three, two, one."

The music filled the tiny studio and Jeanette could feel a light sweat break on her brow. Then came the break they were waiting for and in perfect unison everyone did as had been planned; after which Billy Fairelane tore into a solo that would peel the skin off of a grape. Everyone stood and listened as this incredibly talented guitar virtuoso made his instrument sing, talk, scream and wail with a brand of blues that would make Buddy Guy blush.

When he finished, everyone stood silent their mouths agape at what had just transpired.

"Yeah, I think we got it kid. That's a print." Terry croaked.

"I told you so." Billy smiled sheepishly. "Can we go home, like, now?"

Nearly two hours later, on her ride home after dropping Billy at his apartment, Jeanette was exhilarated. This kid was it. He was the best she'd ever heard. He took a back seat to no one. Not King, Clapton, Vaughn, Allman or anyone else. He was her ticket out of her job at WHTS and straight into the big time.

She was as happy for him as she was for her herself. She loved him like a brother and could think of no one who deserved it more than he did.

*****

As Billy tiredly climbed the stairs to his apartment he heard the door at the base of the stairwell open.

"Hey, Billy," a voice called after him.

Turning around, he looked down into the shadowy vestibule straining his eyes to see who it had been that followed him in at this hour of the morning. When his eyes adjusted to the light he saw a pair of ice blue eyes looking back at him.

"Hey, Gary," he said nervously, "what are you doin' here?"

"Can I come up?" Gary asked, smiling.

"I don't know, Gary. It's really late. I'm sure Brian's already in bed."

Undeterred, Gary scaled the stairs toward him his smile dissolving a little more with every step.

When he joined Billy on the landing outside the apartment what was left of his smile had turned into an angry scowl.

"Where ya been, Buddy?" Gary asked pointedly.

"I- I was out with Jeanette," Billy stammered.

"Oooo, and what will your boyfriend think of that, I wonder?" Gary said sarcastically.

"Stick it, Gary. What do you want?"

"I know where you were, you little puke. And I know what you've got planned," Gary said, backing him against the wall. "You're gonna dump me and the rest of the band and go out on your own! Isn't that right, you little faggot?"

Billy flinched and covered his face with his arms as Gary grabbed him by the collar and slammed him against the wall. "You were nothin' before you met the rest of us and I'll make sure you're nothin' again if you dump us! Do you hear me?"

"You can't *make* me stay in the band, Gary."

"Maybe not," Gary seethed, "but I can make sure you never play guitar again, you little shit," he seethed; grabbing Billy's fingering hand and squeezing it with a vice-like grip.

"Ow! Come on, Gary. You're hurting me. Please, don't!"

Just then the door behind Gary opened to reveal Billy's partner Brian.

"Hey, leave him alone, Gary, or I'll call the cops!"

"You do, and I'll rip off your arm and beat you to death with it, Chubby!" Gary spit. "Get inside and mind your own fuckin' business or I'll throw him down the stairs right here and now!"

Brian closed the door and Gary returned his attention to Billy. "I know people who would kill you between supper and desert just for the fun of it, Nancy!" Gary whispered malevolently. **"So don't screw with me! You *got* it?"** He yelled.

Billy nodded mutely.

"Good," Gary said his face easing into a sarcastic smile, "I'd hate to have to kill my own meal ticket."

Gary let go of Billy's hand and collar and headed down the stairs. "See you around, kid. I'll be in touch."

When he heard the door slam Billy slid down the wall and sat on the landing, his left hand throbbing and shaking violently. He recoiled slightly when the apartment door opened and Brian stepped out onto the landing.

"Are you ok? Why don't you come on inside?" Brian said sympathetically.

"I'm fine, mother!" Billy said too harshly. "Just leave me alone and go inside!"

"Are you sure?"

"Yes, God damn it. Leave me alone!"

"Fine, suit yourself!" Brian barked back and he re-entered the apartment and slammed the door.

Billy pushed himself up and, taking the stairs two at time,he descended into the vestibule and disappeared into the crisp October night.

PART ONE
SHOCKWAVE

CHAPTER ONE

"Oh come on, Rick, I really need this one...Oh for Christ's sakes, BSN, BSN, that's all I ever hear in this town! Well of course they have the biggest audience in town. That's because you and everybody *like you* give them all the damn first play rights. Not to mention sponsoring rights to every hot band out there... I don't mean anything by people like you. It's just that all the major labels... How much!? Are you kidding!? It would cost us at least that much just to put an event that size on! Look, I'm on my knees Rick. Can you see me on my knees? You're being impossible... Attitude! I'll give you an **attitude**-. Hello? Hello? Damn!"

Jeanette slammed the phone down and fell back into her chair disgusted and dejected. She had just blown what she figured was the last chance W.H.T.S had to host a major concert event this season.

As she sat alone in her office, on the twentythird floor of the Hancock Building in Boston, her mind began to wander. It hadn't been that long ago that she'd had big ideas about what she was going to do with the mass communications degree she'd received upon graduating Emerson College with honors.

First there would be the obligatory internship at a local radio station, then straight into TV. Maybe local at first, but just to get her feet wet. Then it was off to New York and the big time...

Thirteen years later... had it really been 13 years? Well, at any rate she had never made that trip down Interstate 95 from Boston to New York, and it really wasn't her fault. The promotions had come so fast and furious in the first five or six years, she hadn't had the time-much less the desire-to leave.

And now, at the relatively young age of 34, she was station manager at the number three radio station in town. That alone was impressive by anyone's standards in a market the size of Boston. Besides, she reasoned, it is a market second only to the Big Apple itself on the east coast. I suppose I can't complain, she thought. Boston is a hot bed of cutting edge rock and roll and I really do love the business.

Still this life she was leading wasn't exactly what she'd planned that June day thirteen years ago. Look out Diane Sawyer, she'd thought, here comes Jeanette Tolby. She was going to be the hottest investigative reporter on the international beat.

As she sat staring out the window at the city below the door to her office swung open, snapping her back to reality.

"How's it going beautiful?" The tall slender man asked.

"Oh God, Duane, not now. I can't take you right now," she whined, burying her head in her hands. But her protestations did nothing to dampen the man's spirits, or deter him from entering.

"Oh, that's a fine way to greet the guy who's paying for your lunch," he said, feigning disappointment.

"*Lunch*? Is it noon already?" she asked, looking at her wrist. "Where the hell is my watch?"

Duane laughed and shook his head. "1:15, darlin'. While you were downtown you were gonna pick it up, remember?"

Standing up, she walked to the large window that looked out over the city. Peering out into the fall sky, she sighed heavily. "I'm sorry Duane. It's just that I've had the worst morning of my life," she offered apologetically. Walking to her desk, Duane picked up her desk top calendar. Checking the date he saw it was October 28th, only three days until her vacation. Placing it back on her desk, he turned to speak to her. Before he got a chance, she turned to face him.

At 5'7" 126 lbs. she was something to behold. She wasn't a beautiful woman, although, her delicate features were none-the-less captivating.

The afternoon sunlight reflected off her long sandy blonde hair. This coupled with her sturdy yet model-like frame gave her an almost statuesque look that stole the words from his mouth. Forcing himself, he broke the awkward silence. "Just think," he smiled, "three more days and you're out of here for three whole weeks!"

Jeanette looked at him and tried to force a smile of her own. "If I don't cause some promotional noise around here I'll have all the time I need to rest," she said, rounding her desk to take his arm.

"I don't know what you're so worried about," Duane offered. "When you took this place over it was a second rate station with a handful of listeners. Now were number three with a bullet! Relax, old Pinkham knows when he's got a good thing goin'," he concluded in his contagiously optimistic nature.

Shrugging her shoulders, she looked him in the eye. "All I know is if we don't get a break we'll be back to number six with an anvil."

Once they were outside on the street nothing seemed quite so bad, and she was glad she'd kept their lunch date.

As they picked their way through the one o'clock lunch-crowd, she was mildly amused at the looks they got from passers-by. Don't they hate to see an attractive white woman on the arm of a black man, she thought. For all of their pompous moralizing, and so called, northern liberalism, they were still scared to death of blacks. *Hypocrites*.

As the two approached the Prudential Center she wondered why it was that Duane always brought her here, to the Top of the Hub, for lunch. At first she'd thought he was trying to impress her, but now she knew him too well for that. At any rate, she hated it. Especially the revolving dining room, as it spun slowly she could never locate the bathroom, particularly after a two martini lunch, and today was definitely going to be a two martini lunch.

Stepping out of the elevator at their destination the Matre`d rushed to their assistance. "Ahh. Mr. Avon and Ms. Tolby, so nice to see you. We weren't expecting you and-" Duane discretely slipped the expected twenty dollar bill in the man's pocket. "We saved your favorite table, just in case," the man finished without missing a beat.

"Could you show Jeanette to the table?" Duane asked. "I'd like to go freshen up a bit." Nodding dutifully, the man offered Jeanette his arm.

Upon entering the dining room, she was instantly reminded of why it was Duane liked coming here so much. The view from up here was nothing less than(suggestion: nothing short of) breath-taking. You could see the whole city and half of the suburbs from up here, especially on a clear, crisp fall day like this.

Once seated at the table, she ordered her extra dry Vodka Martini and slipped back into her reverie. Duane was a good and loyal friend, she thought. Always upbeat, always supportive, just a nice guy, plain and simple.
She was glad she'd insisted that they hire him when he lost his job as a bartender for, as he liked to put it, "Teaching that fool a lesson."

The "fool" in question had been a drunken regular at his former place of employment. One evening, just before closing, she had stopped in on her way home after a particularly long night of work, a ritual that had become increasingly regular since her promotion to Station Manager at W.H.T.S "The Hits of Boston".

The moment she'd entered, the drunk had started on her, becoming considerably abusive when she ignored his primitive advances. After numerous warnings from Duane, the man became increasingly agitated at the bartender, at which time Duane decided to show the gentleman out the back door. Only to return, shortly thereafter, with a small mouse under his right eye and a swollen left hand.

"You're really out there aren't you?" He'd said, with a wink. Wait a minute, that isn't what he'd said!

"I said you're really out there aren't you?" Duane laughed, in his best attention getting, bellicose way.

"Oh, sorry," she apologized.

"A penny for your thoughts," he smiled, taking his place across the table from her.

A full hour and a half later they were on their way back to the station, and work, and not a moment too soon, Jeanette thought. She loved Duane dearly, but, what with his constant needling and attention grabbing nature, an hour and a half was more than *anyone* could be expected to take. Opening her office door, she pecked his cheek. "Thanks Duane, I feel a lot better now." The moment the words had left her mouth she knew she'd said the wrong thing.

"Well you should!" he began, loud enough for everyone in the office to hear. Jeanette winced, awaiting the sexual implications of his next barb. "Four double martinis are enough to put a smile on a corpse!" He finished, mercifully giving her a break. Winking, he turned and headed for his cubicle, laughing, as usual, too loud at his own joke.

Jeanette's secretary looked up at her and grimaced. "He's such a jerk!" She said, acidly.

"Yeah, I know." Jeanette answered, with more than a little bite in her own voice. "But when was the last time a jerk dropped sixty bucks on *your* lunch?" she finished, slipping through the door to her office and closing it softly behind her.

The moment she sat down behind her desk all the self-doubt and disappointment she'd felt that morning settled in on her again. Noticing a piece of paper stuck to her phone, she picked it up. It was one of those, "while you were out", messages.

"Bill Forest?" she said aloud. "Who the hell is Bill Forest?" Snatching up the phone, she dialed the number. "Rock Pile." was the abrupt answer on the other end of the line.

"Yes, this is Jeanette Tolby. Is-"

"Hold please." the faceless voice ordered, and the line broke into strains of Nirvana's Come As You Are. It all came back to her now. Bill Forest was the owner of "The Rock Pile." One of the premiere rock and roll clubs in Boston. Not to mention, a royal pain in the ass.

Who was slated to play there? She thought. "Aha, Billy Fairelaine!" she said out loud. *Now* what was Forest's problem?

"Tolby? Bill Forest here! What the hell are you gonna do about this mess?"

God, did she hate it when people talked down to her. "What mess, Bill?" she asked in a resigned tone.

"The Billy Fairelane mess, that's what mess!" He snapped.

"Listen Forest," she began, sliding to the edge of her chair. "Why don't we just cut the guessing game short? What's your problem?" The silence on the other end of the line caused her to smile victoriously.

"Y-You mean to tell me you haven't heard?" the man stammered.

"Heard what?" She demanded, now in complete control of the conversation.

"Billy's dead," he offered apologetically, the harsh edge in his voice now a thing of the past.

The shock of the news caused her jaw to fall limp. Then, after a long and awkward silence, he continued. "Jesus, Jeanette, I had no idea you didn't know. I hate to be the one to give you the news, and I don't want to sound cold, but he was slated to headline next Friday night. That's only eight days away and we've already sold eight hundred and fifty tickets. This showed signs of being our biggest weekend this fall. We have to have a comparable replacement..."

As his voice trailed off, Jeanette reached down and summoned all the professional detachment she could muster for the awkward situation. "Listen Bill, let me make some calls. I'll get back to you in an hour or so," she blurted. "I'll see what I can do about getting a number one for you by then."

Without waiting for an answer, she dropped the phone into its cradle and sank back into her chair. Her head was spinning. Billy had been more than just a business acquaintance. He had been a close and valued friend.

Their working relationship had started two years ago, but since then it had blossomed into much more. She thought back to that day when she had first met him. Being in the business she'd heard his name and made it a point to find out where he was playing so she could get a look at this prodigy.

Finding him in a dump of a club in the Fresh Pond district of Cambridge, she was floored by this brashly self-confident, 22 year old, guitar virtuoso.

In the next six months she'd found out more than she'd ever wanted to know about him. Becoming totally immersed in his rise to fame and fortune, she had turned him into, what he liked to call, her "little project." And what a project he'd turned out to be. In that first half year she'd weaned him off the cocaine and booze and worked with him on behaving in a more businesslike (p r o f e s s i o n a l) manner. She'd drilled into his head that, after all, this was a business like any other, and pointing out that his braggardly fashion of self-promotion was fine for the radio and in the papers, but when dealing with people in the industry, nobody liked a stuck up brat.

All it had taken was to point out several remarkably talented musicians and writers, who as a result of attitudinal short comings, were pumping gas, or worse.

So he'd changed his style and let his softer, almost self-effacing, side be the one for which the people in the business knew and appreciated him. He was a good student, and an unbelievably talented musician and writer. Although his stage presence had some rough edges, he was one of the best at his craft that she had seen in a long time, including the big names in the business. His bitingly realistic lyrics, coupled with his knife sharp back to basics rock and roll style, would be the vehicle of his inevitable impending stardom.

At one point she'd actually thought she was experiencing the sensation of falling in love with her creation. That situation was remedied quickly by his declaration of his homosexuality. And there was the other thing. The thing they didn't talk about to anyone else, which drew them together.

So much for a companion, a business partner would have to do. Just two months ago, with her acting as his manager, they had inked him a deal with Top Flight Records for two releases. The first of which was due on the stands in less than two months. And as far as first play rights were concerned, a conflict of interest for sure, but could it be any other station than W.H.T.S. That much had been their little secret, and now it seemed it would remain as such.

"Jesus, he's dead," she said aloud, hoping the sound of the words would drive home the reality of the situation.

Picking up the telephone she rang up Duane at his desk. "Avon answering." he said. Usually his play on the cosmetics slogan solicited at least an obligatory chuckle on her part, but not this time.

"Duane, Billys dead, I have to talk to you, now!"

As she hung up the phone, her first tear of grief crawled out of the corner of her eye. But by the time Duane entered her office she was just barely keeping up her professional appearance.

Upon seeing him, she immediately dissolved into the emotion that churned in her stomach. He held her for a moment while she regained her composure, then walked her to the chair next to the window that looked out over the city.

Drawing a large breath, he spoke. "Listen, sweetie, I know you don't want to be thinking about this now, but you've got some calls to make. You have to find someone to cover that gig a week from Friday. Any ideas?"

- 18 -

Jeanette squirmed a bit, uncomfortable with the job at hand. Then, cinching up her business-like manner, she spoke, "I don't see any problem replacing Billy for that Friday night; he's got a lot of friends in this town. Besides any one of them would jump at the chance for the publicity."

Duane watched as the woman, who two minutes ago seemed so incapable of dealing with the situation in a detached manner, stood, straightened her skirt, and headed deliberately for the telephone.

"Would you excuse me for a minute?" She said with a half-smile and a wink. "I've got some phone calls to make." Blowing him a kiss she picked up the receiver. "Valerie, get me Jim Freitas at Blue Note please. Ring me when he picks up. Oh Val, don't take no for an answer. This is an emergency! Thanks hon."

Duane smiled and shook his head as he watched her drop the receiver back into its resting place. Looking up, she seemed surprised to see him still standing there. "Duane, don't you have something to do?" She asked, only half joking.

"Yes Ms. Tolby, I do," he smiled, backing out the door.

"Oh, and Duane, could we make it something remotely related to-brace yourself-work!"

"Yes Ms. Tolby," he said, and the door swung closed between them.

She sat for a few minutes, straightening her compulsively neat desk, and then the phone rang. As she'd expected, Jim Freitas was well aware of the situation, saying, "Bad news travels fast in this business." After offering his condolences, he assured her that, yes, he would have a number one for her, possibly several, by the weekend.

"You know how these folks long for a cause," he said, and he was right.

"Listen Jim, I think it would be better if you got directly in touch with Bill Forest over at The Rock Pile. You know, too many cooks, and all that."

Freitas chuckled. He knew exactly what she meant. He didn't want to talk to Bill Forest either. But being the nice guy that he was, he said yes.

"I'll give him a call right now," he said.

Thanking him she hung up the phone and prepared herself for the call she dreaded making. She had to call Brian, Billy's partner. She had to know how it had happened. Did he fall in the bathtub? Was it a car accident? Could it possibly have been a suicide? No, not a suicide. A year ago maybe, but since then he had been so centered, on such an even keel. He'd had his eye set on his goal and nothing was going to deprive him of it. What, then? She wondered, as she hesitantly reached for the phone. Reluctantly, she dialed Brian's number, holding her breath until he answered.

"Hello, Brian, Jeanette here. I just heard. I'm *so* sorry. Is there anything I can do?" His answer came subdued and uncertain over the phone.

"No, Jeanette. There's nothing anyone can do."

The finality in his voice helped drive home the helplessness of the situation. Still, there was something in his voice that didn't sound right. It wasn't the obvious pain he was feeling, that was to be expected. Though she didn't understand their relationship, much less the attraction, it was quite evident to her that the two were very much in love and quite happy with their choices. His voice carried with it an uncertainty, a near befuddlement in its tone. Before she even asked the next question she felt foolish. But she didn't know any other way to address the man's apparent puzzlement. "Is there something else bothering you, Bri?" She sat and waited for what seemed an eternity for the answer. In the background she could hear the murmuring of voices, and the distinct sounds of more than one person moving about in the apartment.

"Jeanette, hon, there are a lot of people around here, police and all, could I call you later, once this place is all cleared out?" He asked, his voice showing signs of breaking.

"Oh, oh sure, Bri. You've got my number, if there's anything I can do, anything at all, you be sure to use it. If I'm not here, you call me at home, and you've got my cell, right?"

"Yeah, yeah I do," he choked.

"Anytime, ok?"

The man on the other end of the phone sniffled. "Oh I will, I-I really do need someone to talk to. Thanks, hon, bye," and with that he hung up.

Jeanette sat for a minute, the dead line buzzing in her ear, her feelings of empathy giving way to curiosity. When at last the dial tone clicked in, snapping her back to the moment, she hung up the phone. She couldn't help feeling as though the man, in some subtle, 'roundabout way, had been reaching out to her. He'd been silently begging her to come over to see him. "That's it!" She said aloud. Something's not right here, but he doesn't want to talk about it in front of the police. Hopping up she grabbed her coat and headed for the door. As she did the phone rang. Ignoring it she opened the door to leave. She only made it as far as her secretary's desk.

"Ms. Tolby. Bill Forest on one." the woman said.

"Damn! I'll take it in my office. Val, tell Mr. Avon I want to see him will you?"

"I'm sorry Ms. Tolby, Mr. Avon stepped out," the secretary said.

Jeanette thought to ask where he'd gone but instead just disappeared back into her office.

After she had spent a full forty-five minutes on the phone with Bill Forest, appeasing him, and assuring him that he would have his headliner by the weekend, she thankfully dropped the receiver back on the hook. Falling back in her chair she saw, through her open door, Duane stepping out of the elevator. Getting his attention with a wave, she gestured for him to join her in her office.

Once she'd finished telling him about her strange call to Brian and her feelings on the matter, he looked at her with a hint of skepticism.

"So, you're going over there?" He asked, raising one eyebrow.

Sensing his doubt she nodded uncertainly. "You coming?" She nearly begged. Duane rubbed at his chin and rolled his eyes. "Good," she said, grabbing him by his sleeve. He considered protesting, but realizing it would do no good, he decided to go along. The least he could do, he figured, was keep her company. And with any luck maybe he could keep her from making a complete fool of herself.

*****

"North Station please, Canal at Causeway." Jeanette instructed. Then, settling back into the taxi, she turned her attention to Duane. "I-I just can't believe this has happened!" She stammered.

"You can't believe *what* has happened?" Duane asked a bit too callously. "For all you know the guy got hit by a bus. As a matter of fact, you should have just asked what happened. I mean instead of jumping to conclusions!"

Jeanette's jaw tightened slightly, as she eyed him with more than a little contempt. "I haven't jumped to any conclusions!" She shot back. "I just don't know what conclusions to draw from this whole thing!"

Realizing he'd made a mistake in questioning her intuition, his voice took on a softer, almost apologetic, temperament. "That's just what I mean," he began, "there may not be a, *whole thing*, to this."

Jeanette sat, back erect, and looked out the window. The rest of the ride was a quiet one. Duane afraid to speak his mind at the risk of incurring the emotional wrath he saw smoldering behind his boss's eyes, and Jeanette afraid she might have to admit he was right.

The traffic was particularly bad for that time of day, and after a full twenty five minutes they were still two blocks away from their destination.

"Jesus, we could've walked by now for God's sake." Jeanette said disgustedly. "Driver, we'll walk from here." she added, stuffing a twenty into the money tray and hopping out her door.

As she stepped out into the stagnant traffic, a brisk autumn wind whipped at her cheeks, bringing out an instant rosy hue in her porcelain skin.

Duane trotted up behind her slipping his arm through hers, "Hey, wait up will ya. I mean, you dragged me all the way down here, so we might as well walk together."

Jeanette offered a small smile as an apology for her lack of patience, and the two continued their walk into the long afternoon shadows of The North End.

As the two passed North Station Duane decided to opt for the less chilly route and led Jeanette into the railway terminal which ran parallel to Causeway St.

Duane had always loved this hulking mass of concrete and iron; the Station itself and the Boston Garden upstairs. He would be sad to see it go at the end of the current Bruins and Celtics seasons. The building held many fond childhood memories for him and the more distant and unapproachable the general public seemed to get, his faith in his fellow man had been buoyed every time he'd heard the fifteen thousand plus fans cheer a Larry Bird three pointer, or boo a Montreal Canadiens goal, in unison.

As they stepped inside the huge building the sounds of the old arcade buzzed, beeped, and rang in the air, creating a nearly carnival like atmosphere as the throngs of commuters bustled to and from the pre-winter chill of the city streets.

Once inside the terminal, the crowd thinned out as the strains of two street musicians rose above the ancient tile floor to mingle, forming a cacophony of unrelated notes, adding to the arcade's milieu. Duane looked around the bleak and dreary surroundings. It was the people that brought this place to life. Its walls and ceiling soaked up a little of each of them; their characters and attitudes, even their loneliness and despair. Years after it was empty of the street musicians and panhandlers, the homeless, the drunks, and the constant commuters, this place would live on with the energy it had extracted from its diverse patronage.

Turning up their collars, the two friends stepped back out onto Causeway Street, and as they crossed to Canal the wind gusted a little harder and colder than before.

Halfway up the street they entered the hallway that led to Brian's apartment. There had been no police cars out front, a good sign that Brian would now be free to speak his mind.

After making the climb to the third floor, Jeanette and Duane reached the door to the apartment. Jeanette, suddenly feeling a bit intrusive about her unannounced visit, drew a deep breath, raised her hand, and knocked firmly three times on the doorframe.

When no answer was forthcoming, Jeanette leaned closer and listened for any movement inside the apartment. Hearing none, she knocked again, albeit a bit more briskly this time. Showing Duane a look of concerned anticipation, she reached slowly, almost fearfully, for the knob.

Looking back to Duane, she saw him rolling his eyes in exaggerated impatience, and after returning the look with a sneer, she twisted the knob gingerly to the right.

With a click, the door swung freely in, to the surprise of both she and Duane.

"Doesn't the fool lock his door?" Duane asked, shaking his head.

"As a matter of fact," Jeanette whispered, "he's compulsive about it. He's been robbed at least twice that I know of." Leaning her head in the door, Jeanette surveyed the seemingly empty apartment.

"Brian?" She offered tentatively. "Brian, its Jeanette Tolby. Are you home?"

When the man didn't answer, she shot Duane a look which betrayed the knot she felt forming in the pit of her stomach. Smiling, he raised his palm before her, in an effort to prevent her from jumping to anymore wild conclusions.

"Now just hold it a second," he began. "You didn't call and tell him you were coming, did you?"

"W-Well, no I-" she stammered, suddenly feeling a bit unsure of herself.

"Then he wasn't expecting you, was he?" he added in a patronizing tone.

"Well, I-"

Holding his hand up, he again interrupted, "Well, maybe he needed some milk. Or better yet, some scotch. So whaddaya say? Let's get outta here, and you can call him later, ok?"

Jeanette, feeling mildly foolish for the way she'd let her

imagination run away with her let the corners of her mouth turn slightly upward in an apologetic smile and nodded. "Ok, alright, I give up, you win. Just let me leave him a note to let him know I've been here."

Duane squinted narrowly, nodding his approval as the first indication of a reluctant smile tugged at the corners of his own lips. But by the time he'd given his ok, Jeanette had already reached into her pocket and pulled out a pen as she made her way into the empty apartment in search of a piece of paper.

After exhausting her possibilities in the modest living room, she headed toward the kitchen. Looking back over her shoulder, she held up one finger in a futile effort to appease Duane, who obviously, from the way he was looking back and forth between his watch and her, had finally begun to lose patience with her.

Pushing at the swinging door to the kitchen it gave way easily at first, but stopped mid-swing with a thump. As she stepped back from the door, it swung back toward her with another dull thud, causing her to jump back from it, a small, strangled scream erupting from her throat. Quickly she turned to stare at Duane, the blood draining immediately from her face.

Then another thump, this one causing the door to swing slightly open in her direction.

Backing away from whatever it was that was on the other side of the door,

Jeanette backed right into Duane's arms which caused her to scream again.

"Christ! Enough is enough!" Duane uttered, pushing his way by her, headed for the door. Once he reached the entryway though, he stopped and listened for any sign that anyone or anything was in the other room. Hearing nothing, he placed both hands firmly against the door and pushed hard, only to have it stop once again with a loud thump.

The pressure he felt pushing back caused his heart to race. But as the force on the other side of the door increased, Duane met it with more force of his own. "Brian? Open up, for God's sake! It's Jeanette's friend, Duane!" He grumbled.

Then, with a strained groan from Duane's throat, and one final push, the door swung in to expose Brian, suspended from his own tie from the sprinkler system, his unseeing bloodshot eyes protruding repulsively from their sockets.

When his lifeless body cleared the edge of the door, Brian swung through the open entry, spinning grotesquely, and causing Duane to spring backward landing on his rear-end to avoid contact with the corpse.

Scrambling back on his elbows and feet, Duane reached the base of the couch, watching in mesmerized horror as the door swung closed cinching up the tie and causing the body to lurch forward as blood ran from the corners of the dead man's pursed lips.

Sitting traumatized, Duane felt his mind short-circuiting, his eyes transfixed on the gruesome spectacle dangling before him. Try as he might, he couldn't harness the images and thoughts that were assaulting his senses. Then, as he began to recover his faculties, he realized that half of his confusion was being caused by the continuous horrified scream erupting from Jeanette's throat.

Leaping to his feet, he charged at the corpse, both hands extended stiffly in front of him. Hitting the body waist high, he shoved it back through the door. But when he turned to look at Jeanette, his eyes fixed on her just as her scream subsided, her eyes rolling back in her head as she collapsed into the corner unconscious.

Bolting across the room, Duane lifted her into his arms and placed her delicately on the couch. He reached to his belt for his cell phone. It wasn't there. He quickly scanned the room for a land-line... There wasn't one. So summoning all his courage, he pulled himself to his full 6'4" and looked toward the kitchen. A cold shiver raced up his spine causing the hair on the back of his neck to bristle.

As he made his way across the living room, he noticed another door in the same wall, and he opted for the latter, fairly confident that what awaited him on the other side of that door could hardly be as repulsive as what he was *sure* was behind door number one.

Still, he could feel his pulse rise as he turned the knob and peeked into the empty bedroom. Just as he had hoped, there was a phone on the night-stand. And as a sigh of relief escaped his lips, he crossed the room, snatched up the receiver, and dialed 911.

CHAPTER TWO

Jeanette sat cradling her aching head in her hands. The pounding at her temples was almost too much to take.

"Just a few more questions, ma'am. Then you can get out of here and about your business," the middle aged, slightly rumpled, detective offered.

"Look," Duane began, returning from the now corpse-less kitchen with a glass of water and two aspirin for his boss. "I already told you what went on. We just came over here to offer our condolences to the guy and found him hanging there. Why do you have to keep hammering at her like that?"

The cop, who had first taken Duane's statement, and was now in the process of taking Jeanette's, looked up from his place on the couch and leered coldly at the young man.

Taking the look as a challenge, Duane continued. "And besides, the last thing we knew, *your* boys were giving *him* this whole routine! Why don't you go ask them what happened to him? Jesus, you'd think we were suspects or something!" He finished, returning the officers menacing glare.

Standing up and drawing himself to his full height, the detective still gave away a full four inches to Duane; a fact that was seemingly lost on the man. "Listen, palie, I'll be done askin' questions when I find out what I want to know. Now sit your ass down, and keep your smart-ass accusations to yourself!"

The second the spiteful words had crossed the detective's lips, an older officer approached him from behind, placing a hand heavily on his shoulder.

"Take five, Burton. I'll finish up here," the inspector ordered, mercifully winking at Jeanette and smiling.

Detective Burton turned to walk away, but just as quickly, he whipped around and looked Duane straight in the eye. "*Everyone's* a suspect until we find out they're not guilty of anything'!" He said acidly. And spinning on his heels, he stalked off into the kitchen.

The older officer laughed quietly to himself and shook his head. Then, taking a seat next to Jeanette, he took her hand gently in his, and patting it softly, he looked at her compassionately. "Are you ok, Miss Tolby?"

Jeanette nodded distantly, and taking a deep breath, she tried to look anywhere but into the man's eyes.

"You'll have to forgive Sergeant Burton, ma'am. He's fairly new to plain clothes and he's having a hell of a time adjusting to the radical idea that people are innocent until proven guilty," he continued. "I can't see any reason you two can't run along. We know where to find you if we need you. But frankly, I doubt you'll be hearing from us, this looks like a suicide to me."

Jeanette heaved a huge sigh of relief. "Thank you, ah"

"O'Hare, ma'am, Lieutenant John O'Hare."

"Thank you, Lieutenant," she nodded, and headed for the door.

Duane smiled and nodded at the older cop, but as he turned to follow Jeanette, O'Hare took him by the elbow and pulled him aside.

"You just nod and smile, my friend," the officer said, a large grin creasing his weathered face. And once Duane followed suit and did as he was told, O'Hare continued, "Mr. Avon, this fuckin' job is tough enough without smart asses like you bustin' our balls every step of the way. So you best hop down off your high horse, or so help me Jesus I'll make your life a living hell. Do we understand each other now?" The cop beamed.

"Yes sir," Duane smiled, the sweat beading on his forehead. "Yes sir, we sure do."

"Good," O'Hare piped, slapping Duane on the shoulder. "Now you have a nice day," he added, and offering Jeanette a slight tip of his hat, the lieutenant retired to the kitchen.

Duane turned and walked to Jeanette, his manufactured grin still in place, but as soon as the door was closed behind them, his mock smile melted into a tight-lipped scowl.

Looking up, Jeanette couldn't help but notice his sudden change in demeanor. So taking a chance at opening the floodgates, she slipped her arm into his and pulled herself close to him, resting her head against his shoulder. "I'm sorry, Duane," she said innocently.

Duane, reaching into the pocket of his suit-coat, pulled out a handkerchief and dragged it across his sweat soaked forehead. "*Sorry*?"

Sorry don't cut it," he said, shaking his head. "Not after draggin' me around the city all afternoon lookin' for dead queers."

The second the words left his mouth, Duane wished he could take them back. And as he felt Jeanette tense up, her head snapping in his direction, he knew he was in for an earful.

Stopping dead in her tracks at the head of the stairs, Jeanette yanked her arm out of his grasp. Then, stepping back, and as if to size him up, she glowered at him, a look of anger and disbelief distorting her features.

"I- I can't believe you said that!" She stammered, her face screwing up even tighter as she formed the words. "Sometimes you're so callous! Better yet, make that *stupid*! Why don't you grow up!" She finished. And turning, she stormed down the stairs toward the street.

"Oh, damn!" Duane cursed, slapping himself in the forehead. "Jeanette, wait a minute. You know I didn't mean that, I-"

But it was too late. The door at the bottom of the stairs slammed shut and she was gone. Duane, now alone in his shame and embarrassment, grabbed a fistful of banister. Then, sitting down hard, he let the air drain from his lungs with a constrained hiss.

"Son of a b-, Jesus!" he uttered. "Sometimes I can be such an idiot!" Of all days, he thought, I've got to pick this one to come out with that beauty. "Shit!"

Pulling himself to his feet, he figured that if he gave her a while to cool down, she'd surely forgive him his indiscretion. After all, he thought, she always does when I act like a fool. Trudging heavily down the stairs, he made his way to the door.

*****

When Jeanette turned the corner onto Causeway Street, she could see the subway train pulling into the North Station boarding area. If only it hadn't been a full two blocks to the stop she'd have run to catch it. But that was academic. She just hoped that Duane wouldn't try to catch up to her and apologize. It wasn't so much that she wouldn't forgive him eventually. It was more that, right now, after the day she'd had, she didn't feel like forgiving anybody for anything.

Standing on the platform at the station, she had a clear view of the corner of Canal Street while waiting for the next train. Eventually she saw Duane appear at the corner. But to her surprise, he hustled across Causeway Street without so much as sneaking a glance in her direction. Then, just as quickly as he had appeared at the corner, he vanished into the station. She stood staring at the door through which Duane had disappeared, wondering why it was that every time they ended up in this part of town, no matter what the time of day, or what the circumstances of their proximity to the hulking ark of a structure, Duane insisted on walking through it. He never bought anything. Not so much as a paper from the news stand, he never had a shoe shine; indeed, he never even stopped. He simply walked right through. But now that she thought about it, on their jaunts through the antiquated terminal, she always noticed a certain peace, a calm serenity that seemed to wash over him like a waterfall of positive emotion. His manner seemed to soften ever so slightly, he seemed at home there. In fact, he seemed more at home there than anywhere else.

The screech of the air-brakes on the train shocked her back from her reflective state before she could ask herself why that was. But as she boarded she made sure she took a seat on the right side of train facing backward. Then she watched as the shimmying train screeched and rattled, rocking gently as North Station faded into the quickly falling dusk.

*****

Back at the office after having made some phone calls, and finding out the official story on Billy's death, it soon became obvious to her that she wasn't about to get anything else done today. Between the death of her good friend and protégé, and the images of the horrific scene she had witnessed that afternoon, in the hour since she'd returned, she had succeeded only in walking aimlessly from corner to corner - Stopping only every so often to stare blankly out the window at the increasingly lighted city below.

She was having a particularly tough time accepting the official version of what had happened to Billy. An overdose, she thought. Heroin just wasn't his gig, she'd told herself time and again. He had been an intense, driven kind of guy. A guy with his eyes set firmly on what he'd wanted. And now, with everything he'd worked for right in his grasp... No, the timing was all wrong. It just didn't flush. And as far as Brian was concerned, she had known him for almost as long as she'd known Billy, and she didn't even know he owned a tie. So why the hell would he be wearing one around the house? None of it worked. It just didn't make sense. But that was what the police had decided happened, and in Billy's case, they supposedly had the evidence to prove it.

"None of it makes any sense!" She said aloud. But then a thought occurred to her. What with Billy being alone in the world except for Brian, who would claim the body, and who would make the arrangements for his funeral. With Brian gone, the only answer to those two questions seemed to be the same. The answer, as it turned out, was her. She'd be Goddamned if she was going to let him be buried in some pauper's field with a shabby wooden cross and no friends to see him off. So reluctantly, she grabbed her coat and headed off to the morgue to identify the body of her friend.

Duane shifted restlessly in his third floor apartment on Beacon Street. It was only a block from Jeanette's Commonwealth Avenue address just outside of Kenmore Square, and more than once he'd entertained the thought of walking over there to apologize for his tactless behavior earlier. Indeed, he had made it as far as his door twice; each time deciding that she definitely needed more time to cool off before he encountered her face to face.

Snatching up the phone he dialed her number, his fingers pecking quickly at the keys to overcome his rapidly fading nerve. But in the anxious seconds that it took to make the connection, he hung it up before the first ring.

He felt a little foolish for his childish insecurity. After all, he and Jeanette were good friends, and had been for some time, now. She wouldn't let a little thing like this come between them. But just the same, he thought, peering out the window in the direction of her apartment. What would he say to her? Shaking his head, he realized that she was only a block away; but since he'd known her, he'd never felt quite this far from her.

By the time Jeanette got back to her brownstone it was eight thirty. It had been a full fourteen hours since she'd left for work that morning. As she dragged herself up the front steps her exhaustion clung around her legs like runner's weights. It wasn't so much the physical weariness that weighed on her, it was the mental fatigue brought on by the stressful day she'd had that made her doubtful of her ability to reach the second floor.

Her fingers failed her miserably as she fumbled numbly with her keys, and before she knew it they were jangling between her feet and coming to rest on the top step.

When she bent to retrieve the runaway keys, she heard a man's voice.

"Please, allow me."

Startled, she snapped to attention and whipped around to face the disembodied voice, and then fell back against her door. The man who had spoken was a mere silhouette, his head framed by the glow of the street lamp directly behind him, his face a featureless patch of threatening anonymity.

"Wh-Who are you, and what do you want?" she stuttered, her eyes burning with fear.

" Man oh man, you really are spooked, aren't you?" Duane said, stepping aside as he bent to pick up the keys.

"Damn you! DAMN YOU!!" Jeanette growled, clutching at her chest as she whacked him in the head with her purse.

"What are you nuts sneaking up on a person like that? You're lucky I wasn't carrying my mace!" She scolded.

"Now hold on a second," the man pleaded, ducking the second swipe of her pocketbook. "I wasn't even on my way over here. I was just headed out to pick up a newspaper. Hell, I even slowed down up the street so we wouldn't bump into each other by accident. But when I saw you drop your keys. Well, I thought I'd do the right thing and pick them up for you … so here you go," he finished. Softly tossing her the keys, he turned and started dejectedly down the stairs.

"Duane, w=wait. We should talk," Jeanette heard herself say. Originally she hadn't really wanted to talk to him at all, at least not until tomorrow. But now that she thought about it, she realized that to let this thing fester wouldn't do anyone any good.

Duane stopped on the bottom step, his head falling to rest on his chest. Then, turning slowly, he forced a wide smile. "I'd like that. I'd like that a lot," he agreed. So climbing the final three stairs, he took her keys, found the lock, and pushed the heavy oaken door in on its hinges.

Once upstairs behind a warm brandy, Duane felt a little more confident than he had outside on the stoop. But still he felt like a teenager on his first date. He wasn't quite sure where an acceptable place to begin was, or even if he should say anything at all for fear he might say the wrong thing.

Looking up from his drink, he saw pain and exhaustion hanging like a veil on Jeanette's face. The blank look she wore convinced him that he had to say something. Wrong or right, he had to make an effort.

"Look," he began haltingly, "about this afternoon, I- I don't know. I just want to apologize. I know how close you and Billy were..." his voice trailed off as he checked the bottom of his glass. "Sometimes my timing is terrible," he admitted, looking up into her tired eyes.

Shaking her hair back, Jeanette straightened up, doing the best she could to look less worn out than she was. It was no use. "No, forget it. I mean, after what I dragged you into this afternoon... Christ, what normal human being wouldn't react resentfully." She offered, shaking her head. "But you are right about one thing. Your timing *sucks*!" she added, the faintest smile dancing at the corners of her eyes.

"You know," Jeanette blurted, "they say Billy overdosed on heroine. I just can't buy it. Heroine was never his thing; he was too hyper, too intense. It just doesn't fit him at all."

That said, they sat in tense silence at her breakfast bar. Both of them sipping at their drinks and avoiding eye contact until neither of them could stand it any longer. Then, just as Duane was about to speak, Jeanette cleared her throat and beat him to it. "I don't know. I just can't believe that, Billy, after all this time, and all his hard work, just when things were starting to open up to him, would get into anything like this. I mean, if he had relapsed on the coke, or even the booze, that I could understand. But all of a sudden, out of nowhere, *heroin*? No. Something isn't right about this. Something isn't right at *all*!"

Duane let his head drop into his hands. This is it, he thought, peeking between his fingers. He recognized the look in her eye. It was that famous look he, and everyone else at the office, had come to refer to as "battle stations". It was the look she got every time she was about to go on a crusade, or hop up on a soap box. Not that there was usually anything wrong with her motivation. To the contrary, her crusades were usually carefully chosen, and reserved for such gallant causes as, the homeless, social injustice, or governmental improprieties. But this time he was worried. This sucker hit a little too close to home. This, to her, was personal.

"Now don't you go getting any crazy ideas about solving the crime of the century, here. If the cops say it's an overdose and suicide, that's good enough for me, and it should be good enough for you, too," he finished, choosing his words carefully so as not to make it sound like a challenge

Jeanette stood, looked down at the hardwood floor, and slowly shook her head. "Sorry Duane, this doesn't flush," she said, just above a whisper. And looking up, her eyes, deep and brown, burrowed into the deepest recesses of his soul. Immediately, he knew he was along for the ride. What else could he do? Not only was she his closest friend, but someone had to look out for her, and who better than him?

Getting to his feet, he swirled the last sip of brandy around his glass, waited for it to stop, and threw it back. This would be his last shot at dissuading her from pursuing this thing, and regardless of how feeble his chances, he felt obligated to try once more.

"Okay," he started, formulating his case as he spoke. "Let's just say, for arguments sake, that there *is* something to all of this. Just what is it *you're* going to do about it all? I mean, if one or both of them were murdered, what's going to stop whoever killed them from doing the same to you?" It was weak and he knew it, but it was the best he could do on such short notice.

Pushing back her sandy mane, she regarded him wearily. "As far as them doing the same to me, well, who the hell would expect *me* to get involved? And for all we know, they don't even know I exist. And as far as what I'm going to do about it... I'm not exactly sure. But whatever it is I'm sure it can wait 'til morning. I'm exhausted," she declared. And draining her snifter, she placed it firmly on the counter.

Gracious in defeat, Duane walked to her, put his arms around her, and gave her a hug. "I'm on your team champ, you know that," he assured her. "Anything I can do?"

"Yeah," she yawned, "you can start by letting yourself out so I can get some sleep!"

Duane reached out, and giving her shoulder a squeeze, he headed for the stairs. As he made his descent, he smiled to himself and shook his head. Then, locking the door behind him, he sniffed the cold evening air and shivered slightly from its bite. The crispness of the night was just as he liked it. He always thought easier when he walked. And when it was cool his thinking seemed all that much clearer. But on this walk home he felt his smile fade as his pace picked up. He couldn't help but wonder what it was he'd let himself in for.

CHAPTER THREE

Jeanette slipped under the covers, the soothing waves of the waterbed rocking her gently as she immediately began to nod off to sleep. As she floated into her subconscious, the rocking began to feel more like a rolling motion. A motion much like she was being transported somewhere, somehow. Her eyes snapped open, and in a blur of revelation she saw the lights on the ceiling whipping by above her. She tried to sit up, but couldn't. She was immobilized. What the hell is going on here! She thought.

As she lay there helpless, she could hear the squeaks from the wheels of her transportation reverberating off the tile walls of the corridor through which she was being pushed. She tried to lift her head, but that too proved a futile effort. The lights still whizzed past at an ever increasing clip. Then, using only her eyes, she looked down toward her feet, and there, at the end of her seemingly self-propelled bed, was a masked figure.

She tried to speak, tried to ask what was going on, but could not. How much brandy had they drunk? She felt drugged. Everything looked so sharp and clear, yet somewhere between her eyes and her mind, the pictures seemed to lose meaning. Nothing made any sense.

Suddenly the lights above her stopped short, and the masked figure walked to the side of her bed and spoke to her. But the words made no sense. At first she assumed that it was the mask that was muffling them. But quickly it became obvious that it was her. The words made perfect sense, she just couldn't understand them. She was becoming terrified. Where the hell was she, and why?

With a thump, the figure pushed on the side of her bed, and again she was moving. Then, again she stopped; this time beneath a brightly glowing orb. The brilliance of the light seemed infinite, causing the rest of the room to fade into oblivion. Suddenly she heard more voices, more gibberish. She was beginning to panic, now. Again she tried to speak, and then scream, but nothing came. Then, as if by divine providence, she heard a single word she understood. **Doctor.**

Amidst all the disjointed words, and the sounds she knew she should understand, that one word stood out. Then she heard it again. **DOCTOR.**

As the figures converged above her they continued to babble incessantly. Jeanette tried to look into their faces, groping for the eyes that she knew must be there, but the dazzling radiance of the beam above her caused their faces to melt into mere silhouettes. Featureless forms of a nameless evil.

There were four of them. Or was it five? Now she couldn't even count. She felt a sharp searing pain in her right forearm, and almost immediately her eyes began to become heavier by the second. Then the word again invaded her consciousness **DOCTOR.** Her mouth was so dry she couldn't even swallow. And as she began to lose consciousness, she looked down toward the pain in her arm. But wait a minute, that wasn't *her* arm that the I.V. was in. That arm belonged to some child. As a tear of confusion and fear ran down her cheek, one of the figures bent over her, and clear as a bell, said "Now don't you worry, dearie, you just go back to sleep."

When she lost consciousness, the room began to spin as though she were caught in a swirling tempest. Then, with a rush of confusion, a loud beeping sound caused her to spring up erect into a sitting position. Why was she no longer immobilized? Where had her abductors gone? My good Lord, what the hell did they do to me?

Her eyes darted around the room expecting to find unfamiliar surroundings, her hand covering her gaping mouth in near hysterical panic.

As she sat on her waterbed, in her darkened room, the last vestiges of her tortured sleep, along with the fractured half memories, half pictures, of her vividly horrid nightmare, dissolved into the endless blackness of the pre-dawn morning.

Reaching back to the headboard she hit the kill button on her alarm clock.

The interminable screeching stopped immediately, and she fell back against her pillows, wiping the remainder of the sweat from her forehead. Grabbing the clock she checked the time. "Damn!" She mumbled. It was 5:12. Already time to get up. Not that she wanted to go back to sleep. Right now, that was the last thing she wanted to do.

*****

As she sat at the breakfast bar finishing her Pop Tart and black coffee breakfast, she couldn't help wondering why the recurring nightmare had returned. It had been so long since she'd had it. Indeed, it had been a good eight months; long before she'd stopped seeing Sidney, the analyst Billy had suggested when the dreams had originally begun to resurface after almost six years of dormancy.

Why now? Could it be the stress over Billy's death? But, as Dr. Bernhard had said, they had never really found out what it was that was causing them. They could only assume that the catalyst for their recurrence was the stress she'd been feeling lately over her job and having all her work scrutinized so closely by Mr. Pinkham, her boss. But even that was no more than enlightened speculation.

Well, whatever it is, it has to wait, she thought. Duty called, it was time to get to work. And if there was anything Mr. Pinkham hated more than her, it was her when she was late for work.

CHAPTER FOUR

Jeanette's purse caught on the door handle, yanking her to a jolting stop as she ran into the ground floor of the Hancock Building. Shaking it loose, she checked the clock. The train had been late, but mercifully she was still on time.

"Hold that elevator!" She shouted above the din of arriving workers. Much to her surprise, someone did. She was going to make it with one or two seconds to spare. For a day that had begun on such a bad note, things were really beginning to look up.

Just as the doors slid closed before her, a voice from the back of the car rose above the mumbling sardines who, more often than not, were her faceless morning companions on her ride upstairs. "Well, good morning, Jeanette!" The voice piped.

Trying to turn around was no use. But it was obvious who the owner of the voice was. Who, but a politician could be that chipper at this time of the morning. "Good morning, Senator. What brings you out at this time of the morning?"

"Oh, please," the man chuckled, "you want to drop the formalities? And besides, I didn't know it was *early* in the morning. I've been up for hours, now. This is my third appointment!"

"Well, well, you busy little politician, you." Jeanette teased. "But I'm terribly sorry, we're fresh out of babies for you to kiss."

Jeanette's quip caused even their groggy companions to let go a barely stifled laugh. But as usual, the Junior Senator from Massachusetts laughed louder than any of them. That was one of the things that truly endeared him to her. Aside from the fact that he was just a regular guy, he loved a good joke, even if it was at his expense.

The overloaded elevator jerked to a stop and Jeanette was pushed out the door by the crush of people exiting on the seventh floor. Slipping back in just before the doors eased closed again, Jeanette extended her hand to Dean Tunney.

"So, to what do we owe the honor?" She asked innocently.
"I'm cutting my commercial in the sound studio this morning," he smiled genuinely.

"Oh, that's right! I heard the demo tapes they ran off yesterday morning. Barry and Steve are wizards, I think you're going to love the ideas they came up with. A couple of them are really you."

"Well, I don't know for sure if I should take that as a compliment or not," Dean smiled.

"Oh, don't be silly. If I didn't like what you stood for, what makes you think I'd campaign for you?" Jeanette offered.

Dean's eyes sagged in a boyishly cute look. "You mean it's not my matinee idol good looks? Damn!" Dean joked, referring to an article in Boston Magazine, describing him as 'The most eligible bachelor in Boston'.

Oh, Damn! Jeanette thought, I hope he doesn't bring up our date. But no sooner than the thought had crossed her mind, did the young Senator's eyebrows rise as he picked up the conversation. "So, we're getting down there. Only a month and a half to go!" He began. "And the day after tomorrow the big push starts. Ah, you *will* be there, right? And before you answer, the Junior Senator from Massachusetts would like to point out that you did promise to be there to walk the carpet with him at the festivities."

Jeanette, looking toward the floor as if searching for the answer on her shoe tops, shifted her weight uncomfortably. Reaching out, he took her chin gently in his hand. The stress of the previous day and her virtually useless night of sleep were evident, not only in her appearance, but in her uncharacteristic failure to speak her mind as well.

"Dean," she began apologetically, haltingly searching for the right way to let him down. "It=it's just that these last few days have been a real mess, and then, on top of it all, yesterday I lost a very close friend," she confided, a tear welling in her eye. "I-I'm just afraid I wouldn't be very good company, is all. The funeral will be this Saturday, and then I was going to head directly to the Cape for a week or so. I *really* need this vacation."

The sting of the rejection was clear in his eyes. However, summoning his best politician's sympathetic smile, he gave her shoulder a gentle squeeze as the bell rang for the eighteenth floor. "Of course you do. I understand," he lied, as the doors peeled back. "And I'm terribly sorry to hear about your friend," he added. Then, patting her cheek softly, he stepped out of the elevator and turned to offer a small wave as the doors crawled closed between them.

She felt terrible. She truly liked Dean Tunney, which was quite unlike her. She usually hated politicians. They were always spending all the wrong money on all the wrong things. But Dean was different. Oh sure, he was from old money, some of the oldest in Boston. And he did come from a long line of crooked politicians, so what was new. That was exactly what impressed her, *he* was new, a fresh drop in an otherwise stagnant pool of political corruption that went back to the dawn of democratic government. You scratch my back, I'll stab yours.

She liked to believe that the difference was solely a byproduct of being from her own generation; a generation which she considered a more caring and intelligent one. Not to mention a more enlightened and ethically sound one. He had all the right ideas about the things she cared about; the homeless, the drug problem, government spending and social injustice.

Yup, if she didn't know him better, she'd think he was too good to be true.

Looking to her wrist, she cursed. "Shit! I've **got** to pick my watch up!"

The bell rang again, and when the doors opened on the twenty- third floor the first thing she saw was the clock above the receptionist's desk. 8:05, she was late. As she hustled toward her office, she nodded her good mornings with a finger to her lips to discourage any verbal evidence of her late arrival.

Once in her office she pushed the door silently closed, a sigh of relief escaping her throat. She'd made it again. Smiling wearily, she turned around. There, sitting behind her desk, in her chair, was Mr. Pinkham.

"Good morning, Jeanette," he said coolly, a wry smile wrinkling his thin lips.

Leaning back in her chair, he looked at her over the tops of his glasses. "I dare say you look like hell," he began.

Before he went any further, Jeanette interrupted to plead her case. "I'm sorry I was late, the damn train was late again. I-"

Standing, the man held up a wrinkled hand. "Come, sit, dear," he offered, motioning to her chair with the other hand.

Making her way around the desk, she couldn't help wondering if that was really compassion she'd heard in his voice. No, she thought, as she took her seat. Not a chance.

Leaning over her desk, he looked her squarely in the eye, and she could feel her stomach muscles tighten as she prepared herself for who knows what.

"Jeanette, you're a valuable employee here. You're much too valuable to be replaced very easily." He began, walking to the center of the room. Then turning, he once again fixed his gaze on her. "I don't want to have to replace you."

This is it, Jeanette thought, I'm canned.

"As I said before, you look like hell," Pinkham continued, "and you've had a rough couple of days-"

"But-" she started to interrupt, but again he held his hand up between them.

"Never mind, young lady!" he snapped. "You have vacation time coming, and I want you to start it today! Do you understand?"

Jeanette sat there flabbergasted, a haze of confusion clouding her exhausted features. As she sat there speechless, Pinkham walked to the desk and pulled three envelopes out of his pocket.

"This week's pay, your vacation pay, and a bonus," he said, handing them to her. "Now disappear. I don't want to see your face until you look like you're in your thirties again! Take as much time as you need, but this time you're going to take at least your allotted three weeks! Do you hear?" Jeanette took the envelopes from him and sat staring at them for a second. Looking up at him, then back at the checks, she wasn't really sure if she was being rewarded or punished. But when her eyes found Mr. Pinkham once more, he was smiling broadly at her. Then, turning on his heels, he headed for the door, stopping only when he reached it to turn and address her again. "I may be a crusty old wind-bag," he began, the smile shrinking from his face, "but I didn't get where I am by burning out my brain trust."

Jeanette looked at him with only half a smile and finally found her voice. "I-I don't... Well, thank you, first of all," she blathered, scratching at her head. "But there are just a few-"

"Nonsense!" Pinkham crackled, "not so much as one phone call! It's about time some other people around here learned to carry their weight and earn their pay!" He scowled. "Oh, and by the way," he continued, his voice softening to a near whisper, "I'm sorry about your friend, Fairelane. I won't pretend I understood him, or even liked him much for that matter. But I know *you* did, and for that, I'm sorry."

Jeanette stood and rounded her desk, walking to her boss. "Thank you, Harry," she said, giving him a peck on the cheek. The old man instinctively pulled his handkerchief from his pocket, blushed slightly, and wiped the lipstick from his face.

"That's Mr. Pinkham," he ordered tersely. And with that said, he disappeared out the door.

Once he was gone, Jeanette walked to her window. She was already picturing herself leisurely strolling the dunes in Sandwich, and spending ridiculous amounts of money on stupid little baubles in the shops of Provincetown. She loved the Cape in the fall. No crowds. No traffic. This, she thought, is going to be a great, and much needed, vacation. As she stood there daydreaming in the early morning fall sun, she felt it caressing her, body and being. But as she closed her eyes to revel in the warm glow of her contentment, an ugly thought fought its way into her mind.

As she came around and opened her eyes, the sun was blotted out by an ominous looking cloud. "Shit!" she said aloud. "I have arrangements to make for the funeral. And there are people to call..." She suddenly felt guilty about feeling so good for that short second. And then more so, for being mad about the responsibilities she herself had assumed. As she reached for the phone, Pinkham's words rang in her ears. "**...not so much as one phone call!**"

"The hell with it," she dismissed, and pushing her blonde hair back off of her shoulders, she grabbed up the receiver, and began to dial.

An hour later, as she hung up the phone, a soft knock on her door broke the silence of the office. "Come," she said routinely. Suddenly, realizing she wasn't supposed to be there, she hastily began formulating an excuse for being in her own office.

Duane stuck his head around the door, smiled, and entered. "What are you still doing here? Didn't the old man send you home?" He asked.

"Yeah, but I still had a few calls to make," she admitted. "But wait a minute, how did you know that? Oh, never mind," she said, waving her hand before him. "I don't want to know Val was listening in on my private business." Slowly Jeanette's face took on a look of mischief, and leaning back in her chair, she began tapping herself on the chin with her pen and squinting thoughtfully at Duane.

"What?" Duane asked tentatively.

"You've got some vacation time saved up, don't you?" His look of uncertainty quickly changed to one of careful appraisal. "Yeah, I might... Why, what do you have up your sleeve?" he asked guardedly.

But before she could answer, Duane began shaking his head vehemently. "Oh no! Absolutely not!! I'm not spending my vacation playing cops and robbers. Sorry, I'm not your guy!"

"Oh come on Duane. Take it now and give me a hand. Please? Besides, what do you have to worry about? There's nothing to this, remember? You said so yourself."

Before he had a chance to reply, Jeanette pushed the button on the intercom. "Val, could you come in here for a minute please."

"But I don't-" Duane began. But Jeanette held her hand up, taking a page from Pinkham's book.

"Listen, I'm your boss, and I say you need a vacation. However, what you do with it is entirely up to you. But I could really use your help, pleeease," she whined.

He hated it when she whined. It gave her an unfair advantage and she knew it. He could never say no when she whined. So, true to form, and against his better judgment, he reluctantly nodded his agreement as he sank into the chair next to her desk.

Seconds later the door swung open, and the secretary entered, smiling innocuously. "Yes, Ms. Tolby?"

"Val, could you have payroll draw up Mr. Avon's vacation pay? As of today he's on vacation."

"Oh, sure. What a coincidence," the girl winked, snapping at the wad of gum in her mouth.

Jeanette couldn't believe the girl was that thick, but she couldn't help playing the game a little longer. "Oh really? And who else do you know who's going on vacation?" She asked, smirking mischievously.

The secretary's jaw fell open. "Um, ah, well..." She stammered, fidgeting nervously.

The young lady had paid for her breach of confidence, and it wasn't like Jeanette to make people squirm. "Never mind, Val. Just have them draw the checks please," she said, letting the secretary off the hook. "Oh, and Val, be careful which buttons you push out there or you may find *yourself* on an ***extended*** vacation," she scolded, adding, "Oh, and Val, lose the gum."

The secretary turned, her face beet red, and hurried out of the office, chased playfully by Duane's needling laughter.

Standing, Jeanette grabbed her coat and headed for the door. "Now I better get out of here before Pinkham comes to check on me. Call me at home, will you?" she said, looking to her wrist.

"9:12," Duane offered.

"Damn! I've ***gotta*** pick up my watch," she agonized. "I'll be home in about an hour. Call me?"

"Yeah, yeah, I'll call. Now get."

Opening the door little more than a crack, Jeanette peeked out. The coast was clear so, wasting no time, she slipped out of the office, leaving the door slightly ajar.

The next sound Duane heard was Mr. Pinkham's voice.

"Tolby? I thought I told you to vanish. What in Gods..."
Duane quietly pushed the door shut. "Busted," he chuckled aloud, and walking to Jeanette's desk, he flopped down in her chair and hoisted his feet up onto it. The more he thought about it, the more he liked the idea of being on vacation. Once Pinkham was finished bawling out Jeanette, and once Val got back with his checks, he would let himself out of his boss's office discreetly and begin his leave.

*****

Jeanette stood in front of her eight foot windows that overlooked Commonwealth Avenue lost in retrospective daydreams of Billy. She was beside herself trying to swallow the fact that she would be burying him in two days.

Picking up the newspaper she had bought on the way home, she stared at the obituary she had ordered the day before. Making the arrangements had helped somewhat, but the sense of loss she felt would take more than that to extinguish.

Her difficulty in accepting Billy's death was obvious, even to the most casual observer. It was the peculiar closeness of their friendship that made it so overwhelming. They had been more than close. They did things for each other that average friends wouldn't ordinarily expect from each other. They acted more like brother and sister, more like core companions, than mere friends. Everyone they knew noticed it, but what they didn't know was why.

Billy and Jeanette were both orphans. And, coincidentally, they had both been brought up in the same state home, Saint Bridget's in Waltham. Although they had been there years apart, the fact that they had that in common caused them to gravitate to one another. Then there was the unfortunate circumstance that neither of them had ever been adopted. Until, of course, they had met each other. And finally, there was the other thing; the thing which they didn't talk about to anyone but each other. That one thing had made them closer than all the common factors which knit the fabric of their friendship. Both of them were sterile. If their common histories were the bricks of their relationship, then their inability to parent children was the mortar that gave it strength. To each other they could talk about their feelings of inadequacy, of not being whole. No one else could really ever understand. Sure, the doctors could comprehend the mechanics of it. But every night they went home to their families, their flesh and blood families.

The phone rang, startling her out of her daydream.

That must be Duane, she thought, crossing the room. Then, snapping up the receiver, she barked into the mouthpiece. "It's about time!"

At first there was a long awkward silence, then a confused voice on the other end of the line asked, "Is this Jeanette?"

"Yes, it is," she said a little annoyed, "and who is this?"

"Ah, it's Dean, did I catch you at a bad time?"

"Oh, God, I'm sorry Dean," she offered, feeling foolish for the way she'd answered the phone. "No, this isn't a bad time. I was just expecting a call from Duane. What can I do for you?"

She waited as he attempted to devise a way of convincing her to accompany him to his fund raiser without seeming as though he was pressuring her into it. When in fact, that was exactly what he'd had in mind.

"Jeanette..." he began haltingly, "I, ah, well, I've really been counting on you to come with me on Saturday night, and-"

Jeanette cut him off there. Much to his relief as he didn't really know what was to come after the **and**. "Dean, I really apologize for canceling on such late notice, but like I told you this morning, I really don't think I'll be quite up to dancing the night away so soon after spending the day burying a friend, I-"

With what he considered his last chance, he opted for guilt. And in a harsher tone than he'd originally intended, he retorted,"Oh, that's just terrific, how selfish of me to expect you to honor your commitment."

His words made their mark, but not quite in the fashion that he'd intended. Until that moment Jeanette had always thought of him as being sensitive and sympathetic; but now, she thought, he was showing his true politician's colors. "Oh, get off it, Dean. You can find a date in ten minutes, and you know that as well as anybody!"

Immediately realizing he'd made a huge mistake, the senator scrambled to effect damage control. "But it wouldn't be the same," he nearly whined. "I really wanted to take *you*. That is, after all, why I asked you in the first place."

He waited anxiously as she wrestled with her guilt, and her agitation at his insensitivity. Unfortunately for him, her agitation won out. "Listen, Dean. This time could be better spent by you finding another date than trying to make me feel guilty about my priorities! The answer is still no! And if you don't like the answer, change the question! The answer to that one stays the same! Goodbye!"

"Wait a minute, Jeanette, I-" The line went dead in his ear, the mocking monotony of the dial tone causing his pulse to quicken. "Shit!" he seethed. And slamming the receiver down, he turned to address the man seated in *his* chair, behind *his* desk. "She's not coming!" He spit.

"You have an incredible grasp of the obvious, son," the old man said, standing on legs long worn feeble from over-use. "Not to worry, though. It's simply a minor setback. Now stop your whining, and help me to my car, we'll talk on the way."

Dean walked to the coat rack, fetching the older gentleman's overcoat. Then, helping him on with it, he took the man's arm, opened the office door, and led him through it.

Standing, Dean's secretary offered the man her arm on the other side, accompanying them to the elevator. As the doors slid closed between them, she smiled, "Good afternoon Mr. Tunney, so nice to see you again."

"You, my dear, may call me handsome," the elder Tunney croaked, grinning widely as the doors crept silently closed. He smiled at hearing the titter of the secretary's laughter fade as the elevator started down.

CHAPTER FIVE

Jeanette stood seething as she looked out her oversized front windows at the constant flow of pedestrians that filed daily by her brownstone. It was strange, she thought silently, but very seldom did she see anyone she'd seen the day before, or ever, for that matter. Were they all really different people? Or was it just that she had become, as most city dwellers do, disinterested and unaware of the rest of the rank and file - unfazed by the masses who roamed the streets of this, at once bustling and desolate, pocket of humanity. The thought made her shiver with a physical sensation of cold, and cringe with the mental anguish of emotional emptiness.

Quickly, she turned away, hoping the lack of visual stimuli would allow the void she felt to collapse in on itself. It worked, somewhat. Like a Band-Aid on a bullet wound.

Looking to the fireplace she saw the jagged shards of what used to be a wine glass as they refracted the light of the glowing embers. How childish, she thought. Exactly what she had expected her little tantrum to accomplish she wasn't sure. But what she was sure of was that now she had to clean it up.

Realizing that Duane should have called some time ago, she looked to her wrist. "Damn! My watch!" She bristled. Then, as she trained her eyes on the phone, a bell sounded. Jeanette jumped slightly, startled by the coincidence of timing, then made her way across the room and picked up the receiver. But to her surprise she heard the dial tone. Again the bell sounded, jolting her for a second time. It was the doorbell. "Jesus, sometimes I'm such a piece of work," she said aloud, and hanging up the phone, she hurried for the door.

Halfway down the stairs the bell rang for the third time. "Hold on, hold on, I'm coming!" She groused, negotiating the last six stairs two at a time.

"Well, it's about time!" She spouted, pulling the door open, then stopped short. She'd expected to see Duane. But instead, the older policeman from Brian's apartment stood in his place, equally surprised by the odd reception he'd received.

"Afternoon, Ms. Tolby. Ah, were you expecting me?"

Jeanette's brow furrowed. "Well, no. I can't say as I was, is there something I can do for you?"

The cop pulled off his wrinkled fedora, wiping at his forehead with the back of his wrist. "Well, ma'am, I'm not sure, but if I could ask you a few questions, maybe you could clear up a few things for us," he offered, a large and gentle smile creasing his weather weary features.

Jeanette balked momentarily, smiled back, and stepped aside. "Sure, Sergeant, come on in. It is Sergeant, isn't it?"

"I'm sorry, ma'am," he apologized. "It's O'Hare. *Lieutenant* John O'Hare," he added, extending his hand as he made his way across the threshold.

As they entered the downstairs sitting room Jeanette offered the cop a chair, seating herself across the coffee table from him on the couch. "What can I do for you Lieutenant?" She asked apprehensively.

Looking up at her, he smiled disarmingly, catching her eyes with his.

Oh, God, she thought, Paul Newman. The prettiest eyes this side of Hollywood. No one, but no one, could lie into those baby blues. They were a bit yellowed from smog and age. But she could virtually see the wheels spinning behind them.

"Well, it's about the Fairelane case," he began.

"The Fairelane case?" She asked the edge of irony clear in her voice. "I thought that was an overdose, case closed?"

O'Hare scratched at his whiskered chin. "Oh, so do we. But you can't be too careful. There are just a couple of things that don't quite jive."

"For instance?" she pressed, leaning forward.

"Well, I shouldn't really say, but, see, it's his arms, and his feet, for that matter."

Jeanette looked at him, obviously bewildered by his vagueness. "You see, it's not so unusual to find a dead junkie with no apparent needle tracks. Sometimes they shoot up between their toes, sometimes under their tongues, or in other inconspicuous places. You know, to hide it from bosses, mothers, girlfriends and the like. Well, it seems the boys at the morgue have been over that body a dozen times if they've been over it once, and not a single track. Except the one the needle was hangin' outta," he added, pointing to his forearm. Then, seeing Jeanette flinch, he shook his head. "Sorry, ma'am," he apologized.

"No. No, go on," she urged, sliding to the edge of her seat.

"Well, there were some other things too," the Lieutenant hedged.

"Oh yeah? Like what?"

O'Hare rolled his eyes and shook his head. "His liver," he blurted.

Jeanette swallowed hard and closed her eyes, "His, his liver..." her voice trailed off.

"Yeah. It seems there was minimal damage to his liver. Junkies, and frankly even heavy drinkers, have obvious signs that show up in their liver. You know, distention, swelling, scar tissue. But not Billy, his liver was better than average. And any damage there was, was old and well healed. This guy was no junkie. Hell, he probably didn't even drink, as a rule..."

O'Hare's voice fell off, but Jeanette new there had to be more. She could see it in those icy blue eyes, and feel it in his deliberate silence. "And?" she pushed, not really sure she wanted to hear any more, but quite sure she had to know.

"And," O'Hare continued, "there were some bruises on his arm, above and below the needle mark. Bruises caused by hands; two hands. So the way I see it, there was someone in that stairwell with him; maybe even two people. Yeah, your friend was either very unlucky, or someone wants us to think he was."

Jeanette fell back against the couch and tried to absorb the information the Lieutenant had just afforded her. The scene drawn by the officer's words was an ugly one. She could picture Billy struggling against some faceless villain as he fought for his life. But the thing that gnawed at her heart most, the thing that caused her the most confusion, was the apparent senselessness of it. "But why?" She asked, tears welling in her eyes.

O'Hare reached into the pocket of his London Fog and pulled out a handkerchief, offering it to her.

"No. I'll be fine," she said, standing and walking to the large front windows. "But I still don't understand what I can do to help."

O'Hare placed his hat back on his head and wrung his hands. "*Why*, we don't know. And as far as what you can do, that's just about as sketchy. But what we have to know is if there was anybody he knew who was a user. Or anybody who would want him dead."

Jeanette turned to face him, a look of resignation on her face. "Oh come on, Lieutenant. The man was a musician. God, if the Emmy presentations last year were any indication... well, just put it this way, I was there, and you couldn't swing a dead cat without hitting someone who was roped out on something," she offered, her voice thick with sarcasm. But when she spoke again, her voice was soft and wistful. "But as far as enemies," she shook her head and turned back to face the windows, "no, everyone loved Billy..." her voice faded as a lump grew in her throat.

"Listen," O'Hare began, "I'm really sorry to have to ask you this stuff, but you're the only one we can find that really *knew* him," he admitted.

Then, walking up behind her, he gently squeezed her elbow, and started a bit when she recoiled from his touch. "You ok?" He asked, genuine concern in his voice.

"Yup," she lied, the tears now running freely down her face.

Sniffling, Jeanette turned around only to see O'Hare, again volunteering his handkerchief. This time she accepted his offer, but avoided his attempt at eye contact as she made her way back to her seat.

"Just one last question, then I'll leave you alone, ok?"

Jeanette nodded obligatorily as she dabbed at her smearing mascara.

"How about," he cleared his throat, "lovers?" he finished, nearly choking on the word.

She eyed him disdainfully. "Oh, sure. What about those fags and their kinky sex games!" she retorted.

"No, no, now hold on. That's not what I meant. I was just wondering if he was, well, promiscuous. I mean, did he have a lot of boyfriends?" The Lieutenant fumbled.

Jeanette squinted, fixing her eyes on his baby blues. "I *know* what promiscuous means," she spit, getting to her feet. "And the answer is no. He and Brian were very happy together, and had been for some time now! Anything else?"

"No, ma'am. That should do it for now," he offered almost apologetically.

The two stood staring at each other uneasily, neither of them wanting to be responsible for the deterioration of their discussion. Then, mercifully, the phone jangled to life cutting through the tension of a very awkward moment. Snatching up the receiver, Jeanette smiled benignly at him. "Oh, hello Duane," she began, and O'Hare, taking advantage of the opportunity, signaled that he'd let himself out, and headed out of the room. "Where the hell have you been?" she asked. But she didn't really listen to his answer. Because at that very moment she heard the door close and realized she was still clutching the Lieutenant's handkerchief. Walking to the window, she watched the officer hustle across Commonwealth Ave. He looked like some perverse cross between Phillip Marlow and Columbo, she thought. All except for those eyes, they were all Newman.

*****

Forty-five minutes later, Duane and Jeanette were seated at her kitchen table. He was sitting slack jawed as Jeanette finished her account of O'Hare's visit.

"So, what do *you* think of all of this?" She asked, smugly pulling the last olive out of her martini glass and popping it in her mouth.

Duane stood up, drained his glass, and walking to the other end of the kitchen he turned to look her in the eye. "I'll tell you what I think," he said, speaking firmly as he crossed the room toward her. "I think you should leave the police work to the police. That's what I think. Just suppose they're right, and someone did kill him, or **both** of them for that matter? I'll ask again, what's gonna stop them from doing the same to you?"

Jeanette smiled, and then chuckled sarcastically. "Well I'm not about to make a citizen's arrest for Christ's sake. I just think I could find out some stuff that the cops couldn't, that's all. I'd more or less be helping them out without them knowing it," she finished arrogantly.

Duane shook his head and wiped away the beads of sweat that had materialized instantly on his forehead when she'd finished her story.

"Oh, come on, Duane," she scoffed, "what would *you* do if it was *me* who was killed for no apparent reason?" She watched his eyes soften under the weight of the question, and when it seemed to her that he was at his weakest moment, she played him like a stacked deck. "I owe this to Billy, Duane. Help me, pleeease?"

"Aw, damn!" he cursed. "You know I will. But you gotta promise me one thing," he said sternly.

"What's that?"

Pointing a finger in her face, his eyes could have burned two holes in her forehead. "Any trouble, and I mean any at all, and we call the cops and get on a plane to Florida."

She chuckled in spite of herself. But his countenance grew all the more serious. She had never seen him like this before. And it was glaringly obvious that this was no joke to him. Swallowing hard, she looked him in the eye. "I-I promise," she barely choked. But even then, she wasn't so sure she actually meant it.

"Ok." he nodded, rolling his eyes, "I'm in."

The two friends sat in an uncomfortable silence for a long time before either of them felt relaxed enough to talk. Then, just as Jeanette prepared to speak, the telephone broke the uneasy stillness.

Boosting herself out of her chair, she crossed the kitchen and grabbed the offensive appliance. "Hello?" She croaked, her throat constricted from her long silence.

There was an extended pause on the other end of the line, and then an uncertain voice asked, "Is this 369-6409?"

"Yes, yes it is. Who's calling please?" She asked suspiciously.

"Well, ah, you don't know me. My name is Skip Phillips, and I'm at a definite disadvantage here."

Jeanette covered the receiver and looked at Duane, shrugging her shoulders. "This is strange."

"Well," the man on the other end continued, "this is gonna sound kinda weird, but see, I found your number in Billy Fairelane's wallet."

Jeanette's eyes widened. "You say you found it in Billy's wallet?" She said, getting Duane's attention and motioning him to pick up in the other room.

"Yeah, see, me and Billy went out the other night and had a couple'a beers, and then we went back to my place to listen to some tunes, and..."

"Please deposit ten cents to continue," a mechanical monotone chimed, and Jeanette heard the man drop the required funds into the phone. "Thank you." offered the computer.

"Listen, I'm outta change, could we meet somewhere to finish this up?" The man asked hastily.

Jeanette stopped and thought for a second. "Sure. Why not? Where are you now?" she prodded.

"Great," the man replied, ignoring her query. "But this isn't the best place. Ah, where are *you*?"

A stomp from size twelve shoe got Jeanette's attention, and turning, she saw Duane motioning wildly for her to keep her whereabouts a secret. Nodding, she complied, sort of . "I'm right outside of Kenmore square," she sidestepped, much to the dismay of her friend.

"Oh. That'll make it easy, then, I can take the subway over there. Do you know the Coach's Box, across from Fenway Park?" He asked.

"I know where it is," she admitted, mildly chagrined at the thought of actually entering the dumpy little watering hole.

"Should we say eight o'clock, then?" Phillips suggested.

"Eight is fine," she agreed.

By this time, Duane was becoming exhausted by his animated gesticulation warning her against what she had already decided on.

"So how will I know you?" he asked, to which Duane again began waving his arm and shaking his head.

Jeanette waved at him in a dismissive gesture, and smiling wryly she turned her back to him. "I'll be wearing a red overcoat, and carrying a white purse. See you at eight," she offered. And turning back to face Duane, she dropped the phone into its resting place.

When she looked back at her friend he was scowling and shaking his head. "Are you nuts?" he asked, barely controlling his anger. "You don't know that guy from Adam! Suppose..."

"Easy there," she smiled. "I don't own a red coat either. I may be crazy, but I'm not stupid."

Duane relaxed, if only slightly, and smiled thinly. "Then you're not going to meet him?" he said with a sigh.

"Oh, I fully intend on being there," she offered coyly. "but he won't know it. And right now, I'm going to take a shower. After all, we *are* going out tonight." That said, she turned and hustled down the hall and into her bedroom.

Duane stood there for a second, stunned by the realization of what he'd gotten himself into. Then, making his way into the sitting room, he plopped himself down in a chair, and sipped at his freshly made martini. This one was a double.

CHAPTER SIX

Looking at his watch, Duane saw that it was 7:15. In the
kitchen he could hear the sounds of Jeanette doing the dishes
they'd used for dinner. As he settled back into the overstuffed
chair a warm and welcomed calm replaced the tension that had
threatened to ruin an otherwise wonderful meal. And as he stared
into the fire, he drifted off into his memory.

As the years peeled slowly back, he found himself in the
living room of his parent's apartment. It was the home that they
had moved to when his father had been transferred to Boston
from a small town in Maryland with a sizable raise. His father
never made it home for dinner anymore. Along with the raise
had come longer hours, and along with the hours had come
bigger headaches.

"D, you get your lazy butt out here and help your sister with
these dishes!" his mother called from the kitchen.

"Can't Mom, tonight's the game. Dad got some tickets for me
and Kevin from work. If I don't get goin' now we'll miss the tip
off."

His mother appeared in the archway that connected the two
rooms. Hands on hips, she was shaking her head, and desperately

trying to scowl disapprovingly at her son. "On a school night, boy? Just wait'll that old man of yours gets home."

"Aw, Mom. It's the Celtics and the Sixers. It's a real important game," the boy exhorted.

"Aren't they *all*?" She said rolling her eyes. "Well, you best be goin', then. But if I have my way, this is the last school night you'll be spendin' on the streets of Boston."

Duane hopped up from his seat in his father's overstuffed chair, bounced across the room, and planted a heavy one on his mother's cheek.

"You got money, boy?" She asked, knowing full well that he didn't.

Sheepishly, he shook his head, all the while staring at the tops of his sneakers.

His mother pulled a twenty dollar bill out of the pocket of her apron, and stuffed it into his front pocket. "Now you keep your hand in that pocket, boy. I didn't give you that so some pick-pocket could buy a bottle with it!"

Giving her a huge hug, Duane grabbed his coat and headed for the door.

"Mama, that's not fair! D' never has to do the dishes!" He heard his sister whine.

"You just hush up, girl. He'll do'em tomorrow night."

As the door slammed behind him, he heard his mother call out one last time. "D, you *wear* that coat, boy. It wasn't meant to be carried."

The words stopped him in his tracks, and slipping on his coat he raced for the stairs. This was going to be a great night. This was the only thing he liked about his father's new job, or living in Boston for that matter. His company always had great seats for all the major sporting events.

It had been that night that he had come home to find his mother and sister sitting in the living room crying. He looked immediately to his father's chair. There was no folded newspaper on the seat. No ever-present highball glass on the end table. And no half smoked cigar left to go out by itself. It was then that he realized something was dreadfully wrong. His father never came home again.

"Ready to go? It's almost seven thirty."

Her voice caused his head to snap in her direction. There, in the archway that connected the living room and kitchen via the foyer, she was standing in her apron, hands on hips. For a millisecond, she was his mother.

His memories instantly retreated into their musty hiding places. The spot reserved for teddy bears, high school love letters, and the smell of Nana's house on Thanksgiving. For a second he was disappointed. But then he realized that the memories that were soon to follow were the ones of the funeral. And those, he could well do without.

"Yeah, I'm ready when you are," he said, prying himself out of her overstuffed chair.

"Nice chair. he offered, patting at the back of the seat. "My dad used to have one just like it."

"I know," she said gently, "You tell me every time you sit in it."

Grabbing his coat, he began to make his way across the room to join her. And at that, she skittered off to get her own. Before leaving the room, he turned and looked back into the barely glowing embers of the fire, and then stole another look at the chair. Pulling a newspaper out of his coat pocket, he folded it once and tossed it onto the seat. Then, shaking out the cobwebs, he walked into the foyer to meet her at the head of the stairs.

*****

The walk to The Coaches Box was only about five blocks. But when they turned the corner onto Brookline Ave., leaving the relatively close confines of Kenmore Square, the crisp fall wind gusted in their faces. The sounds of the roaring engines from the turnpike in the distance added to the wind tunnel effect that would punish them with ever increasing intensity until they made the length of the overpass a quarter mile ahead.

The battering wind died down once they had reached the clutch of squat buildings that make up the area surrounding

Fenway Park; but, once pleasurable, the briskness of autumn had settled in for what, it seemed, would be a long and inconveniently cold night.

When they rounded the corner onto Yawkey Way, The Coaches Box was in view. Set on the ground floor of the buildings across the street from the ball field, the very sight of the seedy little bar caused Jeanette to feel instantly self-conscious for her choice in clothing. This place was definitely jeans and tee shirt apropos. Dressed in a casual skirt and blouse, and what with Duane still dressed in his suit from work, the two would most certainly stand out like a bride at a bullfight.

Upon entering the bar, they could see that they would have little trouble picking Skip Phillips out of the crowd. There were only eleven other people in the place. Twelve by count, but the one passed out in the corner booth almost certainly wasn't him. As they crossed the gritty tile floor, their feet sticking and ripping free with every step, Jeanette scoped out the rest of the patrons. Picking a table at the front of the room, which gave them a pretty good view of virtually every seat in the house, Jeanette took a seat. Only then did she realize that every eye in the house was on them. As she had assumed, their attire lent little credence to their charade as casual customers. Thankfully, and much to the delight of the regulars, Bruin defenseman Ray Bourque picked that moment to drive a slap shot from the point past Canadiens goalie Patrick Roy, diverting all attention back to the T.V. set over the bar.

Duane started to sit before he realized that people didn't
here to be waited on, they came here to drink. "What'll you
have?" he asked. Adding, "Better make it a beer, I don't think I'd
trust the dishwasher."

Jeanette followed his eyes to the other end of the room. There,
the drunk who had been asleep in the corner was making his way
toward a door at the end of the bar in unsteady fashion, totally
engrossed in a futile effort at tying a filthy apron. "Beer would
be fine," she smirked.

As far as she could tell, there were two couples at a booth, and
then four guys at the bar who seemed to know each other.
Having narrowed it down to one of three men seated at the other
end of the bar, they promptly got up and left together. Checking
her wrist for the time she cursed. "Damn!" She whispered,
realizing she had again forgotten to pick up her watch. Oh well,
she thought, if he's not here, I guess it doesn't matter what time it
is.

When he returned to the table, Duane placed a long neck
bottle in front of her; no glass. Immediately he recognized the
anxious look on her face, and looking to his watch, he then
turned it around, sticking it in her face. "It's only 8:04. Give the
guy a chance, will ya?" He said, hoisting up his beer for a toast.

Smiling, Jeanette obliged. But before Duane could put the
bottle to his lips, a flit of motion outside the window caught his

eered out the window into the poorly lighted

man hustling toward the bar from across the

our boy now," he said, motioning to the window

wĩu...   d. As the man approached the doorway to the bar he

stopped short of entering and looked back over his shoulder

toward the corner. The two followed his gaze and became aware

of someone rounding the corner on the other side of the street.

As the person passed under the street lamp, they could hear

the engine of a car fire to life directly across the street. Jeanette

squinted through the smoke stained window to try and get a

better look at the individual who was approaching as the driver

of the car hit the lights, pulled out, and headed down the road.

The woman in the waist length coat was stepping of the curb to

cross, but thought better of it, and she stopped to allow the car to

pass.

The driver of the vehicle hit the high beams and began to

pick up speed rapidly, and the woman lifted her hand to shield

her eyes from the glare of the headlights. But as the vehicle

approached her it suddenly veered to the right, and the woman,

paralyzed with fear, let her hand drop to her side.

When her mouth fell open, Duane and Jeanette could hear a

faint scream, and they watched in horror as the car struck her

with such intensity that it sent her hurtling through the air.

Stopping suddenly when she struck the lamp post, the woman's

twisted body then fell, face first, into the street; only to be crushed and dragged under the wheels of the black sedan as it sped around the corner of Brookline Ave. and out of sight.

The man outside didn't wait around. By the time the victim hit the ground, he had already hit full stride in the opposite direction down Yawkey Way.

Jeanette and Duane, numbed by the brutality of the seemingly senseless act of violence they had just witnessed, sat, their eyes transfixed on the battered body that lay on the avenue. Then, as if on command, they both hopped up and headed for the door. Duane shouted to the bartender, "Call an ambulance, someone's been hit!"

As he hit the sidewalk, Duane shot a look down Yawkey Way. Doing so, he was just in time to see the man who had watched the carnage with them round the corner, a full three blocks away. Realizing that a chase would be useless, he headed out into the street to try and cut off Jeanette before she reached the ugly scene that awaited them.

Halfway across the street he caught up with her, grabbing her by the shoulder and spinning her around. "Get back inside!" He ordered. But shaking him off, she turned and continued to run toward the fallen woman. Suddenly, she tripped, falling hard to the ground, the road ripping into her exposed knees; but scrambling to her feet, she limped to the corner, and leaned against the lamp post. Then, looking back toward Duane,

Jeanette saw what it was she had tripped over. Duane stood in the middle of the street, staring down at the white purse that lay at his feet.

She could feel her body begin to tremble as a small crowd began to gather around her. One of the patrons, claiming that he was a police officer, took charge of the situation. And heading out into the Avenue, he directed a car around the body. Then, almost as an afterthought, he took the woman's pulse then tossed his jacket over her face.

When Duane reached Jeanette, she felt the warm drink of nausea rise from her stomach. Tears were running down her face, as the blood from her knees ran down her legs. She felt as though she was going to faint. And as her knees began to give out, she felt Duane scoop her off her feet, heading back across the street to the bar.

*****

As she came to, she screamed at the horrible vision that lingered before her subconscious mind's eye. Then, realizing she was lying down, she began to sit up, but the pain in her temples caused her to fall back onto the stretcher. The light that hung above her was blinding as she was encircled by a crowd of bobbing silhouettes.

That's it, she thought, this is my nightmare. But, contrary to the pattern of her dream, one of the figures above her leaned down to where she could make out his face. "Don't worry, Ms.

Tolby. You're gonna be just fine," the handsome young paramedic assured her. "You fainted. And I'm not surprised, after what you just saw. Those knees are gonna need some attention though. Maybe just a stitch or two," he added through a forced but well-practiced smile. And walking to the end of the stretcher, the man began to wheel her toward the door.

Jeanette sprung up to a sitting position, her head still pounding painfully. "Wait! Where's Duane?" She asked, the sound of near panic readily audible in her voice.

Suddenly, she felt a large hand grip her shoulder. Recoiling, she looked into the dark eyes that hung faceless amid large patches of blue and green. But once the spots caused by the bright lights dissipated, she saw Duane's face screwed up into a pained grimace, which he was unsuccessfully trying to hide.

"Duane, that could have been me!" she breathed.

"Yeah, it could've been anyone, Darlin'," he lied, putting a finger to her mouth, and easing her back onto the stretcher. "Right now, you just relax and lie back. You're gonna take a little ride and get those knees checked out."

Jeanette snatched at his wrist, pulling his hand to her breast. "Duane, you have to come with me," she gasped, a look of full blown terror in her eyes.

Duane, a bit shaken by her obvious distress, looked to the paramedic for help. "Sure. That'd be no problem at all," the young man offered, evidently misunderstanding Duane's plea for support.

Looking back to Jeanette, he bent down and brushed her hair from her face. But clasping even tighter on his hand, she continued to press. "Please, Duane? I'm-I'm scared to death of doctors," she wheezed, tears now running down her pale cheeks and onto the pillow.

"Of course I'll come," he nodded, "after all, I'm not going to let anyone undress you unless I can watch," he tried to joke. But his feeble attempt at humor couldn't even elicit as much as a chuckle from *him* this time. And as they loaded her into the ambulance, Jeanette, although headed for the dreaded hospital, couldn't help but feel lucky to be alive.

All the way to the hospital, Duane had his hands full trying to keep Jeanette calm. But once they arrived she began trembling like a frightened rabbit. Grabbing him by the wrist again, she begged for a reprieve. "Duane, this is all so silly," she began, her voice cracking. "I really feel much better now. All I need is a couple of Band-Aids and I'll be fine."

Her tears again began to run as they unloaded her stretcher and started pushing her toward the emergency room doors. Her grip tightening on Duane's arm with every step he took, she became more and more agitated.

"Duane, I can't go in there! Please, I'm begging you, you don't understand! **DON'T LET THEM TAKE ME IN THERE!**"

The paramedic pushed Duane aside, and as the doors slid open before her, Jeanette sat bolt upright, swinging her legs over the side of the stretcher. "God Damn It, I said **I- can't- go- IN THERE!**" she shouted again.

The two orderlies, who had been awaiting the arrival of the ambulance, joined the paramedic in trying to restrain her; as in her fear and frustration, she began to become physically aggressive. "YOU STUPID BASTARD, GET YOUR HANDS OFF OF ME!" she screamed, swinging a hard right cross at one of the orderlies, catching him just above the right eye. "LET ME GO, YOU SON OF A BITCH! NONE OF YOU UNDERSTAND! DUANE, PLEASE DON'T LET THEM DO THIS TO ME! HELP ME!"

The two orderlies were joined by another, and two nurses. And as they wrestled her back down onto the stretcher, Duane made a move to go to her assistance. It was a move, albeit well meant, which was stopped short by a night stick planted gently but firmly across his chest by the police officer on duty in the E.R. "Don't worry, friend," the cop soothed, "they won't hurt her."

But as they fastened the straps around her wrists, her tirade continued. "You can't do this to me, you fuckin' bastards! I'll sue every God damn one of you!" She seethed between her teeth, "I'LL SCRATCH YOUR FUCKIN' EYES OUT, YOU BITCH!"

As the orderlies cinched up the final leg restraint, one of the nurses exposed a large hypodermic syringe and jammed it home into Jeanette's shoulder, causing a spine tingling "**NOOOO**...." to escape her lips.

Within seconds the battle was over and Jeanette fell silent. Although Duane could tell she was still at least semi-conscious because her lips were still moving, though no audible sound was coming from them. Then the nurses and orderlies talked quietly among themselves for a moment and dispersed, leaving only one nurse to wheel her to the examination room.

Duane, realizing he'd been holding his breath through the whole shocking exhibition of terror he'd just witnessed finally let the air drain out of his lungs.

He looked around the lobby, only to see that every eye in the place was on him. Some of them looked on compassionately, but most with either puzzlement or disgust. "Probably her pimp!" He heard one woman say to her friend. "Probably gave her some bad dope or something." Glaring spitefully at the woman, he sat down. The woman, shaking her head in disgust, went back to her magazine. And as the noise level rose back up to normal, everyone else went back about their own business as well.

*****

The lights whizzed past above her as the squeaking of the wheels on the gurney echoed back to her off the tile walls of the corridor. She could feel her heart pounding at her chest, the terror of her nightmare so much more intense. But this time it was really happening. She tried to speak, but no words came to her. This is insane, she thought, through a narcotic haze, what the hell are they doing to me? The nurse pushing the gurney said something to her. But it was only gibberish; she couldn't make sense of it.

Walking now to the side of the stretcher, the nurse pulled it to a stop. Then, turning it, she pushed it into a small room, a fully lighted room. This wasn't anything like her dream. The nurse then placed a mask over her mouth and nose. At first she tried to struggle but it was no use, she was far too weak. As she lost consciousness, the nurse leaned down, stroked her hair, and spoke slowly and clearly. "Everything is going to be fine. You just go ahead to sleep, sweetheart."

*****

Duane sat thumbing through an old issue of Yankee Magazine, for no better reason than avoiding eye contact with anyone that might still be looking at him. Then, hearing the sound of footsteps stopping immediately in front of him, he looked up slowly, only to see a shabby trench coat, then a perfunctory smile, and searing blue eyes which hung in an age grizzled face. All of which was topped by a badly wrinkled fedora.

"Evening, Mr. Avon," O'Hare rasped, "mind if I join you?" Without waiting for an answer, he pushed a magazine aside and took the seat next to him.

"Something I can help you with, Lieutenant?" Duane breathed, crossing his legs and resuming his reading.

Reaching over, O'Hare relieved him of his magazine. "Yeah, you can give me your attention for starters," the officer bristled, his smile receding into a lipless frown. "Then maybe you can tell me why it is that every time I try to do my job I see your face? Can you explain that? I sure as hell can't."

Picking up another magazine, Duane smiled sarcastically. "You're just lucky, I guess," he scoffed.

O'Hare reached out and ripped the magazine out of his hands and tossed it into the seat next to him. Glaring at the cop, Duane started to get to his feet. But just then, Officer Burton stepped in front of him from out of nowhere, placing a forceful hand on his shoulder.

Duane immediately took the hint, and settling back down he turned a sardonic eye on the Lieutenant.

"Listen, if you think I did something wrong, then why don't you just arrest me and get it over with?" He said, sticking his fists out, palms up.

"No! You listen!" O'Hare growled, "if I thought you did something, I'd already have your ass locked up so tight you'd need a crow bar to crap!" Then, looking around himself self-consciously and lowering his voice, the cop continued, "all I know is that I got three bodies, and every time I turn around you and that woman are there! Now why don't you tell me just what I *am* supposed to think?"

Duane exhaled heavily, resigning himself to the circumstances. "Look, I don't know any more about all this than you do. I swear it. And besides, what does what happened tonight have to do with *you*? I mean, somebody got hit by a car, unfortunate, sure, but hardly a case for homicide."

O'Hare's expression lightened a bit as he pushed his hat back and rubbed briskly at his whiskered chin. "You know, that's what I thought too," the cop began," but then we get this phone call from some guy in a panic. He doesn't give us a name or anything, just tells us he saw the whole thing. Then he tells us this lady was goin' to meet him, and that the whole thing has to do with the Fairelane murder. *Murder*, he says. Then he gives us this phone number and hangs up. The whole thing happened so fast, we couldn't even get a trace on it." O'Hare fell silent and shook his head as Duane sneaked a look at the phone number on the piece of paper he'd pulled out of his pocket.

"Well I don't know where he got that number, but it's Jeanette's, all right. I just went out for a drink with her, that's all," he lied. "The rest you're gonna have to take up with her."

"Yeah, maybe I'll do that," the Lieutenant said standing up slowly. Smiling what Duane recognized as a genuine smile, he put his hand on the younger man's shoulder. "Listen, Duane. I'm beginning to think I got you all wrong. I don't want to bust your balls any more than I want you to bust mine, but if you hear anything, and I'm not asking you to spy on your friend for me, but if you do, could you give me a call at this number?" He asked, holding out a business card.

Duane looked up into the cops eyes, and taking the card, he stuck it in his breast pocket and nodded.

"Mr. Avon?" A feminine voice called out from the nurse's station. Standing, he stuck his hand out. "You got it, Lieutenant," he agreed, shaking the man's hand. "Right here," he called to the nurse, raising his hand and heading across the waiting room. O'Hare watched intently as Duane made his way across the room.

"Burton," he snapped, never taking his eyes off Duane.

"Right here, sir," the younger officer answered smartly.

"I want somebody on his ass every second. No screw ups!"

"Got it," Burton said, "And the girl?"

O'Hare just nodded slowly, as he turned and headed toward the doors rubbing his chin. Then, turning up his collar, he disappeared out into the parking lot.

"Mr. Avon, we're going to need a little information on Ms. Tolby," the nurse said "Do you think you can help us out?"

"I'll do what I can," Duane smiled. "Is there something wrong?"

"Oh, no, but the doctor would like to keep her over night. It seems she's experiencing some degree of shock. And frankly, after what she saw, I'm not surprised. But just the same we'd like to keep an eye on her for the night, just for safety's sake."

Duane smiled half-heartedly. The last thing he felt like doing was answering more questions. But under the circumstances, he really had no choice. "Shoot," he allowed. And the nurse didn't disappoint.

*****

Once he had answered what questions he could for the nurse, Duane was told that Jeanette had already been moved upstairs to the eleventh floor, and that if he didn't stay too long, he could go up and visit with her briefly. Although, he was told, not to expect too much, for having been sedated she would, at best, drift in and out. Still, Duane decided to go up and wish her a good night and see if she needed anything.

Stepping out of the elevator onto the eleventh floor, he found himself directly in front of the seemingly empty nurse's station. "Mr. Avon?" A voice asked from nowhere.

"Yes...?" he said uncertainly, being instinctively drawn to the abandoned desk.

"Down here," the nurse said, "I'll be right with you."

Rising to his toes, Duane leaned on the counter and looked down on the other side of the desk. There he saw, on her knees, a nurse cleaning up what was left of a shattered coffee mug, a telephone lodged between her hunched shoulder and her ear. "Hi, Tammy," the woman continued, offering Duane a pleasant, albeit stress-filled smile. "This is Donna up on eleven. How are you guys staffed down there? Great! Well listen, Jocelyn just called and she says she can't come in tonight... Yeah, again!... The problem is Rebecca already has the night off, and I'm up here all alone... Yeah, and I've got to pick up my son twenty five minutes ago. Do you think it would be possible for you to sacrifice a nurse to cover the twelve to seven, I'd stay but I really can't. Lord knows I could use the money, bu-... Oh, could you? You're a life saver, I owe you big for this... No, no, nothing serious, a couple of overnights, and surgery preps. All you'd have to do is one round at 1:30 and answer any call-lights... Great! I'll tell you what, if you're going to head up now, I'm going to get out of here... Yeah... thanks a million, hon. See ya... Yup, bye." Cradling the phone, the nurse turned her attention to a somewhat irritated Duane as she stood up and pulled her coat on. "I'm sorry Mr. Avon. They called ahead from downstairs and told me you were coming up. Miss Tolby is in 1109, right down there on the right."

Duane nodded obligatorily, and headed down the hall toward Jeanette's room as the nurse rounded the desk and pushed the down button for the elevator. "Oh, Mr. Avon, please be brief, she needs her sleep more than anything else," the nurse called after him. And half turning around, Duane offered a small wave over his shoulder.

When he reached her door the elevator bell rang once again, and Duane barely caught a glance of the nurse stepping off the elevator as he slipped into the room undetected. Christ, he thought, some security. No one even knows I'm here. Then, turning to face the single bed, he was nearly overcome by the sight of Jeanette. God, she looks like hell! He thought. She was asleep, but her rigid attitude bore the unnerving semblance of death. As he made his way to her bedside, he wasn't sure if it was just the fact that she was in a hospital bed, or if it was that foolish stark white light that hangs above the head of every hospital bed and makes everyone look dead. But, after all, it was just her knee. At any rate, at least it was a private room, that way he wouldn't be bothering anyone else, and no one would be tempted to throw him out. Even if they *did* know he was here.

Sitting down in the chair next to the bed, he reached out to push her hair out of her face. But the second he touched her, her eyes snapped open, and all the terror he had seen in them downstairs was still burning as strongly as it had before. Although it lasted only one agonizing second, that second was one of the longest of his life. Then, thankfully, under their own weight, her eyelids slid to a near closed position.

"How you feeling?" he asked, patting her hand. In doing so, he became aware of the strap which was wrapped snugly about her wrist.

"Duane?" she whispered, staring straight ahead.

"I'm right here, sugar," he said, swallowing at the huge lump he felt forming in his throat. He had never seen her looking like this before. She was usually so competent, so impeccable. Now she looked so weak and frail, so.... deranged.

"Duane," she began again, smacking at her lips for saliva that had long ago been robbed by her medication. "Duane, they want to hurt me, here," she said, a tear falling to her pillow.

"Don't be silly. This is a hospital, they're here to help you," he offered reassuringly.

"But I'm-I'm scared, Duane. I'm scared of doctors, scared of hospitals... very scared."

Suddenly, he realized that she didn't have any hysterical shock. She was, just as she'd said, simply terrified of doctors. That whole scene downstairs, and in the ambulance, was caused by some phobia. It was simply an absolute terror that, no matter how ridiculous to him or anyone else, was very real and life threatening to her.

Leaning over her, he kissed her forehead. "Don't you worry, sweetheart, ol' Duane is going to stay right here with you. I won't let anything happen to you. Now try to get some sleep."

As her eyes fell completely closed, in a tiny and weak voice, she whispered, "Don't let them hurt me. I'm scared they'll hurt me...." Her voice faded away as her chest heaved with a sigh. As her breathing became more rhythmic, Duane pulled his chair closer, never letting go of her hand.

Sitting, back erect, he gave her hand a gentle squeeze. "Don't you worry," he whispered, "ol' Duane is gonna stay right here."

CHAPTER SEVEN

When Duane unconsciously tried to twist his 6'3" frame into a comfortable position in the bedside chair, his elbow found the wooden armrest with a dull thud. With that his eyes twitched open and a sharp pain shot to his shoulder . "Ow, shit! Jesus Christ!" He mumbled angrily, and rubbing frantically at the wounded joint, he felt a prickly, burning sensation rush down his forearm to his fingertips.

While the pins and needles attacking his nerves subsided he blinked the sleep from his eyes only to realize that he wasn't at home. In a rush of revelation he remembered where he was, and why. He also recalled having hidden in the bathroom when the nurse had made her rounds earlier this morning. Then, looking over at Jeanette, and then back to his watch, he found why it was that he had still been sleeping. It was only 4:56.

He stood slowly, so as not to injure any more of his already aching parts, and walked stiffly to the window. Then, pulling back the shade slightly, he peered out over the half sleeping city as the first stirrings of a new day breathed life into otherwise abandoned streets. The black and starless October sky reached out over the harbor, where, on the horizon, night was unwillingly beginning to release its grip on the city, giving way to a slate gray morning.

Slipping into the private john, Duane washed up a bit, and made himself as presentable as possible under the circumstances. Somehow, he thought, I have to get Jeanette out of here. Another incident like last night and they may be inclined to move her into permanent residence over in "Crayola Central."

As he straightened his tie and smoothed his coat, the beginnings of a plan already formulating in his head, he opened the door and stole silently to Jeanette's bed. Prodding her gently, he whispered in her ear. "Jeanette, wake up. You gotta wake up."

Her eyes jerked open as if a bell had gone off inside her head. Looking up at him as though she didn't recognize him, she yanked at the straps that still held her wrists, and set her jaw to scream. Quickly covering her mouth with his hand he spoke softly, but sternly. "Jeanette, it's all right. It's me, Duane! Don't scream sweetheart!" Her eyes flickered madly as she continued to wrestle with the straps on her arms. "Listen to me," Duane implored, "I'm going to get you out of here, but you've got to help me. And you can't act crazy or they'll never let you out. Understand?"

Nodding distractedly, she relaxed ever so slightly, her eyes still burning with fear.

Duane nodded, letting go of her mouth. "Now, I'll be back in two minutes, and when I come back you follow my lead. You with me?"

Jeanette nodded her agreement, albeit pendulously, and Duane, reasonably satisfied that he had gotten through to her, headed out of the room. But as he approached the door, it suddenly swung in toward him, the lights clicking on. And there stood the dictionary definition of a charge nurse. Two-Fifty if she was a pound, she was the living embodiment of Attila the good humor man. Just as her thick lips began to form a word, and as she set her chins to speak, Duane got the drop on her, lighting into a tirade that knocked her back a step.

"Nurse!" he began, summoning every ounce of venom he could muster. "Will you please try to explain to me just what the hell is going on here? If you don't get these restraints off my patient immediately, we'll sue you, this hospital, and everyone even remotely connected with inflicting this... this psychological torture on her!"

"Now wait a minute!" The nurse shot back, rallying her nerve. "What do you mean *your* patient? She's Doc-"

Sticking his finger in her face, Duane gnashed his teeth and cut her off, "Yes, *my* patient! I've been treating this poor woman for three years for an acute fear of doctors and hospitals! Six years ago she lost her mother in a case of proven medical malpractice, and just last week we had a major breakthrough. She went to the dentist for the first time in those six years! Six!" he growled, "And now, you and the rest of your inane accomplices have probably sent us right back to square one!"

Jeanette watched with amazement as Duane walked to the bed offering her a smile and a wink, and began working on one of the straps on her arms. "Let's go," he urged, looking at the badge on the nurse's ample bosom. "Walker!" he spit.

"Doctor, I assure you, no one had any idea she had a psychological problem. She didn't say anything to anyone!" The nurse said working at the other strap.

"Of course she didn't! She was probably hysterical, correct?" The nurse nodded, moving to release the leg strap. "Well that's just terrific!" He railed. "Get her clothes!"

Nurse Walker set her jaw indignantly. "I'm sorry, Doctor, I can't do that. This is all highly irregular."

Duane eyed her with his first look of uncertainty. Then, looking around, he saw the telephone on the table, and picked it up, placing it on Jeanette's stomach. "There you go Jen. Ring up your dad for me, will you," and looking back to the nurse, he offered, "we'll just see about this!"

Jeanette, beginning to enjoy the game, sneered at the nurse and dialed her own telephone number. But as she put the phone to her ear, Duane took it away from her and listened to it ring three times while tapping his foot impatiently.

Then, just as Nurse Walker looked to be questioning his resolve, Duane began acting again. "Hello, Judge Tolby, Stan Jefferson calling. I'm sorry to bother you so early, but it seems we have a bit of a problem down here at Boston City Hospital....

No, no. There's no need of that, she's fine.... Well, frankly sir, I'm not quite sure what she's doing here."

Pulling the sheet down, the nurse pointed to Jeanette's knee, then rushed to the closet, and began taking Jeanette's clothes out and laying them on the bed. Duane turned his back and dropped his voice as the nurse helped her on with her clothes.

"Alright, ready to go," Walker chirped, as merrily as possible under the circumstances.

Duane turned back around and nodded, smiling arrogantly. "Yessir, I'll bring her directly home. We'll see you later. Oh, and sir, Nurse Walker has been a huge help with all of this... No, sir, that's not my area of expertise. After all you're the lawyer. Good morning, sir."

Hanging up the phone, Duane took Jeanette by the arm and led her out of the room, Nurse Walker hot on their heels. "Dr. Jefferson, will you be signing Ms. Tolby out?" She asked sheepishly.

"Oh, no. The judge will be here very shortly to take care of that," he said, pushing the down button on the elevator. The doors opened immediately and stepping in the two turned to face the woman and Duane smiled.

"But-" she said as the doors began to close.

"Good day, ma'am," Duane grinned, draping his arm around Jeanette.

Once the doors had closed, Jeanette threw her arms around his neck and began to cry.

"You just hold on, babe. We're almost outta here," he soothed, pushing the stop button to cancel the stop he had inadvertently scheduled for the first floor. Pushing B, the lift jerked to life and continued down. As they approached the lobby stop, Duane held his breath. But, thankfully they descended right past it.

Seconds later, the doors peeled back on the now quiet E.R. and exiting the elevator, they made a Beeline for the doors and the parking lot beyond. They did so without incident, and when they stepped out into the early morning chill, Duane checked his watch. It was 5:30. The most horrifying forty minutes of his life behind him, he wondered silently if he'd done the right thing.

*****

Twenty-five minutes later, as they climbed the steps of 478 Commonwealth Ave., Jeanette uttered her first words since they'd left the hospital. "Duane, I-I don't know what to say," she began almost apologetically, "I've been scared to death of doctors since I was about 15 and I don't know why, it's just-"

"Wait a minute," he interrupted, "you mean you act like that every time you go to the doctor?" Jeanette just looked down at the stoop and shrugged her shoulders. "Whoa," he said, "you don't mean to tell me you haven't been to the doctor since you were 15, do you?"

"Oh, no, we used to have checkups all the time at the state home. And then, when I was seventeen, I got a physical when I was discharged."

Duane looked at her in disbelief. "You haven't had as much as a physical in seventeen years?" He asked.

"Duane, please just open the door, I'm freezing," she begged.

When he did, Jeanette slipped by him and bounded up the stairs into the bathroom. By the time he reached the head of the stairs he could hear the shower running, so shaking his head he made his way across the hall into the kitchen. The questions could wait, he figured. What he really needed now was a good strong cup of coffee and someplace to stretch his legs out.

As Jeanette finished drying her hair, she looked into the foggy mirror. Then, wiping it clear, she leaned over the sink and looked into the face that stared back at her. "Damn! I thought all of this crap was behind me," she whispered. And after a long look she decided it was inevitable. She had to go back into therapy. If not only so that she could go to the doctor if necessary, but so she could get rid of the damn nightmares.

Bracing herself against what she knew was to come, she threw on her robe and prepared herself for the arduous question and answer session that she was sure Duane had planned for her.

Pasting on a relaxed looking smile, she unlocked the door, and exited into the hallway. Stopping, she listened but heard nothing. So following the smell of freshly brewed coffee, she silently stole into the kitchen, poured herself a cup, and made her way to the front sitting room to confront Duane's curiosity.

Taking a deep breath, she swept into the room as though she were entering a cotillion, only to find Duane asleep on the couch.

Crossing the room, she reached down to shake him. But thinking better of it, she rushed back out into the kitchen and picked up the phone book. Sliding in behind the breakfast bar, she banged her knee, wincing at the painful reminder of the three stitches it had taken to close the wound. And wiping a tear of pain from her eye, she began what she assumed would be a long drawn out process. She had to find Billy's lead singer's number. Gary was a self-important son of a bitch, not to mention the fact that he was a Neanderthal, macho slug, butshe had some questions that he might be able to answer. The first of which was, who the hell is Skip Phillips?

She was pleasantly surprised to find that there were only two G. Stricktlands in the inner city area. Circling them, she picked up the phone, and began to dial. But as the phone on the other end began to ring, her eye caught the calendar on the fridge. In big red letters, she'd written, FUNERAL. "Oh, Christ! It's Saturday!" she gasped. And hanging up the phone, she looked instinctively to her bare wrist. Jumping to her feet, she headed for the sitting room, and as she entered the hallway, the clock chimed seven.

"Duane! Duane, wake up!" she fumed, shaking him desperately. She'd been trying to wake him every ten minutes for a half an hour, to no avail.

"All right! All right! I'm up!" Came the agitated reply, muffled, as it was through a throw pillow.

Grabbing the pillow, she yanked it away from his face. "Oh no! Not this time! I've been trying to wake you for an hour!" She lied. And grabbing him by the collar, she pulled him up into a sitting position. "*Now*, you're up!" She said, handing him a cup of coffee.

Setting the cup on the end table, he rubbed at his eyes and attempted to shake the last trace of another stint of bad sleep out of his head. "God, what time is it?" he asked blearily.

"It's seven thirty," Jeanette said. "And the funeral is at ten."

Standing, Duane ignored her answer, shooting another question at her. "Has anyone called?"

"No, why?"

Before answering, he walked to the window and looked down into the street. "No cops have been here?"

"No," Jeanette chuckled, "what would they want *here*?"

Duane shook his head in disbelief and eyed her derisively. "Oh nothing, It just so happens that you're a witness to what might have been a murder. Not to mention that you practically broke out of the hospital this morning with some guy who was impersonating a doctor."

"Well I'll just call them and tell them where I am," she said in a tone that was much too nonchalant and striding to the phone. "If they want to talk to me, they can damn well do it here."

"Ah, don't bother," Duane said, staring out the window, "if I'm not mistaken, that's our old friend Burton down there in the green Chevy."

Walking to his side, Jeanette followed his gaze to the street below. There, twenty yards down and across the street from her brownstone, sat Detective Burton.

Finishing off his coffee, the cop rolled down his window and deposited the cup in the gutter, then rolled it back up, said something to the young cop sitting next to him, and settled in, glancing up toward them.

"Why doesn't he just come in?" She asked as the two stepped back from the window.

"I don't know," Duane shrugged, rubbing at his temple. "But you best just get ready. We'll try to make it to my place without them seeing us."

Duane watched her limp out of the room and turned his attention back to the green car. Pulling up a chair he re-positioned himself between the window frame and the drapes; there he was out of sight of the street and officer Burton, who rolled his window down a crack to dispose of the wax paper which had held his doughnut.

*****

"So you just let 'em waltz outta here like they were goin' out for coffee?" O'Hare growled at the nurse.

The woman, who until then had been sitting head down to hide her flushed cheeks, looked up and wiped a tear from her bloodshot eyes.

"Well, I didn't think-"

"Oh Christ, call the papers, she didn't think!"

"That will be quite enough, Lieutenant!" Snapped the chief resident. Standing up behind his desk, he glared malevolently at O'Hare. "If you're quite through with Nurse Walker, she *does* have a job to do!"

Turning away, the cop pushed his hat back on his head. "Yeah, yeah, she can go," he conceded. But as the woman reached the door he turned to face her. "Nurse Walker, listen I -" His apology was cut short as she exited the room, slamming the door between them.

The old doctor walked from behind his desk glowering at the Lieutenant. "I know you think I'm just an old man," he spit, "and that I am. But more importantly, it just so happens that I am also Chief Attending Physician of this hospital. And as such, my time is in great demand. So if you'd be so kind as to show yourself out, maybe someone besides you will be able to get some work done today."

Walking to the door, O'Hare turned back to face the aged doctor, who was lowering himself into his chair to give his wobbly legs a rest. Tipping his hat, he smiled. "You have a good day now. And thanks for all your help, Doctor Tunney."

The elder Tunney simply waved him out the door without so much as a glance, and went back to his work.

O'Hare buttoned up his coat against the biting wind as he made his way to his car. He always hated it when ordinary citizens got themselves tangled up in police business. It's tough enough out here, he thought, without a bunch of amateurs tripping over themselves and getting into more than they can handle. The problem was obvious, but there was little or nothing he could do about it. As long as they didn't break any laws, people could put themselves in as much danger as they wanted, and be it simply for the excitement, or just because they were too foolish to know better, they would continue to do so. Unfortunately, it was still up to him to protect them. Not only from whichever scum bag or lunatic it was they decided to pit themselves against; but from their own inability to understand the danger of doing so. The criminal mind, he knew, is a swirling shit-storm of misdirected emotion, fueled in equal parts by greed, desperation, fear, and the exhilaration attained through the commission of a crime. And eventually, when their feet were in the fire, it all boiled down to fear. And fear can make people do some ugly things.

As he pulled out of the parking lot, the lieutenant came to a decision. He would try once more to persuade these two cop wannabes that his job would be a lot easier if they'd just get out of his way and let him do it. After that he would let the chips fall where they may and simply wash his hands of responsibility for their safety. After all, there were innocent people getting killed out there.,ad he couldn't let his investigation suffer because of their disregard for their own welfare. This bastard had to be stopped before he began to enjoy this. Every minute he wasted, every miscalculation or useless piece of evidence he considered could cost another life. A life *he* would ultimately feel responsible for until the son of a bitch was caught.

Detective Burton had just shoved his third coffee cup out through the thin crack above his window, and as Duane watched him, Jeanette, limping more perceptibly now, entered the room from the hallway behind him.

"Well, what do you think? It's not too low cut for a funeral, is it?"

"No. No, it's fine," Duane dismissed, without so much as a glance. "Doesn't this guy ever go to the bathroom? Jesus, he's had that young guy get him about three cups of coffee so far."

As the words left Duane's mouth, Burton turned and said something to his young partner. And opening his door, he got out and leaned back in, pointing up to the window through which Duane had been watching him for the last twenty minutes. Then, closing the door, he crossed the street with a determined gait.

"Come on," Duane prompted, "This is our chance to get out of here." Grabbing his coat, he headed for the stairs.

When they reached the door, Duane stopped and looked back at Jeanette. "I hope you're ready. When we hit the sidewalk, we gotta move!"

Jeanette nodded. "Well, let's go, then."

"Let's wait 'til he gets his fly, down," he smiled sadistically, a glint of mischief in his eye.

Catching her somewhat off guard, Duane suddenly pushed the door open and hustled down the steps with Jeanette only a step and a half behind him.

The younger officer looked totally oblivious at first, but as they neared the street he did a classic double take and began fumbling for his portable radio. With that, Duane and Jeanette broke into a light jog and headed across the street.

They negotiated the Commonwealth Ave. traffic with ease, then sliced diagonally across the greenway that divided it from the one way traffic on Beacon Street. Now, the only way that the officers could follow them, other than on foot, would be to go up two full blocks, then come back through the massive bottle neck that always accompanied the traffic entering the square.

When they hit Beacon Street they were lucky enough to catch the light and continue on to Duane's building less than a block away. And once they'd made Duane's apartment, Jeanette took up a position next to the window to watch for Burton's green Chevy.

"Just give me ten minutes," Duane said, stripping as he crossed the living room toward the hall.

Ten minutes later, as promised, he emerged from the bathroom wearing nothing but a towel. "Two minutes," he piped, holding up two fingers with one hand and his towel with the other as he ran into his bedroom. In five he was back, dressed to the teeth in his impeccable way. "Ready? Let's go," he said.

Jeanette jumped up and followed him into the kitchen, watching as he pulled open a door that looked more like an ironing closet than an exit. Then, waving for her to follow him, he pushed aside the cobwebs and started down the narrow winding stairwell to the back alley behind his building. The ancient stairway was so steep, and each tread so narrow, that every step caused more pain in Jeanette's damaged knee than the one before. So much so, that by the time they reached the bottom of the stairs, what had once been a dull throbbing sensation, had now mutated into a searing stab of pain "Wait," she begged, her face distorted into a twisted grimace. "I have to stop for a minute."

Duane turned to scathe her with a burning stare. "Listen, you got me into this shit, and we can do it one of two ways," he began, the edge in his voice as sharp as his appearance, "we can either try to get to this funeral, or we can just wait here until O'Hare, shows up! The man isn't stupid! I'm sure he knows where I live! And the way I figure it we got until Burton finds a parking space before he and his little buddy stake out both doors! Now let's move!" His words stung Jeanette. In all the time she'd known him, he had never so much as raised his voice to her before. But, she realized, in all the time she'd known him, they had never run from the police either.

"Well, go on then," she spit, not sparing him any of her *own* disapproval.

Ignoring her rancor, he pushed the door open, looked both ways down the alley, and reached back for her arm to lead her out, but pushing his hand away, she gave him a slight shove. "Let's move!" She mimicked angrily. Without looking back, Duane stepped out into the alleyway and began jogging back toward Kenmore Square.

"Where are *you* going?" she asked. "Arlington Street is this way."

Stopping, he turned around and dangled his car keys. "What, do you want to walk the three miles from the church to the cemetery?"

Swallowing a bit of her wounded pride, and feeling more than a little foolish for taking what he'd said so personally, she shook her head. "No, of course not, I'm sorry," she gave in. Besides, she thought, they were in this together; and each of them was all the other had right now.

As they rolled to a stop at the end of the side street that abutted Beacon, she turned to him. But before she could even start her apology, he looked at her and smiled. "Forget it, sweetheart. We're both kind of jumpy. I'm sorry too. Now just sit back and relax. We'll get downtown in a couple of minutes and I'll buy you some breakfast. Then we'll head over to the church. Is that ok with you?" He asked disarmingly. And nodding silently, she looked wistfully out her window at nothing as they pulled out on to the main road.

When they stopped for the light at the intersection of

Commonwealth Ave. neither of them even noticed the large black

sedan that had begun following them as soon as they'd pulled
onto Beacon St. But when they made the U-turn onto the avenue,
and headed downtown toward Arlington St. and the Common, the
black sedan waited at the light for a few cars to sneak in between
them. Then it edged out into the flow of traffic and followed,
albeit at an inconspicuous distance. But follow, it did.

CHAPTER EIGHT

The service at the church had been tough for Jeanette. She hated funerals anyway, but being stuck up front, in the space usually reserved for family, had been even more unnerving. With each show of emotion, she had felt every eye in the sparse crowd on her, some sympathetically; some with the same kind of innocuous curiosity that makes people stare at the hideously deformed or severely mentally challenged. But as tough as it had been, at least one good thing had come of it. For on the way out of the church she had seen Gary Stricktland and asked him to join her for a cup of coffee after the graveside service. He had agreed, despite the fact that the two had never really cared for one another's company. And now, as the priest droned on about the celebration of the death of a twenty four year old kid, or the rebirth, as he so conveniently put it, her mind began to wander.

The wind whipped at her cheeks and the gray skies opened up, delivering the first real snow they'd seen since last winter. She could feel herself shivering slightly, but she didn't actually feel that cold, more numb really than anything else. Suddenly the drone stopped, and the crowd, so much smaller than she'd expected, began drifting away and, realizing the service was over, she snapped back to the moment and felt the single white rose in her hand which Duane had so thoughtfully bought for her. Raising the flower to her lips, she gave it a heartfelt kiss and placed it atop the coffin. "Goodbye, Billy," she whispered, a single tear escaping her eye only to roll down her cheek and drop on the casket as a final testimonial to her friend and confidant.

When they reached Duane's car Gary was waiting for them. "Where should we go?" He asked. " Let's make it somewhere with alcohol," he added, "I could really use a drink."

Contrary to her better judgment, Jeanette let Gary choose the spot, and once he had he looked at Duane sheepishly. "Hey, would you mind waitin' here for a second?" he asked. "I'm not so sure my shitbox is gonna start. No antifreeze." Duane nodded shortly. "Thanks, man. I owe ya," he offered, and headed off for his car, jamming his hands deep in his pockets, against the chill. As they stood in the cold, silently watching him make his way to his car, a noise from behind them caught their attention. It was the unmistakable sound of snow crunching beneath someone's feet. Turning in unison, they met the cold blue stare of Lieutenant O'Hare. "Nice touch," he croaked. "The rose, I mean."

Jeanette walked from the front of the car, but as she made a move to pass him he held out his hand to stop her. Looking him in the eye, she volunteered, "It was Duane's idea."

"Ahh, the good doctor has good taste," he said sarcastically. "I just hope he has good sense, as well." Turning his gaze on

Duane, he winked

"Look, you don't even know what went on there," he began. "The poor girl is scared to death of hospitals-"

"The poor girl?" Jeanette broke in. "God, you make me sound like some shoeless waif."

Duane raised his hand in front of him in an apologetic gesture but continued. " If I didn't get her out of there they would have drugged her silly, and that wouldn't have done anyone any good."

"Look," O'Hare said, "what went on at the hospital is of no concern to me. I don't deal in hospitals, I deal in morgues! And unless you two get clear of whatever the hell is goin' on here... Well let's just say we might be doin' some business!

"Is that supposed to be some sort of a threat?" Duane challenged.

At that O'Hare gritted his teeth and walked around the front of the car. Looking up into Duane's face he waited a second to regain his composure. Then, in his condescending way, he smiled and shook his head. "You don't get it, do you, son? I've got three dead bodies that, in some round the block way, are stuck together like Siamese triplets! I'm not out here playin' cops and robbers like you and the misses, here! I've seen enough dead bodies in the last thirty odd years to fill this place! And I don't feel like lookin' at any more than I have to! No, sir, this ain't no fuckin' game to me! So you two just get the Christ outta my nightmare and let me do my job, *capiche*?"

"You through?" Duane asked coldly.

The lieutenant turned and walked back around the car, stopping as he passed Jeanette and putting his hand on her shoulder. "I'm sorry about your friend," he said genuinely, "but if you want me to catch the son of a bitch that did this to him, first you're gonna have to get out of my way, and second, you're gonna have to talk some sense into your friend, there," and tipping his hat, he winked and headed for his car.

*****

Once they were back on the road, both of them sat silent for a few minutes thinking about what the lieutenant had said. Which was, Jeanette realized, exactly what he'd intended. But what he hadn't counted on was the strength of her resolve. She was going to find out what was going on here, and nothing he'd said was going to change that. Duane had been less than enthusiastic to begin with, and she'd be damned if she was going to let O'Hare talk him out of it.

"What are you thinking, Duane?" Jeanette asked, not really wanting to hear the answer. Shrugging his shoulders, Duane let the air run out of his lungs slowly. "I'm thinking maybe we should take O'Hare's advice and leave the detective work to the detectives," he sighed.

Jeanette felt her face flush slightly, and chewed at her thumbnail as she battled to control her temper. Then, suddenly, and without really meaning to, she challenged his integrity.

"Well forget how much this means to *me*," she began, her voice baring the distinct mark of disapproval, "but what about your promise to me? You did promise to help!"

"Maybe so," Duane shot back, "but I never promised to get *killed* for you."

"You just do whatever you have to do, then," she fumed, "but this is something I've wanted to do all my life, and I'm not about to let him or anyone else stop me!" Jeanette gasped once the words had left her mouth. She could feel Duane's astounded glare bore into her; but she didn't dare turn to meet his stare, humiliated at what she'd just admitted, not only to him, but to herself, as well.

"Is that what this is all about?" He asked with disbelief. "This is all about becoming some crime busting reporter?"

"Well maybe it is! Is that so horrible?" She shot back, still trying to come to grips with her self serving motivation. "And what difference does it make as long as we get to the bottom of this!"

"Well, let me tell you something, honey. Dead doesn't look good on a resume and I'm not going to be a part of it!" When he'd finished his say, Duane set his jaw and looked straight ahead as they approached the bar where they were to meet Gary. Pulling over, he put the car in park, but left the engine running and looked over at her, the anger in his eyes now little more than frustration. "Go ahead, win a Pulitzer Prize. Just don't get killed doing it," he said softly.

She pleaded with her eyes for him to come inside with her. But shaking his head slowly, he patted her hand. "You know I'll always be your friend," he said, "But I can't help you endanger your life for a story. It'd kill me to know I was a party to your suicide."

Nodding, Jeanette wiped a tear from her eye. And for a moment he thought he'd gotten through to her. Then suddenly, as if it were her last chance, she grabbed the door handle, swung it open, and hopped out onto the sidewalk.

"Jeanette, don't do it!" He shouted as the door slammed closed with a thud.

By the time he made a move to get out of the car, she was already disappearing down the stairs into the bar. Slamming at the steering wheel with the heel of his hand, he slapped the car into gear and tromped on the gas. Dumping the clutch, his car slid out into the flow of traffic, barely avoiding the large black sedan that was pulling in ahead of him.

*****

For a place that didn't serve lunch, the bar was surprisingly busy for mid-day on a Saturday. Ignoring the temptation to check her wrist for the time, she scanned the crowd to try and locate Gary. Then, looking to the corner, she saw him laughing and jawing with a group of people, only some of whom she recognized.

"Damn!" She said under her breath. She'd been hoping he'd

come alone. Waving, she made her way to the bar and ordered a Sea breeze, reasoning that at least the two fruit juices were good for breakfast.

When she reached the table, she bent down and whispered into Gary's ear. "I really intended for us to talk alone."

"Oh, sure, no problem, we'll get another table. Excuse us, guys," he said motioning to an emptying table in another corner.

Sitting down, Gary ordered another beer. "Look, I now you're worried about the band," he began. But holding up her hand, Jeanette cut him off mid-sentence. "That can wait, Gary. Right now all I'm concerned with is finding out who killed Billy, and why," she said.

Leaning back in his chair, Gary shook his head, his face a smug veil of condescension. "You wanna know who killed Billy?" He said arrogantly. "Well, honey, it was Dr. Nod and the horse lady did Billy boy in. Junk, heroin, you dig?" The waitress returned with his beer and Gary threw a five on her tray. "Keep it, doll," he said pompously, adding a smile that was made to melt hearts.

"That doesn't flush, and you know it," Jeanette scowled, "and the police know it too."

Her revelation caused Gary to drop the front legs of his chair back on the floor and lean in towards her. "No shit? Who told you that?" He asked with guarded curiosity.

At first Jeanette wasn't sure if the look in his eye was one of surprise or trepidation. But as his features evened out into mere inquisitiveness, she decided she'd already said too much.

"Just never mind. All I want from you is an address for Skip Phillips," she said, hoping that, as she had assumed, Gary knew who he was.

Gary's tight expression of interest slowly faded into a large smile. "Well old Skippy shouldn't be hard to find. He's right over there," he said, pointing to the crowd he'd been with when she first came in. "Well, he was over there, anyway. Hey Tommy," he shouted across the crowded room, where'd Skippy go?" One of the men seated at the table held his hand up to his ear in an effort to hear above the crowd. "Skippy. Where'd he go?" The man nodded and pantomimed shooting drugs. "Who knows?" Gary shrugged.

"Well, where can I find him, how do I get in touch with him?" She asked, the beginnings of anxiety evident in her voice.

"That's easy, babe. He's got a place over on Tremont St. somewhere in the twelve forties. For the life of me, I don't know how he affords it. The guy is in and out of rehab like I change my socks."

Jeanette hopped up and leaned across the table toward him. Gary exposed his cheek, fully expecting a thank you kiss. But instead, he got an earful.

"Listen you pompous ass! This conversation never happened, you got it? Or I swear you'll never work in this town again!

And try to act a little less upbeat. After all, you just came from a funeral!"

Gary took a long draw off of his beer and smiled coolly. "Whatever you say, babe," he agreed, obnoxiously raising his glass in a mock toast.

"And one more thing," Jeanette continued.

"What's that?" Gary smiled.

"Don't you *ever* call me *babe* again, asshole!" she spit. And turning around, she strode out of the bar wearing a satisfied smile.

Gary got up, strutted over to his friends, and, true to form, said, "She wants me. She just doesn't know it yet."

As she reached the top of the stairs, Jeanette looked up and down the street, only half expecting to see Duane's Volvo waiting for her. The snow was beginning to fall harder as she crossed the sidewalk to hail a cab. All of a sudden, she was feeling very alone, and beginning to wonder just what it was she thought she was doing. I'm no cop, she thought, Christ, I'm not even a reporter. As she neared the curb and the black sedan, her self-confidence, along with her conviction was beginning to flag seriously. Maybe I should just go home and forget this whole thing, she considered, or, at the very least, find Duane and try to talk him into coming with me.

Stepping off of the curb, her high heeled foot sank up to her ankle, the ice water closing around her stockinged leg. "Shit!" she squealed, losing her shoe in the puddle of slush. Pawing at the ground with her bare foot like a feeding chicken, she was trying to figure out how she was going to get her shoe back without getting her hand wet. As she got down on her one sore but functional knee, the back door to the sedan opened. After fishing around momentarily, and when at last she'd retrieved her submerged shoe, she felt a hand close around her arm, startling her and causing her to drop it back into the puddle.

"Leave the shoe, Jeanette," a voice said.

Her head whipped around, her mouth opening to scream, only to see Dean Tunney smiling broadly back at her.

"Oh, Dean! You scared the hell out of me!" she laughed nervously.

"Sorry," he smiled, offering her his hand. "You looked as though you could use some help. Billings," he said, summoning his driver, "get the lady's shoe, would you?" Then, pulling Jeanette to her feet, he draped her arm around his shoulder and walked her to his car. And as she sat just inside the opened door, the driver returned with her dripping shoe. "Hey, Billings, what do you say, " Dean asked, "how about drying it out first? You can't expect her to put it on like that."

Dutifully, the driver nodded, used his handkerchief to dry the shoe out, and handed it to her. "So, what do **you** have planned for today. I mean besides ice fishing, that is," he laughed.

Jeanette looked up at him as sourly as possible under the circumstances. Then, slowly, a small smile began to breach her phony scowl. "Not much," she lied, "I'm just headed over to Tremont St. to visit a friend. That is if I can get a cab in this weather."

"Nonsense!" Dean admonished. "Save yourself five bucks and change, and ride with me. I insist, it'd be my pleasure. And after all, you paid for the car, and the driver, for that matter."

Jeanette thought it over for a second, then slowly slid over to let the Jr. Senator climb in, her momentary reservations about continuing with her self-styled investigations now a forgotten second thought. But once under way, she fidgeted nervously as she anticipated the question that she was sure would eventually come. Waiting had never been her strong suit. So, as was her style, she met the matter head on. "I hope this in no way obliges me to accompany you tonight," she said a bit too curtly. Then, feeling out of line for her tone, she smiled apologetically.

Dean regarded her cautiously "Jeanette, my dear, you are in no way obliged to accompany me anywhere. Although I *do* wish you'd reconsider. After this morning I think you could probably use a good night out." She cocked her head to one side, her deep brown eyes at once thanking him for the invitation, and begging him not to push the issue. "Ok, all right. Not another word," he relented. "I'll call you at five for your final answer." Shaking her head, she turned to stare blankly out the window.

"Which block, sir?" the intercom crackled

"You can just drop me at the lights up ahead." she blurted.

Dean set his jaw to object, but the defiant look she was wearing put a quick end to that. So pushing the button on the armrest, the Senator spoke into the air. "The lady would like to get out at the lights, Jacob."

As they slowed to a stop Tunney opened his door and got out, allowing her to exit the car onto the sidewalk. Taking her hand in his, he looked at her with pleading eyes. "Talk to you at five?"

Jeanette rolled her eyes and nodded. Then, thanking him, she limped down Tremont St. toward the twelve hundred block. It wasn't until she'd crossed the street at the end of the block, than did Dean finally turn his eyes forward and wave his hand for his driver to continue on his way.

*****

Duane cursed himself as he mounted the stairs exiting the bar where he had dropped Jeanette an hour and a half ago. When he'd first arrived, after driving around aimlessly and feeling guilty, he'd rushed inside. Upon finding no familiar faces, he'd asked the bartender if he'd seen Jeanette, describing her as best he could. The man had merely shrugged his shoulders, said something about how busy he had been this morning, and gone about his business.

When he reached the sidewalk he anxiously looked up and down the block in a futile attempt to make her materialize and ask him where he'd been "Damn!" he cursed, "I **never** should have let her go alone!"

*****

Jeanette had started at number twelve-forty and continued weaving her way back and forth across the street checking every mail slot and doorbell she could find. So far she had come up empty. She had found a Ms. Sara Phillips who, although she assured her she didn't know any Skip, had stroked lovingly at her hair while looking her longingly in the eye, and invited her in for some tea. She'd thanked the lonely woman kindly, but graciously demurred, the whole time backing tentatively down the hall and out the door. Only two more left, she told herself as she labored across the street one more time. She stood at the base of the steps to number 1247 looking up the height of the building, and then shifted her attention to 1249 next door. The door to the next building was blocked off with a piece of plywood, and on the plywood was a sign that read: Your Tax Dollars At Work For Urban Renewal. Permit #2764 D.T.C Construction: "Well, this is it," she said aloud, looking back to the building that loomed before her. Mounting the stoop, she slowly, painfully, dragged her throbbing knee up the five steps to the entrance. Stopping again, she drew a deep breath as if deciding whether or not to go in. If it isn't this one, I'm out of luck, she thought. Then, bracing herself against what she might find, or not find to be more precise, she grabbed the knob, pushed the heavy door back on its rusty hinges, and entered.

This building, which from the street had looked no different than any of the other dwellings on the block, was anything but

the same. Although the general construction of this foyer was an exact replica of the rest, there the similarities ended. This particular approach was uncharacteristically cold. The built in settees which had graced either side of the threshold in better days, were now no more than a landing spot for accumulated dust. And the door that led to the stairway and the rooms upstairs hung from one hinge, half opened. In the other entryways, even with the doors closed, she could hear the sounds of life seeping through the old plaster walls to reverberate off of the black and white tile floor; but here the apparent absence of sound made her skin crawl.

Looking to the mail boxes, she noticed that the doors to most of them were missing, and the name tags in those that remained were yellowed, cracked, and for the most part illegible. Her eyes began to water. Not so much from the dust, which was partly to blame, but from the stench that emanated from the doorway to the stairs. At first she passed it off as just the musty odor of an unused and obviously abandoned building, but it soon became revoltingly clear what it was. It was the smell of urine. Pulling her handkerchief from her purse, she thrust it to her face, barely choking back the sourness she felt rising in her throat. Silently, she thanked herself for the misting of perfume she'd given it this morning and reached for the doorknob to leave. As she did, an earring which had become enfolded in the hanky dropped to the floor, and as she bent to pick it up she noticed something in the dust on the floor. Besides the distinct marks left in the dust by what were quite evidently her *own* high heels, there were other footprints there, big footprints, a man's footprints. Suddenly, Gary's words from the bar came back to her. **"...He's got a place over on Tremont St. somewhere in the twelve forties.**

For the life of me, I don't know how he affords it. The guy is in and out of rehab like I change my socks." These were Skip's footprints, she could feel it. Standing, she turned and looked toward the door. And quickly, before she could lose her nerve, she stepped warily through it and began checking the deserted apartments for signs of life.

*****

Duane rounded the corner of the alleyway that ran behind his Beacon St. address. Looking in his rearview mirror, he could hardly stand the sight of his own eyes as they stared accusingly back at him. Twisting the mirror sideways, he pulled the car into his parking spot. He sat for a moment, almost motionless, not wanting to get out. He knew that once he did he'd have to make the obligatory call to Jeanette's house, and he was sick at the thought that she might not answer. After forcing himself out of his car and making the uncertain climb to his rooms, he reluctantly fit his key into the lock. As he turned it and entered he immediately began to sweat.

Deliberately crossing the room, he grabbed up the phone and dialed her number.

"Damn! Stupid, stupid, stupid!" He said, slamming the phone back into its resting place. Though he wasn't sure if he was yelling at himself or Jeanette, he was sure of one thing. He had blown it. The repetitive ring that had mocked him on the other end of the line made that point painfully clear.

Apartment after apartment had either been empty, or would have been better off that way. And now, as she made the top of the final flight of stairs, she was really beginning to think she'd been wasting her time. But when she peered around the gray green, cracked, plaster walls, she saw the first sign, aside from burnt matches, scorched bottle caps, discarded needles, and balled up tin foil, that someone had actually been using this place for something other than a shooting gallery and a bathroom. At the end of the hall there was a broken window. And in the window, was stuffed a blanket. Someone was trying to make this place more habitable.

Limping to the end of the hall, she passed the opened and missing doors of the empty apartments. The second to last door was closed, so stopping, she held her breath and knocked on it. "Skip? Skip Phillips? It's Jeanette Tolby, Billy's friend." There was no answer, but she was too close now so, undaunted, she continued. "You called last night. Before the woman was hit in front of the Coach's Box..." When there was still no answer, she

leaned her head against the door to listen for any slight sound of movement from inside the room. At first she thought she heard the sound of running water coming from inside the apartment. But readily she became aware that it was the sound of her own blood pumping through her head.

Realizing that she was wasting time, she closed her eyes and grabbed the doorknob, turning it gingerly to the right. To her surprise, the door unlatched and swung in with ease. She opened her eyes just in time to see a rat skitter under the couch, which seemed to be the only piece of furniture left in this dusty and deeply chilled studio slum. But in this room there was something different. On the floor, just underneath the edge of the threadbare sofa, was an alarm clock. Shaking off her shoes for the sake of stealth, she hesitantly crept farther into the room. There was only one door off of it. The bathroom, she surmised, and silently she stole across the room to it. Holding her breath, she listened, her head tight against the cracked and peeling door.... Still nothing. She let herself breathe and pushed the door gently open. There, on the edge of the ancient pedestal sink, were a razor, a bar of soap and some shaving cream.

As she smiled, self-satisfied for both her investigative intuition and what she considered her gutsy persistence, she made her way back across the room to the couch. Sitting down, she bent over, reaching under the edge of the couch and grabbing the wind up alarm clock that had been put there for safe keeping.

She looked at the clock, which was still ticking, and immediately checked her bare wrist to confirm the time. "Dammit! This watch business is getting to be a real pain in the ass," she mumbled. But concluding that a wind up of this type would rarely run a full day without being tended to, she smiled once again, assuming she'd hit pay dirt. She lifted the clock up in front of her, falling back against the shabby couch to rest, but as she did, something jabbed her in the back. She tried to get comfortable, but it was no use. This decrepit piece of furniture had long outlived its intended use. So standing, she began to pace and wait for its owner to return.

Walking to the window, she looked out across the city. The snow was falling harder now, and for the first time since she had entered the room she began to realize how cold she was. Shivering, she decided to leave Skip Phillips a note and hope he'd get back to her. As she fumbled with the catch on her purse, her hands, numbed from the bitter cold, lost their grip, the pocketbook falling to the ground and expelling the majority of its holdings into a jumbled mess at her feet.

"Oh, *Christ*!" she fumed, leaning to pick up her belongings. But as she did, the rat that had greeted her as she'd entered the apartment darted out toward her from beneath the sofa, causing her to shriek with fright, fall to her rear end, and scramble backward across the floor. Unruffled by her piercing screech, the rat snatched up her broken watch, which had been amongst the other emptied contents of her purse all along, reared up on its haunches, then disappeared into a hole in the floor.

"My watch, you little *bastard*!" She seethed, hopping to her feet. Stamping as she walked, to prevent the rodent from making a return appearance, she made her way back to the pile of her possessions, giving the rat hole a wide berth. But as she hurriedly shoveled the mound of sundry items back into her purse, something caught her attention. Something she hadn't noticed when she first entered the room. Behind the couch, sticking out just slightly was the end of a suitcase.

Jeanette looked around the room self-consciously as she considered taking a quick peek at the contents of the case. But determining that it was too risky to go rifling through somebody's stuff, especially when they might return at any time, she decided to ignore the temptation.

But it was right there, teasing and taunting her. Just sticking out there in the open like that, it was almost too much to take. Walking to it, she poked at it with her foot, bobbing her head back and forth to try to sneak a glimpse of what it contained. "The hell with it," she said. She couldn't stand it any longer, so grabbing hold of the case, she yanked it out of its resting place, at which time it promptly fell open, giving up the few meager effects of what, from the looks of her surroundings, she could only assume was a less than ideal life.

But wait a minute, she thought, this stuff is nice. Silk shirts, designer pants and jeans... From behind her, she heard a click, and every muscle in her body tightened nearly to the point of rupture. Without even turning around, she frantically began cramming the things back into the suitcase; all the while trying to remember if she had closed the door.

*****

Duane hugged himself against the afternoon chill that had set in on the city, and so it seemed Kenmore Square, in particular. He had waited long enough, and called more than that. He was going over to Jeanette's to wait. At first he hadn't considered it such a good move, she certainly wouldn't call him *there*, but for lack of another way to expend nervous energy, he'd decided he would go.

As he approached her brownstone a pair of frigid eyes watched intently his every step from Jeanette's front window. Duane knocked deliberately and rang the bell simultaneously. He waited for a second, but right now patience was one thing that was in short supply, so sticking his key in the lock, he pushed the door open. "Jeanette, it's Duane, we gotta talk." he shouted as he mounted the oak stairway.

Just then, he heard a clamor of motion and the slam of a door, followed by the sound of feet pounding down the back stairway; feet much too heavy, and far too numerous to be Jeanette's. Taking the remaining stairs three at a time in loping long legged strides, he reached the door to the back stairway in no time. Tearing it open, he was met by a tightly black gloved fist holding a revolver. The butt of which made a sudden and undeniably distinct impression on his forehead. The message the fist carried with it was clear, mind your own business! As he crumpled into the corner, amid the stars in his eyes, he saw a ski masked face framing two devastatingly icy, yet smiling, blue eyes. As the blackness of unconsciousness closed in around him, he heard a mocking laugh, the deafening sound of bees buzzing inside his head, then nothing.

CHAPTER NINE

"Stand up, lady!" The deep voice from behind her instructed, just as she finished closing the bag. "Nice and slow," it added malevolently. It became painfully obvious to her almost immediately, that she had indeed left the door open. She had read once in a cheap novel that there was no more unmistakable sound in the world than that of the hammer of a revolver being pulled back; even if you hadn't heard it before. She'd never really quite believed it, but now she found that simple elucidation to be horrifyingly accurate.

She stood up slowly, as advised, then entertained ideas of turning around to face the disembodied voice. But that notion was quickly removed from her short list of ways to deal with the situation when the voice spoke again.

"I wouldn't be turning around if I was you," the man said, "as a matter of fact, why don't you just close your eyes. **NOW!**"

Jeanette's eyes snapped shut, and she stood trembling as she listened to the sound of his footsteps coming up behind her. "Nice. *Very* nice," the man offered appreciatively, as his large hand caressed her firm bottom.

Jeanette could hear his heavy breath right behind her left ear as she felt his fingers lecherously trace the outline of her tensed buttocks. She felt as though she was going to throw up. This man was going to rape her, and there was nothing she could do about it. And quite frankly, she had no one to blame but herself. She had put herself into this position and now it seemed she would pay the price. "Please, please don't," she begged, her voice trembling with fear as a tear ran down her cheek.

"Don't what?" The man asked cynically.

Her mind raced. Don't hurt me sounds like, you can take me, just do it gently. Don't touch me sounds like too much of an order. Don't kill me, makes it sound like anything else is acceptable. "P-Please, let me go."

"Let you go?" The man shouted, walking to the center of the room. "Let you go?! Listen, baby, I ain't the one who been draggin' your cute ass up here, am I?"

Her heart leapt with every word. "Please, don't do anything to hurt me," she pleaded.

"Don't do anything to hurt you?" he said. "Hey, sweet cheeks, I ain't the one who's breakin' the law here."

Summoning her last ounce of composure, she chanced a question. "Wh- Who are you?" she stammered, but instantly she wished she could have the question back.

"Who am *I*?" The man railed, "I walk into my own room, and find you riflin' through my shit, and you have the balls to ask me who the fuck *I* am?! No, that ain't how it's gonna go! I'll ask the questions! Got it?" Jeanette nodded slowly her pulse pounding in her head.

"I'm sorry," she offered feebly.

"All right, who the hell are you?" he spit.

She had originally thought she was in the room belonging to Skip Phillips, but the deep throaty voice which now held her at bay seemed to possess no familiar characteristics what so ever.

"I-I'm Jeanette." she said, hoping that her name would jog the man's memory if indeed it was Skip. But remembering that, at Duane's behest, she hadn't given the man her name, she added. "I'm looking for Skip Phillips."

"Humph." was the only answer she got, but as she started to elaborate, he interrupted. "Well you ain't found 'im. So get your tight little ass outta my place before I change my mind."

She heard the hammer of the gun relax with several mechanical clicks as the man walked toward the bathroom. And wasting no time, she turned being sure to keep her eyes glued to the floor, and bolted out of the room and grabbed her shoes, not stopping until she hit the frozen pavement of Tremont St.

Upon hearing the downstairs door of the dilapidated building slam shut, the man laughed, walked to the couch, and flopped down with a sigh of relief. Then, reaching out, he grabbed the suitcase, fumbled with the locks, and dumped its contents out on the couch next to him.

*****

A dagger of stabbing pain cut through Duane's head, temple to temple, as he began to regain consciousness. Putting a palm to his forehead, he winced at the touch of his own hand and tried to focus his blurred vision on the jumble of shapes and colors that danced before his eyes.

"He's comin' to, Lieutenant," Burton shouted as he came into focus. Duane realized he was soaking wet, then eyed the dripping vase the cop had in his hand. Brushing the flowers off his chest, he made a feeble attempt at standing, but the pain in his head, coupled with the weakness in his knees, prevented it.

O'Hare appeared at the entrance to the sitting room and slowly made his way down the hallway to loom over him. "How ya feelin', kid?" He asked lowering himself down to Duane's level.

The sharp pain in his head had eased to a comparably pleasant dull throb. "Ok, I guess. But the drums gotta go," he seethed, pulling himself shakily to his feet.

"Come with me," O'Hare said, taking him by the elbow. "I have something I want to show you." Leading Duane back toward the sitting room, O'Hare hooked a quick right and led him into the bathroom. Then, turning him toward the mirror, the lieutenant pushed the door closed with his foot. Duane gasped at the purple half tennis ball hanging from his forehead. "Get the picture?" O'Hare asked. "You're lucky it wasn't the other end of the gun." Duane propped himself against the sink and stared into the drain. "Where was the girl when this happened?" O'Hare continued.

Duane spit into the sink and shook his head. "She wasn't here," he offered, then added, "At least I don't think she was."

*****

Skip Phillips lugged his intoxicated body up the third flight of stairs and just barely made the landing. "Cum'on Skibber, awmost home." He slurred to himself, his tongue fat with more heroin than the average junkies system would abide. And making his way to the door of his room, he stumbled in, never even noticing that the door was opened. Dropping his coat in the middle of the room, he bent to pick it up. It was then that the door slammed closed behind him.

Wobbling to an erect position once more, he turned around stumbling back a step. His eyes were immediately drawn to the black leather glove, and the 44 revolver it gripped.

"Hi, Skip." The owner of the gun chirped.

Skip's jaw dropped open as he watched, in slow motion, the muscles in the man's hand begin to constrict around the grip of the pistol. He felt his heart pound in his chest, but only once.

*****

As the cab pulled up in front of 478 Commonwealth Ave. the sunless sky was darkening with the early dusk that accompanies the fall months. The snow had stopped, but the low cloud cover along with the brisk smell that escorts true winter into the northeast threatened an impending command performance of that afternoon. Stuffing a ten spot into the money tray, Jeanette hopped out of the cab, noticing Burton's empty car parked in front of her apartment, as she did. Looking up to her eight foot windows, she was surprised to see the front room so brightly lit. She always left lights on, but this was ridiculous. This could mean only one thing. "They're in my God damned house!" She muttered between her teeth. The two martinis she'd gulped down after her narrow escape from the vacant building had not only calmed her nerves, but they had restored her spirited nature as well. "Those *bastards*!" she flared, stomping up the front steps. Jamming the key into the lock, she did a slow boil, and when she realized the door was unlocked, she swung it open and began to cut loose.

"O'Hare, you son of a b-"

When she reached the bottom of the stairs, she stopped short, seeing Duane coming down toward her. "Duane? What the hell is going on here? Oh, my God!" Her eyes bulged when she saw the massive bruise on his forehead. "Wh-What happened?"

"Oh, *nothing*. Nothing at all," he lied, brushing past her and heading for the door.

"But Duane, Wait. I- I-"

"Forget it, Jeanette. It's all over," he said, turning to rebuke her with a cold stare. Out of the corner of her eye, she saw O'Hare beginning to descend the stairs toward her. Turning back to Duane, she saw the door slam closed. "Evening Ms. Tolby.

Come on up," he beckoned. "Let's us have a little talk. Just you and me, whaddaya say?" Jeanette shot another glance at the door, shocked that Duane would leave her alone now. Slowly she climbed the stairs and took the lieutenant's extended hand to follow him upstairs.

Once seated upstairs in the sitting room, O'Hare smiled his condescending smile and spoke softly, the light reflecting off of his steel blue eyes. "Your cohort, there, Avon, is it?"

Jeanette flung a disinterested look in his general direction, then adjusted the sofa pillow. "You know damn well what his name is!" She replied smugly.

"Damn right I do!" He agreed, standing and raising his voice. "And from what he tells me, he'd like to keep it!"

Jeanette looked at him in confusion and shook her head. "What are you talking about?" she asked, the arrogance in her voice replaced by befuddlement.

"Oh, don't worry, little lady, I'm gonna tell you exactly what I'm talking about. I'm gonna spell it out so simple that even *you* can understand it, you couldn't stop me! It goes like this. Your friend there almost bought it today, looking out for your foolish ass!" Jeanette shifted nervously in her seat. "It seems old Duane was worried about you when you disappeared downtown. So bein' the good friend that he is, he decided to come over here looking for you. Well, he didn't find you, of course. You were out playing cops and God damn robbers. But what he did find was one Mr. Gary Stricktland, and ba-bam! Old Gary tries to dispose of your buddy with a butt shot to the head! Are you with me, here?"

Jeanette nodded mutely. "Well, luckily we followed Avon over here, and caught Gary and a bunch of his drunk buddies piling out the back door with these." Reaching into his inside pocket, the lieutenant pulled out a plastic bag containing a bunch of papers and CD's and tossed them in Jeanette's lap. "Case closed!" He finished with a flourish of his arms.

Jeanette picked up the bag and recognized the contents instantly. "That son of a bitch! That no good, back stabbing... These are the contracts Billy and I had drawn up two months ago and the demos he'd cut for the label!"

O'Hare sat down across from her and lowered his voice again. "Yeah, it seems Gary didn't appreciate Billy getting a contract that didn't include the rest of the band. Thought he got a raw deal, I guess. I can't say as I blame him. It's hardly worth killing a bunch of people though. I guess it's all where your priorities lie."

Jeanette sat there dumfounded momentarily and then found her voice. "I can't believe he'd kill Billy and Brian over this. Did he admit to it?"

"Nope. He denied it like hell. Wouldn't you? Now all we have to do is fit that woman on Yawkey Way into this. See, there are two reasons that otherwise normal people will commit murder," he continued, before she could tell him about the phone call from

Skip. "One of the most common is love, and that's out. From what I understand the guy is straight, and damn good at it if you know what I mean. And number one, and the all-time favorite, is money. Bingo! Billy's squeeze told us that the night before Billy bought it, he heard him and Gary arguing about it in the hall outside their apartment. When he opened the door, Gary had your friend jacked up against the wall ready to feed him his fist. All we gotta do is put it all together. So you can go back to being a disc jockey, and I can go home and get a good night's sleep!" Jeanette just sat there with her mouth hanging open. O'Hare stood up and put on his wrinkled hat. "Burton, whaddaya say. Let's go," he shouted. "Oh, and one more thing. They may be calling on you to testify in court. But as far as you and me go, I guess this is aufwiedersehen. Good night, Ms. Tolby, and have a wonderful life," he said, and joined Burton, who was in the process of trying to cram a whole sandwich in his mouth, at the entrance to the hallway. "Whaddaya got, Burton?" asked the lieutenant.

"Roff bff," garbled the detective. And the two disappeared down the stairs.

Jeanette sat for a long time trying to digest the chain of events as portrayed by O'Hare. She knew she should feel better about the whole situation, but something still didn't feel right about it to her. Call it a sixth sense, call it women's intuition, the mere thought of the words made her cringe, but none the less, she still didn't buy it. Had Skip Phillips simply been setting her up for a fall when he'd called? And if so, why had Gary been so willing to tell her where he lived? Or had Gary simply been sending her on a wild goose chase to get her out of her apartment? No! It doesn't work, she thought, Gary may be king of the scum bags, granted. But murder? "He doesn't have the guts for it," she mumbled, as she poured herself a double martini.

As she took a long intimate sip of her drink, the phone rang ruining the moment. And as she made her way into the hallway to answer it, the clock chimed in striking five o'clock.

Her steps quickened when it occurred to her that it may be Duane.

"Hello?" she breathed, sounding, what she felt, was a bit too desperate.

"Hi, Jeanette, Dean Tunney, here. And right on time I might add," he pointed out, taking particular pride in his punctuality. "So, are we on for tonight?"

Biting at her bottom lip, she winced at the sound of his voice. But before she could think of any more excuses for not going, and without even meaning to, she heard herself saying yes; adding only the stipulation that she be allowed to leave as early as she liked, having had an extraordinarily exhausting day.

"It's a deal," he agreed, "But exactly what does *early* mean?"

She couldn't believe she'd accepted. She wasn't really sure if it was the liquor, or the fact that she didn't want to be alone, but it was too late. Now there was no getting out of it.

"Early means when I get too tired to have a good time. Let's say tenish," she offered coyly.

"Well, ten *is* early," he sulked.

"And that means home by ten thirty," she added.

A heavy sigh leaked through the line and he hesitantly agreed.

"Ok, you win. I'll have my driver pick you up at 6:30 on the dot! See you then?"

"See you then," she agreed, and hanging up the phone, she ran to her closet and began the endless job of finding something to wear.

Holding up the first dress in front of her, she looked at her reflection in the mirror. Then with a look of disgust, she tossed it on the bed. She would have hung it back in the closet, but what was the use? She always ended up wearing the first thing that had caught her eye anyway. Setting her drink on the headboard, she dived back into her closet determined to find something truly glorious, which, she was quite sure, she didn't own.

She could barely hear the clock strike six from the shower. Cutting off the water, she hopped out and wrapped herself in a thick cotton towel. Turning, she looked at her fog obscured image in the full length mirror, and grabbing a face cloth, she wiped the majority of steam away and dropped her towel. At first she peered distastefully at her reflection, but turning sideways, she patted at her firm and flat tummy as a faint smile betrayed her satisfaction with, what she considered, a fine example of a female shape. Again turning to face the mirror, she winced. "Except for my breasts." she mumbled. "I hate my breasts. They're too small, and they point out to the sides like who knows what." Turning around she looked back over her shoulder for a rear view of herself. It was then that the memories of that afternoon came flooding back to her. **"Nice, very nice."** she heard him say. She could almost feel him touching her, running his fingers along the contours of her backside. "Son of a bitch!" She spit, and shuddering, she grabbed up her towel and wrapped it tightly around her torso as she exited the bathroom.

By the time she was halfway to the fund raiser, she was feeling much better about having come. Free booze, free eats, free music. Yeah, I'm looking forward to this, she thought. And after all, this gathering was to be held at The Felton Towers Hotel, located just outside the city limits of Boston in ritzy Cambridge, a quickly growing, and politically influential metropolis in its own right. Parked just off of the finely groomed city common, the hotel was as prestigious and beautiful as any that existed in town, and maybe even more so. All the old money mingled there. And it had been the scene for the kick-off of many a successful political career.

As they approached the hotel, she readied herself for her grand entrance. She felt like some debutante making her entry into society. She just wished Dean could be with her to escort her in and introduce her into this foreign, and somewhat frightening, fraternity.

Just before they reached the front door of the hotel, they hooked a quick left, then a right, then another. And as they pulled to stop at a chain-link gate, a security guard walked to the driver's window. The two talked briefly, the guard attempting to shine his flashlight through the deeply tinted windows of the limousine. Then, Billings' window eased up, the guard stepping aside and speaking into his walkie-talkie as the gates rolled back.

Picking up the microphone to his radio, the driver began speaking to some unseen person, and as he did, Jeanette nosily hit the button on the intercom.

"Yes, I've got her, sir. And she was glad to come. Yeah, she's all excited," she heard Billings chuckle. And having heard enough, she let her finger slip off the button as they pulled to a stop just short of the loading dock that serviced the hotel.

Just then, up on the dock, a large metal fire door swung open, and an equally large man stepped through it. He was carrying his own portable radio, and wearing a suitably large weapon.

Billings hopped out to open Jeanette's door, but by the time he had, she was already halfway out. "Never mind, driver!" she fumed, "I can open my own doors! After all, I'm all excited!" she mocked, glaring into his shocked eyes. Brushing past him, she strolled leisurely up the steps. She took her time with the sole purpose of infuriating, not only the driver, but the security guard, as well.

The guard shifted nervously from foot to foot as he checked behind every tree and eyed every car in the parking lot. And as she passed him, she realized just how big the man was. Turning her head to avoid the man's look of obvious disapproval, she heard him speak.

"Come on! Get your tight little ass outta my face!"

The words made her shudder, her head snapping around just in time to catch a glimpse of his eyes as the door slammed closed between them. Deep was an understatement. The eyes were black and bottomless, expressionless and threatening. Even the light from the bare bulb that hung on the dock didn't reflect off of them. Instead it just disappeared into them as though it were being sucked into two miniature black holes. She shuddered again, suddenly uncertain about whether she should have accepted Dean's invitation and frightened for her very well being. Am I over reacting? She asked herself. Suddenly she didn't feel like a debutante anymore.

As she backed down the dimly lit corridor, the incident of that afternoon played back before her mind; complete with the thoughts and fears that, at the time, she had felt may be her last. A sudden flurry of motion, noise, and light, from behind her caused her to wheel around on her heels and shriek.

"Jeanette, hurry up!" Dean barked, fixing her with a scowl. "For god's sake, they're introducing me!"

Grabbing her by the elbow, he led her through the doorway through which he had appeared and into another more brightly lit hallway. But shaking him loose, she pulled back.

"No, Dean!" She said. "I just want to get out of here! I want to go home!"

In the background, she could hear the Master of ceremonies introducing him. "And now, with no further ado, let me introduce our guest of honor." With that the crowd whipped into a rousing round of applause, accented with hoots, hollers of appreciation, and whistles. "Please, put your hands together, and help me to welcome a man who has been described as one of the finest young political minds in the country, the face of our future in Washington, and the best hope for our state, the Junior Senator from Massachusetts, and the next Governor of the Commonwealth, Dean Tunney, and his escort Miss Diane Blake."

Jeanette Backed away slowly, her hand to her mouth. "Diane Blake?" she shouted, "Who the hell is Diane Blake?!" But it was no use, above the crowd she couldn't even hear her own voice.

Looking frantically back and forth between her and the stage, Dean waved his hand at her in disgust and decided to go on without her. Then, as he passed the only other door off of the corridor, it flew open. And through it appeared a man accompanied by a young woman. A woman that looked too much like her for it to be a mere coincidence.

Leaning in toward the man, Dean shouted something at him, pointing a trembling finger at Jeanette. The look in his eye was a mixture of absolute frustration and rage.

After fixing her with another stone cold stare, he locked elbows with Ms. Blake, whipped around, and continued on toward the stage and the waiting throng of his frenzied supporters.

As she watched herself walk away with the Senator, the man who had so unexpectedly burst through the door began walking deliberately toward her speaking aggressively into a hand held radio. She could no more make out his words than she had been able to hear her own, seconds before. But from the look on his face she could tell he was anything but happy.

Wheeling around, she took off down the hallway past the door through which she had just entered. Just as she cleared it, it swung open, Billings and the owner of the threatening eyes entering. Turning, the two began following her at twice her clip. At the end of the corridor was a door. She had to make it to the door. As she neared what seemed her only avenue of escape, it too swung open, a man with a trash hamper fighting his way through it.

Lowering her shoulder, she knocked him solidly aside and bolted through the door. Then, slamming it behind her, she fell against it gasping for breath and shaking uncontrollably. She listened through the door, and could hear her would-be abductors yelling at the man with the trash to open it; to which, in broken English, he tried to explain that he couldn't he didn't have the key. She backed away, her hand held tight to her trembling lips.

And quickly turning around, she gasped to see the entire kitchen staff staring blankly at her.

A bell above her head broke the relative quiet of the kitchen, and immediately two of the crew made their way toward her, obviously intent on answering it.

"No!" She screamed, the terror in her voice stopping the two dead in their tracks. "They have guns! They're trying to kill me!" She added.

The crowd that had been watching her quickly scattered, including the two men who had been headed for the door, and Jeanette picked up a service tray and made her way into the dining room. Holding the tray up between herself and the stage to prevent herself from being recognized, she slipped through the crowd and out into the lobby. Then, handing the tray to the doorman, she fought her way against the flow of the entering patrons, and outside into the frigid night air.

Only when she had crossed the street and disappeared into the protective cloak of darkness that enshrouded the common did her pulse begin to slow to its regular pace. Still, every tree she passed, every statue, trash can and monument seemed an ideal hiding spot from behind which any one of her pursuers could easily overtake and overwhelm her. So every few steps she anxiously checked her back until she had reached the comparative safety of the Harvard Square subway station. She was reasonably sure she hadn't been followed.

Soon she was back in Kenmore station, standing at the bottom of the stairs to the street. Slowly, she mounted the stairs and began to climb, still checking behind her every few steps to be absolutely sure she hadn't been followed. Hearing another train pull into the station below, she felt her adrenalin rush with restored vivacity, and raced up the remaining stairs to street level.

Once she'd made the sidewalk she continued to run until she reached the steps to her brownstone. As she took the first step, she turned and looked across the street. There, in what had become its customary resting place, she saw Burton's green Chevy. At first she thought it odd, considering O'Hare had declared the case closed. Who cares, she thought. She didn't know why it was there, but for the first time since she'd met the man, she was glad it was.

Once inside, she collapsed into her overstuffed chair, her head spinning as she tried to make sense of what had happened to her less than an hour ago. But it didn't make any sense. Nothing made sense anymore. In the last twenty four hours, she had seen a murder, had her life threatened at gunpoint, and been chased by a Senator's gang of henchmen. Was this really happening? Or was it all some kind of bizarre nightmare? No. A nightmare it wasn't. She was all too familiar with what nightmares were all about. This was all real. Or, as Dr. Bernhard had so often said, **"Reality is relative. If you believe something to be true, who's to say that it isn't true for *you*?"** As she felt her life unraveling, and her grip on sanity becoming precariously slight, she could hear herself sobbing as if she were listening from the other room. She could feel the tears running down her cheeks, and taste the bitter salt on her lips. But oddly enough, she felt little emotion; just the unyielding necessity to cry.

The phone next to her rang to life, startling her, and causing a small scream to escape her throat. Instinctively snatching it up, she spit a course "Hello!" into the receiver.

"Have you all together lost your mind?" She heard Dean Tunney ask, his voice filled with all the anger and frustration she had seen on his face at the hotel. Before she could answer, he continued his tirade. "Just what the hell was that performance all about?"

"*Me?*" She shot back with more conviction than she was feeling. "What about the little show your goons put on. And why did they introduce Miss Diane whoever the hell she is. I'm on to you!" She cried, losing control.

"On to me?" he laughed humorlessly. "My God, you have lost your mind." Diane was my official escort. *You* were supposed to be my date!" This time he didn't laugh.

"Well, what about those men you sent after me? she sobbed.

"I wanted them to bring you back! But quite frankly, Jeanette, I think I'm kind of glad they couldn't catch you." Her head was throbbing as fast as it was spinning. This is it, she thought, I *have* lost my mind. "Jeanette, do me a favor wi... no, on second thought, do both of us a favor. Get some rest. I kind of feel like this was my fault for talking you into coming. Listen, ah, I'll give you a buzz sometime, huh?"

"Dean, I'm sorry," she heard herself say. And she listened as the connection was terminated.

She sat in her confusion and humiliation for she wasn't sure how long, crying sometimes, simply staring at others. On and off she would swear at herself for being such a fool. But mostly she'd just cry and stare. Finally, when she had composed herself sufficiently, and sorted things out as best she could, she got up and headed for the bathroom. She was going to do something she hadn't done in a long while. Indeed, she never thought she'd do it again. She was going to take a couple of Valium; the ones Dr. Bernhard had given her to alleviate her nightmares. This, after all, had been the most nightmarish evening she had ever spent in her entire life.

Her pillows were set just so as she settled back against them, reaching for the remote control. She noticed her bare wrist, and immediately thought of Duane. She would have felt guilty for going out after what had happened to him. But right now, she was feeling very little, if anything at all. "I should really call him," she said to herself, placing her drink on the headboard. So picking up the phone, she punched in his number and let it ring seven times.

Just as she was about to hang up, he answered.

"Duane, please don't hang up!" she pleaded.

"Oh, no! No, no, no. Not this time, Darlin'. I've been perfectly happy, soakin' my head in a cold bourbon compress," he said rather drunkenly. "And, as a matter of fact, I was just about to dive into the bottle, and pull the cap on after me. The last thing I need is anymore of your harebrained schemes."

"Duane, please. I just called to check on you... And, and I need someone to talk to," she admitted. She listened as he took a long pull on his drink.

"Ah, well, how are you?"

"Listen, Jen, you know I love you like my own." It was the booze talking. He always called her Jen and told her he loved her like his own when he had a brain full. "But damn, girl, I almost got my ass blown off today 'cause of you. So my ass and my brain had a little pow wow, and my brain told my ass not to let me talk you- I mean, talk- I mean, you know what I mean."

She could tell that this conversation was going to go nowhere and getting there in a hurry, so she stopped him there. "Ok, Duane. I get the picture; you don't want to talk to me again. I can understand that." It was a dirty trick to play on someone in his condition, but oh well. Besides, it would never work on someone who wasn't in his condition, so she might as well use it.

"No, no, wait a minute, babe. That ain't it at all," he said.

Jeanette felt a little guilty about her method, but what was important was her motivation. "Then will you promise you'll call me first thing tomorrow morning?"

"Yeah, yeah, I'll call," he promised.

"Ok. Now write yourself a note so you don't forget. Remember, first thing."

"Yeah, I'll do that," he slurred, and began fumbling for something to write with. "Lemme see. Pen, pen- Oh, *shit*!!" He screeched, the sound of breaking glass coming clearly through the line. "I dropped my damn drink!" He whined.

"Good night, Duane," she purred, and dropped the phone into its cradle. Then, hitting the lights, she sank down into her pillow and kept on sinking.

Seemingly seconds later, she awoke to hands, lots of hands. The hands were lifting her out of her bed. She was soaking wet, but why? The hands lifted her like a rag doll, plopping her onto a cold table, and strapping her down; so many hands. They were touching her where she didn't want to be touched. As panic wrapped its unrelenting fingers around her pounding heart, she saw a glint of reflected light bounce off of a shiny metal object. Almost simultaneously, she felt a sharp pinch on the inside of her forearm. "Did she eat?" a voice whispered in monotone. "Nothing but a little water." The answer reverberated from the darkness that surrounded her. She opened her mouth to scream, but a hand plunged down out of the darkness to cover it.

Then, suddenly she was in the hallway. It was the hallway of her house, but it wasn't. Now it was tiled. The squeaks of the wheels were deafening. She squinted her eyes into tight slits in an effort to protect her senses from the screaming wheels. Now she was under the orb. A pair of the hands pulled her nightgown up to her chest, and then strapped her feet into stirrups. Then a sharp pain in her other forearm, the child's forearm. The garbled voices were dissolving into no more than a disjointed symphony of grunts and moans. They were going to kill her this time, she was sure of it. "**DOCTOR,**" That damned word again. She was trying desperately to cling to consciousness. She felt someone slipping something up inside of her between her legs. As the wavering shapes huddled around her, she thought to herself, they shouldn't be touching me there. They shouldn't be doing this to me, I'm just a little girl. But wait a minute, she corrected herself, I'm not a little girl. She could stand it no longer, she was passing out. But before she did, she let out a scream that would curl a tire iron. Immediately, someone covered her nose and mouth with a mask, and leaned down and whispered. "You just go back to sleep, dear," the nurse said. And as if on cue, she spiraled into oblivion.

She woke up much more slowly this time. She was in a fetal position, both of her hands cupped tightly between her legs. She was soaking wet, and naked from the waist down. Except for her pajamas; which still clung to her left foot her underwear lost somewhere in the tangled mess. The first thing she smelled was gin. Her bed clothes were nowhere to be found.

She heard a faint yet distinct ringing sound. "The doorbell." she mumbled, pressing herself to her knees to look at her clock. "8:10, Jesus, who the hell is that?" she mumbled. Next to the clock she saw her upended glass from the night before. The smell of gin was so strong it caused her to gag. Again the ringing, so tumbling out of bed, she woozily stripped what was left of her dripping night clothes off of her martini glazed body, and grabbed a robe out of her closet.

"I'm coming for God sakes," she hollered as she pounded uneasily down the stairs. Opening the door a crack, but leaving the chain still secured, she saw, through the haze of a narcotic hangover, Duane's bloodshot eyes staring blearily back at her.

"Can I come in?" He asked warily, adding. "Wow! You look as bad as I *feel*! And that's a tall order."

Nodding mutely, she slid back the chain and stepped aside to let him enter. As he passed her, he caught a good whiff of the gin that laced her body. "Oh, God!" He breathed, his hand going instinctively to cover his mouth and nose. "What the hell did you do, take a bath in gin?" His once bleary eyes were now as sharp as daggers. And as she stepped closer to him to swing the door shut, he had all he could do to contain the dam of nausea that inched its way up his throat.

Without a word, he spun around, bounded up the stairs in what seemed two steps, and raced into the bathroom slamming the door behind him.

When Jeanette mounted the stairs, a wave of dizziness started at her head and corkscrewed down her body as if her brain was going to roll out the bottom of her bathrobe. Grabbing hold of the banister, she sat down hard, her head reeling as the Valium from the night before pumped with renewed vigor through her

veins. "Damn," she groaned, "how many of those did I take?"
Then, fighting her way to her feet, she lugged her torpid frame
up the stairs, her mind apparently lagging well behind.

In passing the bathroom, she could hear Duane growling at
somebody over the porcelain telephone. Whoever it was, she
surmised, they must have done something truly awful to make
him roar like that. Her little joke, coupled with the lingering
effects of her tranquilizers, caused her to chuckle as she wove
her way toward the kitchen.

After starting the coffee, she plopped down in the seat next to
the window and stared out at the considerable amount of snow
that had fallen overnight. Funny, she thought, but she hadn't
even noticed it when she'd answered the door. She tried to run
her fingers through her hair, but it was a futile effort. They
stopped almost immediately on a huge sticky tangle. "You better
take a good long shower," Duane said in a nasal voice as he
entered the kitchen. Looking up, she saw that he was hanging
onto his nose for dear life. Giggling, she stood up and pulled her
robe open. "Do you think my breasts are ugly?" she teased.

Duane's jaw dropped open, and he stood staring for seconds
that seemed more like hours. Even in this state, she presented an
alluring form which was a delightful sight to behold. Reaching
out, he grabbed her by the collar of her robe and pulled her
toward him, then past him and out into the hallway. Holding the
garment closed around her neck, he led her, at arm's length, to
the bathroom. "Now I *know* you need a long shower," he

inferred, shoving her in and pulling the door closed. "Now I know *I* need a long shower," he mumbled to himself as he walked to the kitchen.

"Prude!" She sulked, staring at her bedraggled aspect in the mirror.

A full twenty five minutes later, Duane heard her sneak from the bathroom to her bedroom. He was tempted to tease her for her uncharacteristic lack of inhibition, but charitably, he let it slide. Standing, he walked to her bedroom door and knocked softly. Inside he heard a flurry of movement.

"Don't come in! I'm not dressed!" Jeanette shouted, pulling on her panties and running into the closet.

Again he let the opportunity for a joke pass. I must be getting soft, he thought.

"Don't worry. I was just wondering how you're feeling."

"You mean besides humiliated? Like hell. How about you?"

He tried to restrain himself, but the words just leapt from his mouth. "Well, when I first got here, I felt lousy too," he began, "but since then, things are definitely looking up." He just couldn't help himself. If he hadn't said anything he would have had to check his license to make sure he was him.

"Drop dead, Duane. I'll be right out," she called to him.

Smirking mischievously, he walked back into the kitchen and poured himself another cup of coffee.

Jeanette thought she would handle the situation like an adult,but the second she entered the kitchen, her face turned as crimson as an embarrassed school girl's. She walked to the coffee pot somehow avoiding Duane, who was standing in the middle of the tiny room.

"No, I don't," he said.

"Don't what?" She asked, looking, if just for a second into his smiling eyes. "Oh shit, can't we talk about something else?" She said, her voice laced with a tone of self-deprecation.

"Hey." he said, "it's only me."

Sitting down across the table from him, she finally looked him square in the face. "I know," she whispered, "and I'm lucky you're such a good friend. Thanks."

Pursing his lips, he smiled wryly, as if to say all is forgotten, and your secret is safe with me. Staring down into her coffee cup, she was still confused. Not so much by her earlier indiscretion, but by the fact that at that moment, she had actually wanted him to take her. But even stranger was the fact that she still did. It was a strange feeling for her. A feeling she had seldom let herself feel in her entire life. There had been the handful of times at the orphanage as she got older and began to wonder about her sexuality. Lord knows, there were enough boys there to take care of her introduction to the joys of normal teenage sexual experimentation. But since then, just like all the other times she had been attracted to a man, for whatever reason, she wouldn't allow herself to give in to her desires. And the worst part was that she didn't even know why. All she knew was she couldn't stand to be touched intimately, for any reason, by anyone.

The morning slowly drifted into afternoon as the two took turns telling their versions of what seemed the latest in a growing list of the worst day either of them had ever spent. When both had finished their stories, Duane hoisted himself out of the overstuffed chair and crossed the room to sit next to her and put his arm around her. At first she tensed up. But as she relaxed she realized how long it had been since she'd had someone to hold her. It felt good, she decided, and the two sat, staring into the fire, as the snow blanketed the city and Burton's green Chevy.

Jeanette had read somewhere that there are times in life when the silence that surrounds you whispers to your soul. And at others it screams with the rage of unfelt feelings and unspoken words. The former can be soothing, almost therapeutic. The latter is always explosively disquieting. Jeanette wanted to scream.

CHAPTER TEN

Later that evening, once Duane had gone home, she realized that the time was approaching that she should think about going to bed. She dreaded the idea, but she'd really run out of ways to avoid it. Duane had offered to stay in one of the spare rooms, but after careful consideration, Jeanette had sent him home with a peck on the cheek and a hesitant goodnight.

As she readied herself for bed she came up with one more stall. There was a telephone call she really should have made earlier. She'd put it off all day, but it was something she really should do, and today. So lifting the phone out of its cradle, she dialed Dean Tunney to make a formal apology.

"Senator Tunney's answering service," a tired voice on the other end of the line breathed. Jeanette held her breath then spoke. "Hello, my name is Jeanette Tolby. Would it be at all possible to let me ring through, I really need to talk to Mr. Tunney."

"Hold please," the operator instructed. But within seconds she was back on the line. "I'm sorry Ma'am, I can't do that."

"You don't understand I'm a good friend of his."

The operator broke back in, "I said I'm sorry, Ma'am, I have a list of names here that were left with me, and you're not on it. The Senator is out for the evening and can't be reached. If you'd like to leave a message, I'll be sure he gets it."

Jeanette felt the hair on the back of her neck stand on end. "What If I were the President?" she spit.

"Well Ma'am," the woman answered, "if you were the president, then your name would be on the list. Good night."

Jeanette sat and seethed into the dead line. The thought crossed her mind to call back and say she was the president, if for no better reason than spite. But what would be the use of that. "Screw it!" She cursed, slamming the phone down.

There was no more putting it off. It was bedtime. She dreaded closing her eyes, fearful of what she was now sure would come. She turned down the sheets of her waterbed and slipped hesitantly between them. She thought of taking a valium, but after the embarrassing scene of that morning she thought better of it. Tonight she would just tough it out. Tomorrow, she promised herself, I'll call Dr. Bernhard and begin to get on with the rest of my life.

Sleep came easy, brought on by the state of emotional exhaustion she was in. Within seconds she was spinning out of control into the inner most regions of her tortured subconscious. Twisting and tumbling out of control, down into the places where her most silent secrets were stored. Some of which she never knew, others she'd rather forget.

She was awakened from her vividly terrifying nightmare by a sound she couldn't place. As the fog of sleep lifted from her senses, she realized what it was. It the sound of her own hoarse voice screaming at the top of what was left of her spent lungs. Looking around the room she was disoriented. In a flood of revelation she realized where she was. She was lying on the bottom landing of her back stairway, curled in a ball, shivering and naked.

The sun poured through the singular grimy window, pale, and bitter cold. She could hear the sounds of the morning traffic as it crawled through the snarled bottleneck of Kenmore Square mingled with the speeding cars on the freeway behind her apartment. Had she gone outside last night? Gone out naked? How did I get down here? Did I walk in my sleep? Her mind whirred with unanswered questions. She felt another scream rising in her throat but fought off the urge. Leaning back she shook her head in a last ditch effort to find out that this was some sort of bizarre dream. It wasn't.

Pushing herself to a standing position against the wall, she wrapped her arms tightly around her exposed breasts to fend off what cold she could. Then, in some primal exercise of self control, she calmly, slowly began her ascent to the warmth of her inner rooms.

*****

"I swear, I don't know nothin' about any of this stuff. All I wanted was what was rightly mine," Gary Stricktland whined.

O'Hare's eyes wrinkled into threatening slits as he pushed his beat up fedora back on his head. "Stop your blubbering, you mealy mouthed little shit!" He barked, staring down on him. "So, let me get this straight, you were just there taking back *your* contract with a dead man's name on it from a house that you broke into, and this guy surprised you so you cracked him in the skull with your revolver. Well that's perfectly understandable. Don't ya think so, Burton?" The detective covered his mouth, turning away to hide his smile and nodded.

"Get this puke outta my sight!" O'Hare growled through his teeth.

The guard, grabbing one of Stricktland's cuffed arms, dragged him to his feet, leading him toward the door. As the two passed O'Hare he stuck out his arm to stop them. Leaning in to make his point he stared his prisoner level in the eye. "Your ass is mine anyway, kid." Holding up his weathered hand he counted off the charges. "Assault with a deadly weapon with intent to commit larceny! Breaking and entering! Larceny of a legal document with intent to defraud! Shall I go on?" There was a knock on the door before he could answer, and another officer stuck his head in the door.

"'Scuse me, Lieutenant, Stricktland's lawyer is here and on his way down. We stalled as long as we could."

"Well take Jesse James here with you. I can't stand the stink of him."

Once the two cops escorted Stricktland out the door, O'Hare slammed it closed. Twisting the lock, he walked to the center of the room and looked at Burton, his blue eyes burning into the man's forehead. "What do *you* think?" He asked, not wanting to hear the man's answer.

Burton shifted on his feet uncomfortably for a second, and clearing his throat he answered. "I don't think he iced the other three. I don't think he's got the balls."

O'Hare nodded, rubbing furiously at his three day growth. "I don't think so either. And that means we still got a killer out there somewhere. So let's get the hell out there and find him!"

Grabbing his coat off the rack he headed for the door. Stopping, he turned back to look at Burton who hadn't moved. "Come on Burton. **Jump!**" he shouted. At that the Sergeant ducked his head and followed him into the hallway.

*****

Jeanette sat and stared at the telephone. It wasn't that she didn't think she needed to see Dr. Bernhard. After what had happened this morning it was obvious that she did. It just seemed that actually making the call was admitting just how badly she did. Rallying her nerve she quickly snapped up the receiver and began to dial before she could change her mind.

Once the appointment had been made she felt a little bit better; better in the way a person's tooth stops hurting on the way to the dentist. As she made her way to the kitchen for another cup of coffee, the doorbell rang. Hustling down the stairs she yanked the door open, fully expecting to see Duane. Much to her surprise, Dean Tunney looked back at her, apprehension nipping at the heels of his nervous smile.

"Hi," he blurted awkwardly, and sticking out his hand he pushed a bouquet of flowers under her nose. "Listen I'm really sorry for the way I talked to you the other night, but I was just floored by the way you acted. I mean, I should have listened when you said you didn't think you were in the proper frame of mind to go."

At first she was going to refuse the flowers. But instead she accepted them, and made an apology of her own. "No Dean, there's no reason for you to apologize. You only reacted like any sane person would who was confronted by the actions of a raving lunatic. It's me that owes you an apology. You want to come in?" She asked.

Shaking his head he declined her invitation. "No. No, I can't. I have a meeting in a half an hour clear across town. I'll be lucky to make it on time as it is," he said looking back and forth between his watch and his limo. "I-I do wish you'd let me make it up to you though, say for lunch?"

Jeanette stood dumbfounded. "You mean after what happened the other night you want to take me to lunch?"

"Well, what do you say?" He pressed.

Remembering her appointment, she cursed. "Damn! I'd love to Dean, but I have an appointment at twelve thirty. I can't really say what time I'll be free."

Frowning, he furrowed his brow. "Well how about dinner? Come on, somewhere nice and quiet, just the two of us?"

Jeanette couldn't believe her ears, and she listened as somehow, without any help from her brain, her mouth accepted the unexpected invitation. "I think I'd like that," she said.

"Great!" Dean sighed, his apprehensive expression inching its way into a smile. "I'll call you later to work out the particulars. I gotta run. See you tonight," he smiled, as he backed down the steps, turned, and hopped into his car with a boyish wave.

Closing the door she drifted up the stairs to find a vase for the flowers. Is it possible that what happened the other night wasn't as bad as I thought? Well, she supposed, anything is possible. Still, somehow she didn't believe it. But what other explanation could there be?

Painfully, she ran the events of the fund raiser through her mind. Nope. Just as she'd thought she had acted like a certifiable lunatic. What in the world was Dean thinking? Why would he possibly take the chance of subjecting himself to that insanity again? Well, I'm sure I'll find out later, she figured, and placed the flowers in the vase.

Walking to the front windows, she looked out onto the street. As she did Detective Burton's green Chevy pulled up to the curb. "Oh, terrific, just who I wanted to see," she said aloud, her voice soaked in sarcasm.

As she watched, Burton heaved himself out of the car and looked up to meet her cold stare. When their eyes met Jeanette glared at him momentarily then turned away in contempt. As she did Burton chuckled to himself and headed for the steps to her door.

Jeanette puttered around the kitchen doing nothing as the doorbell rang, Two, Three, Four times. Finally she casually headed down the stairs to answer it. And pulling the door open, she gasped in mock surprise. "Oh! Detective Burton. Why, I wasn't expecting you. *Please,* come in."

The sergeant forced a smile that looked more like indigestion and stepped through the door. "Gee whiz, Ma'am, it sure is a good thing you answered the door when you did, I was just about to give up. I figured no one was home," he lied, returning Jeanette's condescending tone.

Immediately she dropped the charade. The last thing she wanted was to share a joke, no matter how mean spirited, with an ill-tempered doughnut junkie in a bad suit. "Ok, knock off the bullshit, Burton! What do you want?"

The cop's false smile disintegrated into a very real scowl. "The lieutenant wants to talk to you and Avon. He's over there getting him now, they should be here any second," he groused, adding, "I'd make myself comfortable if I were you. This could turn out to be a long day."

Jeanette appraised him spitefully, and walked into the downstairs sitting room. "I hope this doesn't take too long," she shouted back over her shoulder. "I've got an appointment in an hour and fifteen minutes!"

Burton's head appeared in the doorway. "Well maybe you better cancel it, then!" He baited."

Jeanette plopped down on the couch. "Not a chance... Asshole," she said, the last word little more than a whisper.

Burton's round face brightened into a genuine smile. And turning, he walked back into the hallway, clucking heartily at her involuntary agitation.

The sound of the doorbell brought her to her feet. As she entered the hallway she saw Burton letting Duane and O'Hare in. "Hey! It's *my* door, *I'll* answer it, damn it!"

O'Hare slipped through, smiling widely. Good morning, Ms. Tolby, sorry to bother you again," he said, in an effort to smooth over the obviously tense situation. "This'll just take a minute. There are a few things I think you ought to know; both of you." he added, shooting Duane a half smile.

Without a word Jeanette led them into the sitting room, where she retook her seat. Duane snatched the seat next to her, O'Hare across from them, and Burton stood.

The lieutenant leaned in toward the two, his once icy blue eyes taking on a new quality. They were no longer the penetrating weapons they had seemed. Now they were just the cloudy, tired eyes of an old man. Not softer, just less piercing, maybe; but less riveting? Not a bit.

Taking off his hat, he began. "We couldn't hold Stricktland," he said, almost apologetically.

Duane's eyes peeled back in shock. "**What!**" He screeched.

O'Hare raised his hand. "Don't you worry, kid, you'll get your chance in court. He made bail, is all. It's kind of tough to hold someone with no prior record. Even in an open and shut case like this. But that's another story. What I came by to tell you is he's not our murderer." Jeanette smirked to herself, and Duane jumped to his feet to tower over the cop.

"Well he isn't exactly Captain Kangaroo either!" He shouted. "He sure gave *me* one hell of a whack!" At that point Burton walked toward him. "Sit!" He barked. Duane did as he was told, gingerly fingering the welt on his forehead.

"That's just it," the lieutenant continued, "The man *hit* you with a gun. A person who's already killed three times would've shot you, surer than.... Well anyway, he has an alibi. It seems old Gary fancies himself somewhat of a star. He's broadening his career branching out into films. Probably nothing *you'd* want to see."

"Yeah, but you have to admire his motivation!" Burton chirped.

O'Hare turned on his steel eyes like a flashlight, training them on the younger detective. "Well, at any rate, he was filming the night Billy Fairelane was murdered. But all that means is, there's someone out there who doesn't mind killing people who get in his, or *her*, way," he finished, nodding in Jeanette's general direction.

Jeanette felt her body tense as she and Duane exchanged concerned glances. She waited a second for Duane to come to her defense. When he said nothing, she did. "Just what the hell is that supposed to mean?" She fired back, throwing Duane a pained look.

The lieutenant held up his hand and shook his head. "Whoa, hold on there. What I mean is you could be on someone's list. If I thought you were guilty of anything, I'd lock your butt up-"

"Unless of course you didn't have enough to hold someone who had no prior arrests," she interrupted, mimicking his own words.

The cop sighed and continued. "Look the only thing I want you two to do is lay low for a couple of days, preferably together, until we can get this thing sewn up." Jeanette crossed her arms indignantly and walked to the front windows.

Duane shifted nervously in his seat. Feeling guilty for his failure to defend her, he cleared his throat. "Well, I'll have to get some stuff from my place, but it sounds good to me. Whaddaya say boss?" He shrugged, adding a nervous laugh he instantly wished he'd omitted.

Standing up O'Hare took a deep breath and smiled. "Thanks," he offered, extending his hand for Duane to shake. Hesitantly,

Duane obliged. Then, turning on his toes, the cop tipped his beat up hat to Jeannette, who was now facing them. "Good afternoon Ms. Tolby. Don't bother, we'll show ourselves out."

As Burton followed his boss out of the room he turned to face them. "Be seein' ya, kids," he said with a mocking little wave. Simultaneously, they gave him the finger.

O'Hare's voice echoed from the hallway. "Burton! Let's hit it!" He shouted. The sergeant, proud of the way he'd gotten under their skin, chuckled all the way to the door.

Duane fumbled nervously with the magazine on the table. "Ah, listen, Jeanette," he began haltingly. "I-"

"Oh God!" she blurted, looking at her wrist. "What time is it?"

"It's 11:50. Why, what's up?" He asked suspiciously.

"I have to get out of here!" Jeanette said, bolting out of the room. She headed for the stairs with Duane close on her heels. "I-I have an appointment," she shouted back over her shoulder.

"Oh no, not without me you don't," he admonished.

Jeanette turned around halfway up the stairs. "Listen, you're just going to have to trust me on this," she said, a slight hint of exasperation in her voice. "You just go over your place and get what you're going to need for the next couple of days and I'll meet you back here in an hour and a half. Deal?"

Duane stared blankly at her, rubbing his chin as he assessed the situation.

"You aren't gonna to go sticking your nose in any trouble?" He asked, his eyes narrowing slightly.

"Scout's honor," she offered, holding up three fingers on her right hand.

"All right, but just remember, you promised," Duane agreed.

Jeanette blew him a kiss. "Thanks, Sweets. See you then." And turning, she finished her mad dash up the stairs.

As Duane pulled the door of the brownstone closed behind him, a frigid gust of winter wind swept through Kenmore Square causing him to shiver and pull his collar tight up against his cheeks. Looking first one way up the street, then the other, he loped down the steps and jogged across Commonwealth Ave.

Minutes later, Jeanette locked the door to her home and hustled down the steps to the sidewalk. As she approached the entrance to the subway station, for reasons she couldn't explain, she stopped and turned to face the green across the street and behind her. There, leaning up against one of the barren trees, looking quite nonchalant was Duane. He smiled widely and waved, blowing on one hand for warmth. Jeanette returned the gesture, and then waited for him to leave. But he just leaned there and continued smiling. Just then, the sound of the arriving train rolled up the stairs. Waving quickly, she spun around and ran down into the station. God, she thought, most people would be embarrassed if someone caught them spying on them.

CHAPTER ELEVEN

Gary Stricktland made his way through the North End toward Causeway Street as a subway train rattled and swayed to a stop at the station.

When Duane exited the train and made his way through the crowd to the sidewalk, Gary could pick him out like a single cornstalk in a freshly plowed field. Ducking into the doorway of Sully's Tap, he watched as the man he had pistol whipped just days ago crossed Causeway Street and disappeared into North Station. Up until now he had never noticed just how big and fit Duane was. But after seeing him among a crowd of average human beings, he was glad they hadn't met by chance.

Stepping out of the doorway, he continued on his way, his eyes riveted to the door Duane had just entered; but as he reached the corner, he felt a muscular hand grab him by the shoulder and yank at his jacket. Throwing his hands up to defend himself, he whipped around, and found himself looking into his own eyes.

"How's it goin' Gary?" O'Hare smiled. "Why so jumpy?"

Stricktland dropped his hands and shot another look to the door of the station. "What do *you* want?" he spit.

"Just want to have a little chat, is all," the cop chuckled. "You know a fella by the name of Skip Phillips?" Gary looked harshly into his eyes. "I might.Why?"

O'Hare's smile disappeared instantly, and he grabbed the punk by the collar, slamming him up against the wall. "Listen, wise ass, you can either answer me straight, here and now, or we can go down to the station! We still have your room reserved!"

"All right, all right!" Stricktland sputtered, as he peeled O'Hare's gnarled fingers out of his collar. "Yeah I know him. Why?" The lieutenant released his grip on the man and pushed his hat back on his head.

"I'll ask the questions, you just answer them. That's the way this works. When was the last time you saw him?"

Gary scratched his head and thought. "I dunno. Two days ago I guess, right, after the funeral. Listen, I ain't no rat, if you wanna bust Skippy get someone else to do it for you. If you leave him alone he'll probably just die of AIDS or an overdose sooner or later anyway."

The cop shook his head. "See that's our problem. Skippy's already dead, not from an over dose, or AIDS. Seems he developed an acute lead imbalance in his forehead, killed him on the spot," the lieutenant sneered.

"Wait a minute," Gary said, backing away. "I didn't have nothin' to do with it. I'm no murderer!" As he continued his retreat, he backed right into Burton's waiting arms.

"I'd really like to believe you, Gary," O'Hare squinted, shaking his head. "But you just gave me all the wrong answers. Cuff 'im."

Burton grabbed Stricktland by the wrists, applied the handcuffs, and led him to their waiting car.

As the sargent took the back of Stricktland's head into his hand to direct him into the car, Gary looked across the street. There was Duane standing in the doorway to North Station, looking a little confused, but obviously enjoying himself.

*****

"Jeanette, I'd like to ask you a personal question," said Dr. Bernhard, looking up from his notes over the top of his half glasses.

"Sure, shoot," Jeanette agreed with more confidence than she was feeling.

The doctor shifted in his chair to lean in toward her. "If you think I'm out of line just tell me to mind my own business," he smiled blandly. Jeanette nodded with even less conviction. "Have you ever been pregnant or had an abortion?"

Jeanette's back stiffened. She looked at the doctor as though he'd asked if she could fly. "No! Of course not! Haven't you been listening? Christ, I came here for two months before! Half of the reason I came is because I can't stand to have anyone touch me, for any reason!"

The psychiatrist sat back and scribbled something on his pad. "Easy Jeanette, I'm just exploring here. I can't help you if I don't know what's bothering you. And I can't find out what that is, if I don't ask questions." With that the timer went off in his head, and he stood up. "I guess that's it for today. But until next time, why don't you try and work out some of that anger I'm sensing."

"Fine Doc, I'll be seein' you," she said, her tone matching the coolness in her eyes. Grabbing her coat, she left, avoiding the doctor's extended hand.

"Will we be seeing you next week Ms. Tolby?" asked the receptionist. Jeanette walked to the door fully intent on leaving without a word, but thinking better of it she turned on the woman, and with as much distaste as she could summon, said, "Thank you, **no**!"

Jeanette fumed all the way to the subway station. God, I hate shrinks and their pompous attitudes, she thought, "I should work on my anger," she muttered under her breath, trying to come to terms with her thin skinned behavior at the doctor's office.

The subway ride was a long one, the train was packed to the limit, and with the way everyone was pushing and shoving, Jeanette had all she could do to hold her temper. She could hear her pulse beating in her head, as her blood pressure rose and her anger deepened. To stand the whole way home was bad enough, but if that bastard behind her touched her ass one more time...

The train screeched to a stop in the Kenmore station, and not a moment too soon.

As the man behind her nuzzled in and began pushing her toward the door, she lifted her high heeled foot, bending her leg at the knee. Then, as she straightened her leg and twisted her foot, the agonized string of obscenities that flowed muffled through his clenched fist assured her that her spiked heel had indeed found the top of one of his untied sneakers. And without a word, Jeanette pushed her way through the cattle drive for the door.

Once out of the train, the crowd immediately dispersed. Everyone, that is, except the owner of the sneakers, or in this case sneaker. As his mother helped him limp off the train, the large, but obviously young boy's sneaker looked none the worse for wear. It was the big toe protruding from the half cast on his right leg that was bleeding profusely. Gulping so hard she thought she'd swallow her tongue, Jeanette attempted an apology, "Oh my God did I-"

"You most certainly did!" The woman interrupted. "And don't act so damn innocent, it was quite obviously intentional!" She finished, dabbing at the boys toe with her kerchief. "Oh, Ma, take it easy. She didn't mean it!" The boy said through his teeth. "It's ok lady, go on," he tried to smile, wincing as his mother dabbed again at his toe. Jeanette felt a knot develop instantly in her throat. She turned just in time to prevent the boy from seeing the tears begin to run down her face.

Bolting up the stairs to street level and her brownstone, she couldn't believe what she had done. What in God's name is wrong with me? She thought. Have I really lost my mind? When at last she had reached her steps, she rushed up them and inside. Then, slamming the door closed behind her, she leaned back against it and wept the bitter tears of guilt and emotional turmoil.

The rest of the day was painfully tedious. Jeanette spent most of it staring out her front windows at the people passing by. This simple act was devastatingly unnerving. As she watched them pass she realized just how disassociated she had become with the world around her. She felt solitary and insignificant, unable to affect, or even interact with, the rest of humanity.

The clock chimed four as it first occurred to her that Duane should have been back hours ago. Grabbing the phone she dialed his number, but after six rings she gave up and dropped the receiver back onto its resting place. She walked to her front windows and stared into the ever increasing twilight of the green across the way as if by will alone she could make him appear. Then, there in the murky half-light, she saw a shape. It was bobbing and weaving its way toward her, a mere silhouette against the white backdrop of the snow covered greenway. As the specter drew closer, she could make out that it was carrying something. And as it stepped into the artificial light produced by both the store front signs, and the street lights, it became obvious that it was Duane, suitcase in hand, and ready to move in. She heaved a sigh of relief, and directly began to make herself comfortable with a magazine. It would never do for him to know that she'd been worrying about him like some mother hen.

*****

O'Hare watched intently through the rapidly gathering dusk as the officers under his command went over every inch of Skip Phillips' digs, determined to find even the minutest clue that would tie Gary Stricktland to his murder. "Burton! Where the hell, are those lights?! We're cops not coal miners, dammit!"

Burton shrugged his shoulders. "They're on their way, Lieutenant. But once they get here they're still gonna have to drag 'em up seven flights of stairs. O'Hare cursed under his breath as he chewed at his thumbnail.

"Sir, we got a hole in the floorboards over here," One of the younger cops said.

O'Hare made his way across the room and lowered himself down on his haunches. "Anything in it?"

"Don't know. Nothing I can reach anyway," the young cop said between his teeth, still fishing around with his arm stuck into the hole up to his bicep.

"No rats, huh?" O'Hare teased.

The young cop yanked his arm out of the hole and hopped to his feet, wiping his hand furiously on his coat as he shuddered. "Jesus. I never thought of that."

O'Hare's gravelly laugh afforded the rest of the investigative team a moment of levity, and a snicker at the involuntary reaction of the rookie. "Get a pry bar and rip it up, son," the lieutenant chuckled, patting the youngster on the shoulder.

*****

"…and you're going to go?" Duane said in amazement.

"Yeah! And why not?" Jeanette said, sounding a bit more defensive than she'd intended.

"Well, after what you said went on the other night..." he considered, his voice trailing off.

"Well maybe I was just over reacting; After all, it *had* been a perfectly awful day. And besides, if you could have just seen him. All apologetic, flowers, the whole bit. I could hardly have said no."

Duane shook his head, as if rattling the idea around a bit would make it magically fall into perspective and make sense. "Let me get this straight. Two days ago you thought the guy was trying to kill you, but tonight you're perfectly content to go out to dinner with him. Ya know, sometimes *I'm* not so sure you're *not* crazy!"

"Well maybe I am, then! Christ, Duane! Sometimes I wonder whether you're my friend or my father!" That said, she whirled around and stormed into the bathroom, slamming the door.

When Jeanette returned to the living room after getting dressed Duane was either asleep on the couch, or he was pretending to be in order to avoid another round in their disagreement over her decision to go out. She supposed it was just as well, but she really had intended to apologize for her insulting little tirade. So, in lieu of a formal apology, she covered him with a blanket and then slipped down the stairs and out the front door to Dean's waiting car.

CHAPTER TWELVE

Jeanette awoke refreshed and well rested for the first time in nearly a week. There had been no unpleasant occurrences last night at dinner, nothing to keep her awake wondering if she was indeed insane, as Duane had wondered aloud, albeit rhetorically, last night. And best of all, there had been no nightmares. No faceless specters haunting her dreams, no garbled tongues mumbled through the hidden mouths of menacing revenants, and no doctors. Yes, this morning was shaping up very nicely. And she hadn't even gotten out of bed yet.

Last night hadn't been perfect. There was the awkward moment at the beginning of the night when she'd, just in conversation, mentioned to Dean that Duane was spending a couple of days with her. At first she'd actually thought she could read anger on his face. And for a time he had become a bit cold and aloof. But then she'd realized how uncomfortable it probably made him. After all, it *was* an unusual situation. And then there was the whole thing about the fragile male ego. That was what she disliked most about men. The second a woman came into the picture, no matter what the circumstance, they immediately began to compete for her affections; sometimes blatantly, but usually just in some latent and unconscious form of instinctive displaying. And besides, she had rather enjoyed his petty jealousy; even though that was the thing she disliked most about women.

None the less, Dean had eventually warmed up nicely. The food was excellent, and the conversation and company stimulating. All in all, the night had been quite enjoyable, and she could finally look forward to a full day of emotional serenity and physical relaxation.

*****

"Listen, Lieutenant! This whole thing is starting to stink of harassment! You found nothing, I repeat, ***nothing***, to implicate my client in any way, shape, or form, in any of this. Everything you have is circumstantial! You can't prosecute, Christ, you couldn't even get an indictment with this garbage! Kick him loose, and do it now, or I'll file an injunction!"

O'Hare gritted his teeth and swallowed his first reply. "You through?" He asked with calculated passivity.

Gary's lawyer nodded pompously, offering up his palms in a gesture more befitting a Pope than an attorney.

"Ok, Counselor," O'Hare conceded, "now let's take a look at the facts. Your boy was caught in the act threatening a person who turned up dead the next day. Then, the person who saw him threatening the victim gets iced. Not to mention the fact that his alibi for the first night is a bimbo who'd say she went to the moon with him for fifty bucks. And now we have another corpse who somehow around the corner and over the hill is connected to a woman who was murdered over in the Fens the other night. And old Gary admits he was one of the last people to see him alive. That doesn't even include the assault with a deadly weapon we caught him red-handed in. Let's face it. It's only a matter of time."

The lawyer repeated his pretentious gesticulation and shook his head. "Fifteen minutes, Lieutenant, no more. I'll be waiting out front." With that, he nodded good day and walked out the door.

As soon as the door closed behind him, O'Hare looked questioningly at Captain Antonucci. "Sorry, John," The man apologized. "You gotta let him walk."

"**SHIT!**" O'Hare cursed. "This is twice in a week, Jerry. How much do I need on this punk before I can get his ass off the street?"

"Put it this way. You can either let him walk now, or you can forget about ever getting enough on him," the Captain pointed out.

"Yeah, right," O'Hare offered, his voice dripping with contempt, "but this son of a bitch does anyone else, and you and that lawyer can go to confession, cause I'm washin' my hands of all responsibility from here on in!" He finished, storming out the door.

"John, wait a minute. John…" The captain's voice was cut off, first by the slam of the door, then by the clamor of telephones, disjointed conversation, and the customary sounds associated with day to day business.

The lieutenant made his way across the busy station to the booking desk and plopped his hat down on the counter.

"What can I do for you, Brother John," the officer seated there asked.

O'Hare let his head drop and stared at the counter top for a second. Then, lifting his eyes to meet the other officer's, he winced and forced out the words he dreaded saying. "We gotta let Stricktland walk. Do your thing and I'll fill out the paper work later."

"You're kidding! Again?" The man empathized. "Jesus, we bust our balls out there gettin' scum like him off the street, and their high priced suits waltz in here and set 'em loose faster than we can book 'em. No wonder this city is filled with lunatics. They oughtta just build a wall around the whole stinkin' cesspool and be done with it!"

O'Hare nodded his agreement, picked up his hat, and headed back to his desk.

Once seated, the lieutenant surveyed the station with a pained expression. Around him he saw a bunch of dedicated young men. Many of whom, had yet to realize what the future held for them. The years of banging their collective heads against the wall trying to save the same people who would be the first ones

to tell them they were violating some madman's civil rights for
locking him up.

"I'm gettin' too old for this shit," he mumbled. And he leaned
back in his chair, closed his eyes, and began to massage his
throbbing head.

Just then Burton bustled into the station carrying a large
manila envelope, and wearing a large self-satisfied smile.
"Lieutenant, wait'll you get a load of this stuff," he blustered,
dangling the envelope in front of himself across the room.

O'Hare hopped up and walked slowly across the office toward
the detective. "You finished up, over there?"

"Yeah. You wouldn't have believed it. We were all standing
around finishing up, and this big ol' rat comes outta that hole in
the floor, with all six of us there. And, bold as hell, the sucker
runs right between us, grabs a piece of tin foil, then scoots back
down the hole. We had to rip up just about half of the floor, but
we hit the mother lode.

"Anything to tie Stricktland into all of this?"

"I don't know, but we found all kinds of stuff in this rat nest.
Must'a been a pack rat or somethin'."

"Lemme see," O'Hare urged, his eyes widening with
anticipation. Burton reached into the envelope and produced a
numerous selection of zip-lock plastic bags, each containing
their own piece of evidence. Most of the stuff seemed of little
interest. There was a toothbrush, a sock, some wire: A spool of
thread, a colorform of Bambi, enough tin foil to build a small

foreign car, burnt bottle caps, and other assorted debris. But there were a few things that caught O'Hare's attention. One was a skull earring. It was the type of thing that may have been worn by any man who, while he wanted to wear an earring, still wanted to avoid looking effeminate. That piece had Gary Stricktland written all over it. Another was a pair of wraparound sunglasses, again something he could picture Gary in. The third was a watch; a woman's watch. Although it wouldn't have belonged to Gary, from the looks of it, it was in fairly good shape and appeared reasonably new. "Get this stuff down to forensics. I want 'em to lift every print they can off of all of it," the Lieutenant ordered. "These three first!" he added, plucking the three most interesting items out of the pile.

"Yessir," Burton chirped. And gathering up the evidence, he headed for the stairwell.

"And Burton," O'Hare yelled after him, "Do it quick. Tell them it has priority. Stricktland's lawyer was just up here, and we're supposed to cut him loose. This may have bought us some time, but not much."

The detective nodded agreeably as he backed through the doors to the stairs.

"Thomas!" O'Hare shouted to the man behind the booking desk. "Stricktland gone, yet?" The man nodded. "Just let him go. If you hurry you might be able to catch him out front.

The lieutenant raced back to his desk, grabbing his hat. Then, dodging bodies like a running back in his twenties, he headed

out front to try and stall Gary and his lawyer for as long as he
could. If indeed, he could stall them at all.

*****

"...So I step out the door down at the other end of the station,
near that pizza place, and there's our buddy Burton. He's got
Stricktland in cuffs, and he's putting him in the car! Christ, I
laughed my ass off," Duane finished with an exuberant smile.

Jeanette considered him with a puzzled look. "They picked
him up again, right after they let him go?" She asked, licking a
stamp and sticking it on her electric bill. "I don't get it. O'Hare
himself told us he wasn't the killer."

"Yeah," Duane smiled, falling back into the overstuffed chair.
"I don't get it either. But I enjoyed the hell out of it."

Duane watched as Jeanette's face tightened into a thoughtful
frown. "I still don't buy it," she volunteered. "If Gary didn't kill
them two days ago, then he didn't kill them today either."

"Well, maybe they got some new evidence or something. Th-"

"No, Duane! I'm telling you, he didn't do it. I know it," she
said, leaving little room for argument.

Duane sat forward in his chair, his smile melting rapidly
away. "Now don't you start again," he said, shaking his head.
"Just get off of it. If they think he's guilty, that's good enough
for me. Besides, I'm not takin' any more lumps. Not for Billy
Fairelane, and not for anybody else," he finished adamantly.

"That's fine!" Jeanette said. "But look at this whole mess. I'm the one in the middle here."

"That's only because you put yourself there!" Duane offered, getting to his feet.

"No, Duane. I mean **really** look at it. I was closer to Billy than anyone right?" Duane rolled his eyes. "And I knew Brian better than most people, right? And have you forgotten about the lady that should've been me outside of the bar. I don't pretend to know who's doing this, but I'll be God damned if I'm going to sit around and wait for them to finish the job! Duane, don't you get it? I'm next!" Filtering through the front windows, the sunlight glistened off of the single tear which had escaped her eye. She quickly wiped it away. If he was going to help her, he was going to do it because he believed her, not because he felt sorry for her. She watched as his expression softened into one of contemplation rather than defiance.

"So what do you plan on doing about it?"

Jeanette shrugged her shoulders uncertainly and paced to the fireplace, then turned around to face him again. "I don't know. But I get this feeling that it all has something to do with my nightmares. It seems like everything is tied together by some obscure thread. Call it a sixth sense if you want, but I think if I find out what the nightmares are all about, I'll find out who's trying to kill me, and why."

"So where do we start?" Duane smiled.

Jeanette bit her lip for a second, then shrugged her shoulders. "At the beginning, I suppose; at *my* beginning."

*****

Lieutenant O'Hare dragged himself down the stairs to the forensics lab. He had caught up with Gary and his lawyer as they were getting into a car out in front of the station. He'd done his best to stall them with double talk, but was told, in no uncertain terms, and with a finger thrust in his face, "Listen, Lieutenant, as soon as you get something concrete, give me a call. But until then, you stay away from my client!"

As he pushed his way into the outer office of the lab, he saw Burton, seated and reading a magazine. Looking up from his reading, the detective put down his *Sports Illustrated* and stood up. "Didn't catch 'em, huh.?"

"I caught 'em alright," the lieutenant said disappointedly. "But I couldn't very well handcuff the two of them to a parking meter, now could I?"

Burton just shook his head, sat back down and picked up the magazine again. But dropping it back on the table he looked up into O'Hare's cloudy eyes. "We'll get him, John. I mean, you know we'll get him eventually. The son of a bitch has the brain of a gnat. He proved that over at Tolby's place."

"Ah, bullshit, Burton. You know as well as I do that was pure luck, and suppose we don't get him; just suppose for a minute that he's not even our guy. What do we have, then? We have a pair of God damned sunglasses that could've come out of any apartment in that stinking tinder box we found 'em in, a friggin' earring that could belong to any junkie or punk in the city, and some woman's watch that was probably stolen. All that, and some nut running around the city thumbing his nose at us. In case you haven't been keeping score, that all adds up to squat!" the lieutenant finished, kicking a wastebasket across the room with a crash.

Just then a light went on behind his eyes like the sun burning through a coastal fog. "Get off your ass Burton," O'Hare grinned, "We're gonna pay Ms. Tolby another little visit."

"The watch!" Burton beamed, "You think it's hers?"

O'Hare was already out the door and on his way up the stairs. "Come on, Burton, move it!" he shouted back over his shoulder.

*****

As they pulled up in front of Jeanette's brownstone, the sun was swallowed by a very large, and very ominous, black cloud. Pushing himself out of the driver's seat, Burton hustled up the steps and rang the doorbell, the lieutenant lagging behind and straightening his tie.

After ringing the bell six times both officers were ready to give up.

"Damn!" Burton cursed.

"Where the hell did they go?" The lieutenant didn't even hear him. He was busy looking around the stoop thoughtfully.

"Whaddaya thinkin'?" Burton asked.

"Forget it. Never mind. All we need is something with her prints on it." O'Hare said, almost to himself. Then his eyes went to the black cast iron mailbox next to the door. Protruding ever so slightly from the top of it was the corner of an envelope. Smiling, the lieutenant looked up and down the street, then grabbed the corner of the letter between his fingernails and wiggled it out of the box.

"Jeez, I don't know John, that's...

"Don't worry about it, Burton. We lift a couple of prints, just to see if they match, then we drop it back in the mail."

"But-"

"But, nothin'. You got a better idea?"

The detective shook his head, and looked guiltily around them.

"Fine," O'Hare offered, dropping the envelope in his pocket. "So let's go, then."

As the two officers made their way back to the car, a pair of interested eyes watched them from behind the tinted windows of a large black sedan. And as they pulled away, the sedan headed off in the other direction.

*****

The drive to Waltham was only about thirty minutes. But as apprehensive as Jeanette was about going back to the state home, even if it was just for a visit, it seemed as long as a weekend in hell. Originally Duane had wanted to take the highway, but Jeanette had felt compelled to follow Brookline Ave. through Brookline, Belmont, Watertown, all the towns in between, and finally into Waltham. It had been sixteen years since she had traveled these roads, riding to and from her first year at Emerson College, which was her last time at the home. But even after these many years, there were several landmarks which remained the same. Most of the highly developed areas, such as Watertown Square, Belmont Center, and the like, were much the same as she remembered, and expectedly so. But it was the more rural areas, and the residential streets that gave her the feeling that they had been waiting for her return. They had remained constant and unchanging as the world around them grew and hardened into its present shape. So many times as she'd passed these homes and streets she'd wondered what it would have been like to be a part of a real family, and to live in a real home on a real street in a real neighborhood. And now she found herself doing it again. She'd always fantasized about the "real" home she and her prince charming husband would make for their children. It would be a home with a beautiful sprawling back yard, fenced of course, and the children laughing and playing in their own little piece of paradise, safe and loved.

Suddenly, and without warning, the sun was engulfed by a huge dark cloud, and she shuddered with the revelation that the last twelve years of her life had been a lie. Her devotion to her work, and her excuse that she would have those things "all in due time" had been a cruel and misguided invention born of her denial of her infertility. It had never been as obvious to her as right now. She would never have those things she coveted most. Her emptiness was absolute. And as the clouds had devoured the sun, so did her own barrenness consume the last of her wounded and writhing dreams.

"So, which way?" Duane asked, retrieving her from her self imposed torment.

"Huh?"

"I said, which way? We're in Waltham Center!"

"Oh. Ah, let's see. Take the next right. It's about two miles up on the right hand side," she said, rallying her game face. She had lived the last sixteen years well aware of her sterility, at least logically, if not emotionally. And now was not the time to work it out. There would be plenty of time for that when, and if, she came through this with her sanity intact.

As they pulled onto the grounds of the orphanage, and up the long tree lined drive that separated it from the road, rushes of memories flooded back to her; memories of her and her roommate, getting up after curfew, and blocking the crack under the door with a blanket to stop the telling light from escaping. Then they would sit up, sometimes until nearly dawn, talking about the cutest new boys that had arrived, trying new hair-styles, and, in general, being teenage girls. She tried to think back further into the past, but before that the memories got hazy. There were dribs and drabs of innocuous recollections. But nothing concrete. The feeling was frustrating. She knew damn well she had been here since she was four, why was it that her memories of the early days were so faint. Years, she assumed, too many, and too much time between.

Duane pulled the car to a stop in front of the stairs, but as they got out Jeanette noticed something odd, or more to the point, she didn't notice something. As they climbed the stairs, the feeling gnawed at her. Something wasn't right. Something was missing. Then she realized what it was. Stopping, she turned around to look at the small playground that sat on the sprawling frontage of the large brick structure. It was the children. The children were missing. She quickly went back to her memory files and tried to recall a time during the day, when she'd lived here, that the playground was completely empty. She couldn't. Be it spring, summer, fall, or winter, there was always someone out there during the day. She distinctly remembered that different age groups had their daily outdoor activities at different times, in order to reduce the number of children to a manageable number.

"They're not here," she breathed nearly inaudibly.

"What?" Duane asked. "Who's not? What's wrong?"

"The children..." She answered with a whisper. 'They're gone. They're all gone."

Shaking his head, Duane turned around and tried the door. It was locked. He tried again, jiggling the handle as he wiped the accumulated grit of off one of the window panes. As he peered into the darkened foyer of the abandoned building, he realized she had been right; they *were* all gone. Looking downward, he noticed a thick steel chain interlaced between the two panic bars which operated the doors from the inside. And from the cobwebs amassed on the chain, he could tell that they *had* been gone for some time. Then, from behind him, he heard the slam of a car door, and turned to see Jeanette seated in the car, her head in her hands. It was going to be a long ride home.

As he slid himself into the car and fastened his safety belt, he looked sympathetically at her. It was then that he noticed that she was laughing. At first he began to smile, but then he realized that her laugh carried with it a humorless, chilling quality. It was the kind of nervous tittering that is usually reserved for times of great emotional discomfort or stress. "Sorry, sweetheart," he offered. "You gonna be ok?"

Jeanette lifted her head and glared at him, her mouth twisted up in an anguished half smile.

"Am I gonna be ok?" She asked, her voice trembling. "Sure, why not, all this means is that I'll probably never get another decent night's sleep in my entire life. Why shouldn't I be ok? And besides, I probably won't live that long, anyway," she finished, her voice cracking as she fought back a fresh set of tears.

Duane leaned over and took her in his arms. "Hey, that doesn't sound like the *you, I* know. This doesn't mean anything. So they're closed down, so what? They have to have kept the records somewhere. All it's gonna take is a few phone calls. We'll find out where they are."

Jeanette fell back against her seat and wiped clumsily at her eyes with the back of her hand. "I hope so, Duane," she said, "because I don't know how much longer I can hold out like this." Then she fell silent and trained her attention out the window. He had been right. It *was* going to be a long ride home.

*****

Lieutenant O'Hare and Sergeant Burton sat waiting semi-patiently outside the forensics lab. O'Hare looked anxiously at his watch and stood to pace the room again. Just then, the door to the inner office swung open, and the head lab technician stepped through, carrying a box containing all the evidence that Burton had obtained at Skip Phillips' apartment. And there, right on top of the pile, was the envelope O'Hare had acquired at Jeanette's.

"I got a few matches," the tech acknowledged. "The earring didn't match up with anything, but the sunglasses had the deceased's prints all over 'em. No matches on Stricktland's prints, but the prints on the watch and the letter had the same basic form and contour."

"So what does that mean?" O'Hare asked, "I mean contours and forms. Do they match, or don't they?"

"Well, the watch is so small I couldn't get a full print off of it. But let me put it this way, the chances that they didn't come from the same person are infinitesimal."

Burton's eyebrows raised in an apparent fog, and the tech smiled wryly, adding, "Teeny weeny." holding his thumb and forefinger less than an inch apart.

O'Hare stifled a laugh for Burton's sake, but his levity was short-lived. These were not the answers he'd wanted to hear. In one fell swoop, the man had not only dealt their case against Gary Stricktland a near fatal blow, but he had created more questions than answers.

"So, do you want me to do the paperwork and enter this stuff as evidence?" The technician offered,

O'Hare reached out and plucked the bags containing the envelope and the watch out of the box. "Yeah, you might as well. But I'll watch these, and you never saw this," he informed him, holding up the envelope.

"Right," the tech winked. And he disappeared back through the door.

"So whaddaya think?" Burton asked, as they climbed the stairs back to the squad room.

O'Hare pulled off his hat and massaged at his temples with the other hand. "To tell you the truth, I don't know what to think. On the one hand we got this guy who has every motive in the world, plus opportunity. And on the other hand we have this woman, who wasn't only a close friend of two of the stiffs, but had every reason in the world to want one of them alive and healthy. But now we find out, she, at the very least, made contact with one of the victims, some junkie she otherwise would have had no possible interest in knowing. So you tell me. What the hell does it all add up to?"

Burton's brow furrowed with thought. In all the years he'd known John O'Hare, he had never seen him so baffled. Sure there had been cases left unsolved, and the ones that had ended up in court, only to be thrown out, or lost on some technicality. But up until now he still had always seemed in control of the situation. Never flustered, he had no self-doubt. Everything was always just business as usual. There had been some rumblings lately in the ranks. Talk about how maybe he was getting too old, had been at it too long. That he had lost his edge, as they put it. But they weren't his partners. They hadn't worked with him as closely as he had for the last three years. He'd gladly stack O'Hare up against any one of them. He was the best he'd ever met at figuring out what made the criminal mind tick and staying one step ahead of it. But suddenly, he seemed to be falling behind. And now that he thought of it, it seemed it had started longer ago than he'd realized. Were the bad guys really getting that much smarter? Or was it just that everyone else had been right, and he'd refused to see it.

CHAPTER THIRTEEN

On their third call Duane finally made some progress. Jeanette had attempted the previous two. But seconds into the first one it became painfully obvious that they weren't going to get anywhere as long as she kept sobbing and screaming at people. Then, after the second call had failed just as miserably, Duane convinced her to let him handle the rest of the phone calls while she took a shower.

Immediately after she left the room he began to have some success. Once he'd found out from the Waltham Police that all the records from Saint Bridget's Home for Dependent Children were kept at the Child Welfare offices in Brookline, he knew he was on a roll. So, lifting the receiver off its cradle, he quickly dialed the number he'd been given. The phone rang five times before someone picked up.

"Child Welfare Offices, Can I help you?" A flustered voice answered.

"Yes. Well, I hope so anyway. My name is Duane Avon, and I'm looking for some information on a young woman. She was in the custody of the state about sixteen years ago. Her na-"

"I'm sorry, Mr. Avon," the woman interrupted, "We're not allowed to give out information of that nature over the phone."

"Oh... Well, how about if I pop down there, then."

"You're welcome to stop by tomorrow between eight and four thirty, but as a matter of fact, I was on my way out the door when the phone rang," she said, her voice slightly strained with annoyance. "We're closed for the day.

"But it's only just four, now." Duane said, his own voice bearing a hint of agitation.

"Like I said, you can stop by tomorrow. But If you do, you'll need one of the following; either verification of your relation to the woman, written and notarized permission from her personally, a court order providing you with the authorization for obtaining the information, or a form from the police department in the town where she was housed allowing you access to the information," the woman rapped off with practiced precision.

"How about, if I just bring the young lady with me?" Duane said smugly."

"If you have the woman," the receptionist questioned, just as arrogantly, "then why don't you just ask her for the information?"

Duane fumed for a second, then, in a calm and calculated fashion, he volunteered, "The information isn't for me, it's for her." Then, without waiting for an answer, he said "You know what, we'll be in tomorrow. Thanks a lot!" With that he disconnected the call and swore to himself.

"Duane," Jeanette said from behind him. "Who were you talking to?"

Duane turned around wearing a forced smile. "It was just some lady who needed an attitude adjustment," he said. "Actually, it was a lady at the Child Welfare office," he admitted. "What an attitude, though. She said we could stop by tomorrow to find out where the records are."

"*Tomorrow*? What if tomorrow's too late?" She complained, her voice trembling.

"Just relax," Duane said, "They're closed for the night. There's nothing we can do. You'll be fine 'til the morning. Then, first thing, we'll head down there and see what we can find out, ok?"

Jeanette crossed the room, put her arms gently around Duane's neck, and pulled him close.

"Thank you, Duane." she breathed, "I don't know what I'd do if I didn't have you."

"Yeah, neither do I," he agreed. "Where else are you gonna find someone stupid enough to get messed up in something like this?"

Jeanette smiled blandly and headed for the kitchen, "Extra dry?" she asked over her shoulder.

"No, not me. Not tonight," he answered. He wasn't exactly sure what it was that was going on, or if, indeed, anything was.

But one thing he was sure of was that he didn't want to find out there *was* something going on when he was half in the bag.

"Well, I'm gonna have one before bed. Then it's lights out. I am just drained." He kind of half heard her say from the kitchen.

"Humph," he grunted back as though disinterested.

As he stood and stared into the fireplace at the spent remains of this afternoon's fire, his mind was buzzing with questions to which he wasn't even sure there were any answers. The most troubling of them, and the one that worried him on the whole, was the one he'd asked, albeit rhetorically, last night. But now, after thinking back over the last week, he wasn't so sure she *wasn't* a little crazy.

Jeanette returned, her drink in hand and made her way toward the couch to sit down. But, as she placed her martini on the end table, the doorbell rang causing her and Duane to exchange uneasy looks.

Getting to his feet, Duane headed for the stairs. "I'll get it," he offered cautiously. "You just stay up here."

When he began descending the stairs toward the first floor, he could feel the sweat begin to bead on his forehead. Again the bell rang, startling him slightly once more and bringing him to a full stop on the last step for just a second before continuing on to the door.

Through the elaborate cut and opaque glass of the window, he could barely make out a single dark figure hovering on the other side of the door. Less than a foot apart, they were separated by no more than a thin pane of fogged glass. As he reached for the knob, he could feel his pulse rise and his heart crawl up into his throat. Before turning the knob his eye caught the latch chain, and slipping it into its slide, he then confidently turned the knob and pulled the door open until the chain was taught.

"Oh, it's you," Dean Tunney frowned. "I was really expecting to see Jeanette. Is she here?" Duane returned Tunney's distrustful glare and pretended to think for a second.

"I think she's in bed," he answered curtly. "Wait here, I'll check."

"Hey, it's a little cold out here. Can I come in and wait?" Tunney asked pointedly.

Duane considered the Senator's request, then smiled sheepishly and volunteered, "No. I'll be right back," and closed the door in Dean's face.

When he turned around he saw Jeanette standing halfway up stairs, her arms crossed and her foot tapping impatiently. "I don't believe you did that, Duane. Sometimes you're such a child," she said, brushing by him and reaching for the door.

Grabbing her by the elbow, he turned her around to face him. "Before you do that, think about the other night in Cambridge. Then, if you still want to let him in, do it yourself. And if you do, you're on your own," he sighed, shaking his head and mounting the stairs.

*****

The phone rang, causing John O'Hare to curse as he pushed himself out of his favorite chair. Crossing the room, he turned down the volume on his ancient black and white television set, then ambled to the hallway and lifted the phone off of its hook. "Hello?" He exhaled heavily.

The Lieutenant listened for an answer, but couldn't make one out for the popping and interference that buzzed over the line. "Hello!" He tried again.

When still he got no reply, he was about to hang up. But just then, through the sound of crackling and static, he heard, "pop.....Garrison.......ab....crack....ician.....we.....zzzzzz....et....atch...ssssss....let."

"Garrison, you lazy bastard," the lieutenant growled. "If you've got something to tell me, hang up that God damned cell phone, get off your lazy ass, and call me on a real phone!" He said, slamming the receiver down. "Jesus Christ!" He mumbled, "if that's modern technology, I'll take a God damned telegraph."

Just as he began to lower himself back into his chair the phone rang again, giving him a perfectly good reason to swear and complain some more as he crossed to the hallway to answer it. "Hello!" he practically shouted into the mouth-piece.

"Hi, John, Garrison here. Sorry abo-"

"Why don't you junk that piece of crap?" O'Hare interrupted. "The damn thing never works right, anyway."

"Yeah, yeah," the lab technician sighed. "and when are you going to by a color T.V.?" He teased. "Listen, I just thought I'd

- 211 -

call and let you know that the boys in ballistics didn't get a match between the bullet they pulled out of Phillips and your boy Stricktland's gun.

"Damn!" O'Hare winced. "Now I got nothin'."

"Sorry about that, John," Garrison offered.

"Yeah, yeah. Well, thanks for the call. I'll see you tomorrow," the lieutenant barely whispered, and he dropped the phone onto its pedestal.

Walking to the closet, he pulled the door open, grabbed his coat, and stuffed his hand in the right hand pocket, fishing a plastic bag out of it. He attempted to hang the jacket back using only one hand, but frustrated, he tossed it to the floor of the closet and kicked the door closed. Then, turning and heading back into the living room, he retook his seat and held the bag up before his eyes. What the hell has Jeanette Tolby gotten herself mixed up in? He asked himself as he stared at the woman's watch. In all his years in this town, there had only been one other collection of murders that had been so obviously connected, yet still so baffling. In the 60's it was Albert Disalvo, the so called "Boston Strangler." He took out seven ladies over a two year period, and was caught purely by accident. It was the case he'd really cut his teeth on nearly thirty years ago. And not since then had he felt so totally inept. He just hoped it wouldn't take seven deaths this time before the bastard made a mistake.

*****

Jeanette wished Dean Tunney a good night, and then quietly slipped up the stairs and into her bedroom. It wasn't so much that she wanted to go to bed. But she really didn't want to explain to Duane why she had so readily accepted Dean's visit; mostly because she really wasn't so sure herself why she had. It was just something about the man that made her trust him or, more to the point, "everything" about him. He was just a nice guy. Pleasant, intelligent, thoughtful, and best of all, just because a woman spent an evening with him, he didn't always expect it to end in the sack.

After brushing her hair, she crawled into bed and clicked off the light without even considering the journey that awaited her, as always, just on the other side of sleep.

The state of emotional exhaustion she was in caused her to drift off almost as soon as her head hit the pillow. And there, her increasingly regular sojourn began, but this time it was different. This time it began in the treatment room, at the point where, up until now, it had usually culminated.

As she looked up from the treatment table, she could feel the mind numbing poison pumping up the vein in her arm. With every beat of her heart, she could feel its warmth inch closer to her brain as it carried with it the weight of unconsciousness. Everything was happening in slow motion now. The voices, which before had been merely unintelligible, now had become no more than drawn out groans, exaggerated and magnified by the tile walls which seemed to be pulling away from her. She felt a tiny twinge between her legs, but only for a second. Then, summoning all her strength, she forced herself to a sitting position. Everything was still in slow motion, which was seemingly to her advantage. She watched the looks of terror and surprise leap from the heretofore light obscured eyes of her tormentors.

One of the nurses lunged toward her in an effort to grab her and force her back down. But before she could, Jeanette's hand flashed out before her and grabbed the doctor's mask, pulling it down to expose his face. She felt a scream well in her gut as she realized who it was behind the mask. But the bloodcurdling screech died in her lungs as she lost consciousness, Dean's twisted and sadistic smile danced mockingly before her fading subconscious eye. Then, just as his visage began to flicker like a failing candle, she saw his mouth begin to move. Her body began to involuntarily convulse, and she felt panic clawing at the fringe of her senses. Yet still, she listened with all her might to try and make sense of what he was saying. When she finally made it out, what she heard was the sound of her own name being anxiously repeated, over and over.

"Jeanette... Jeanette... Jeanette!"

It was then that she heard herself scream.....

"Jeanette! Jeanette!" Duane said as he shook her gently. "Jeanette, wake up!" He pleaded, one hand partially covering her mouth to muffle her earsplitting scream.

Suddenly her eyes snapped open and she stopped screaming. The terror that he saw there made his stomach wring and his heart jump a beat. As she peered back at him through the thinning semi-conscious fog of awakening, she did so with panic unmistakably etched in the deepening lines of her face. But fear wasn't the only emotion he saw in her eyes. It was accompanied by a time suspending look of loathing. A loathing that surpassed any the likes of which he would have believed her capable. Then, just as quickly, her features softened. And as a rim of moisture began to form around her fluttering eyes, she slowly became increasingly aware of her surroundings.

"Are you all right?" Duane asked as she pushed herself up onto her elbows.

Jeanette looked around herself, her eyes flicking franticly from one corner of the room to the other in a paranoid frenzy, as though she wasn't quite comfortable with her surroundings. But just as Duane was about to ask again she slid herself into a sitting position, wiped at her eyes, and hung her head, shaking it subtly.

"Yeah," she answered breathlessly. "Yeah, I'm ok, I guess."

Duane stood, putting a hand gently on her shoulder. "Jesus, that must have been one hell of a nightmare."

"Yeah, it was," she groaned, swinging her feet over the edge of her bed.

Duane waited a moment in the hope that she might elaborate, but when it became obvious that she wouldn't, he took the liberty of prodding her for a more in depth explanation of her obviously terrifying dream. ""So, what was it about?"

Looking up at him, she brushed her hair out of her eyes and shook her head. "What difference does it make?" She asked. "It was only a stupid dream."

Standing, Jeanette made her way to the bedroom door, her flannel nightgown swishing along the floor. Once she reached the doorway she turned, offering Duane the hallway with the palm of her hand. "I'm ok now," she said, "thanks for waking me."

"You're sure you don't want me to stay?" Duane teased. "What if your nightmare comes back?"

"Just don't you worry about it," she said, smiling half-heartedly. "I wouldn't count on that happening."

"Ok, I get the hint," he grinned. "But you know where to find me if you need me," he added, passing her on his way into the hallway.

"Thaanks, Duaaane," she offered swinging the door closed between them. But as the latch caught with a click, she leaned in, closing her eyes and resting her forehead against the cool oak of the door. She knew all too well, that regardless of what she'd said, the nightmares were just about the only thing she *could* count on lately.

*****

John O'Hare crushed out his cigarette and reached for the chain on his bedside lamp. Instead of shutting off the light, as he knew he should have, he picked up the baggie containing Jeanette Tolby's watch. Reaching over, he grabbed another cigarette, lit it, and lay back, dangling the baggie over his face. For all of his experience, and for all of his years spent guessing just what move to make to stay one step ahead of the career criminals, it just didn't figure that he should be completely baffled by a case that involved nothing but rank amateurs. Squashing out his cigarette, he sighed.

As was usually the case when he was embroiled in a particularly tough investigation, this was going to be a very long night. A night that, at his age, he was sure he could well do without.

PART TWO
THE DESCENT

CHAPTER FOURTEEN

The moment Jeanette awoke, she slowly began to experience an emotional weight that seemed as though it would crush her chest to the point of suffocating her. She wasn't exactly sure which possibility worried her more. Was it the fact that she may not find out anything at all at the Child Welfare Office? Or was it the very real chance that she may find out something she didn't want to know?

The thought of lingering in bed to delay the inevitable confrontation with her fears occurred to her, but she could already hear the muffled morning sounds of Duane puttering around in the kitchen. So with the smell of the fresh brewed coffee to reinforce her nerve, she reluctantly dragged her unwilling body out of bed and headed toward the door and what, she was quite sure, was going to be, at best, a difficult day.

The second she pushed open the door to her bedroom and stepped into the hallway, Duane poked his head around the corner of the kitchen entryway. "Morning, bright eyes. Feel like some breakfast?"

"Not really," she answered with a lukewarm smile, but, seeing the disappointment on Duane's face, she added "Maybe just some toast and coffee," as brightly as she could, then disappeared into the bathroom.

Twenty minutes later, once she had finished a very long and extremely hot shower, she finally reappeared at the entrance to the kitchen and greeted Duane with a much more convincing grin.

"Coffee's in the pot, toast is on its way," he offered over the top of the sports page. "Damn! Celtics and Bruins both lost again! I think it's gonna be a *long* winter!"

Jeanette poured herself a cup of coffee and sat down across from him. She picked distractedly at her nails for a second, but unwilling, as well as unable, to feign disinterest; she cut right through the phony small talk and made her point. "What do you think we'll find out, Duane?" She asked.

"I think we'll find out the Celts need a point guard, and the Bruins need a goal scorer," he smirked.

"You know what I mean, wise guy," she said, grabbing the newspaper out of his hands and tossing it on the counter.

Suddenly, a severe look wrinkled his forehead. "I don't know, sweetheart. What do you *expect* to find?"

Jeanette shrugged her shoulders, and as quickly as it had appeared, the taxed expression lifted from his face.

"I do know one thing, though," he pointed out. "If you don't get a move on, we won't find out anything."

"All right, all right! Just give me fifteen minutes," she said, pushing herself out of her chair.

"I'll be waiting patiently," Duane smiled, rolling his eyes.

Returning his sarcastic smirk, Jeanette headed for her room.

*****

"Oh, Christ, you're kidding! When?" John O'Hare rubbed furiously at his eyes with his thumb and fore finger as he listened to the news from the station about yet another corpse which had turned up overnight. He could hear his stomach bubble like a water cooler, and winced as a burning sensation began to run up his esophagus. "Any I.D.? Ok. Call Burton and have him meet me there. I'll be there in about a half an hour.... Right, and see what you can do about gettin' me an I.D., will you..... Yeah, yeah, see ya."

The Lieutenant dropped the phone back on the hook and continued to massage his bloodshot eyes. Though he'd already been awake for quite a while, the three hours he'd actually spent sleeping last night, or more precisely, this morning, had been less than adequate to prepare him for tending to yesterday's business, much less more of the same today. But regardless of whether or not he was prepared for it, or whether or not he'd gotten enough sleep, his job was still his job, and right now he had to go to work.

As he fetched his coat off of the floor of the hall closet it reminded him of the thing that had been responsible for keeping him up all night. So, hustling into his bedroom, he snatched the baggie that contained Jeanette Tolby's watch off of his nightstand. When he looked up, he realized, thanks to the mirror on his dresser, that his thinning hair was standing on end. At first he attempted to flatten it with his hand, but finding that futile, he settled for covering it with his wrinkled hat and rushed out the door.

Twenty five minutes later O'Hare was walking the distance from the Park Street subway station toward the Washington Street alleyway which contained the latest victim of Boston's increasingly dangerous streets. There had been a time when this area of town had been the host to most of what was considered the seamy side of life in blue blooded Boston. Known as everything from the bowery to the combat zone in its heyday, from the mid-forties until the mid- seventies, it housed the majority of strip joint bars, prostitution, and porno flicks, which had to be kept somewhere. At one time this seamy collection of erotic specialty stores and peep shows stretched from just outside the theater district, a block off of Boston Common, all the way to the border of Chinatown. But since the 70s, what with the surge in both urban renewal and politically convenient artificial morality, what was left of the old red light district had decreased in size to a little more than two blocks. Although, now that he thought of it, he wasn't so sure if it had really dwindled, or if the questionable commerce offered there had simply become so readily available everywhere that it eventually had seeped into every alleyway and dimly lit spot in the whole city.

When he rounded the corner of Washington Street he could already pick out Burton's green Chevy two blocks down on the right. It was accompanied by two cruisers and another unmarked car. As he approached them, he spotted his partner jotting down whatever facts he could glean from what must have been the youngest uniform he'd ever seen.

"Burton!" He called out. "What's up?" When the younger detective looked up, O'Hare saw a look on his face that was nothing short of bewildered frustration.

When he saw O'Hare, Burton's fog seemed to lift, and gesturing with his finger the detective preceded him into the alleyway. "Wait'll you get a load of this shit!" Burton said over his shoulder.

About halfway down the alley, the lieutenant saw two other uniforms along with his boss, Captain Antonucci, and two attendants from the coroner's office. The Coroners orderlies were loading a black body bag into what was jokingly referred to in the department as the meat wagon.

"Why don't you give the Lieutenant a look?" Burton asked as they approached the scene; but before the attendant could answer, Antonucci whipped around and fixed O'Hare with a less than pleasant expression.

"Do you see that, O'Hare? That's a body, and might I add, *another* body, in my precinct! I don't like bodies in my precinct, O'Hare! Now, it's up to you to find out who's makin' 'em, and make 'em stop, am I correct?!"

"That's right," the lieutenant admitted sourly, and leaning into the truck, he unzipped the bag, and flipped back the flap to expose a sightless pair of ice blue eyes. Gary Stricktland's fledgling movie career was over.

"Oh, for Christ's sake!" O'Hare spit. "You *gotta* be pullin' my chain here. What the hell is goin' on?"

Burton just shrugged his shoulders and shook his head. "I don't know, John."

"That's right, Lieutenant, none of us know!" The captain interrupted, "but I know one of us who better get his act together and find out! This shit has gone far enough, it's got to cease! And **NOW**! You've got 48 hours, and then you're off the case, and the street! Do we understand one another?"

O'Hare nodded curtly, and watched as Antonucci pounded to his car and squealed around the corner and out of sight. When he turned his attention back to Burton, the younger Detective picked up right where he'd been interrupted.

"The lady on the third floor on the right, one Mrs. Veronica Cole, called it in. Said she saw him this morning when she let her cat out on the fire escape. Of course nobody saw or heard anything. At least nothing they'll admit to, anyway."

"I suppose we can rule out natural causes," the lieutenant grumbled.

"That'd be a pretty good bet," Burton nodded, "his damn head was twisted around nearly 180 degrees. And there were no signs of any injuries from a fall or a beating."

"Well, if there was no struggle, then that could only mean one of two things," O'Hare observed, looking up above himself to the fire escapes, then up and down the alleyway "One," he began, kicking a can down the alley way and listening to the echo, "somebody sneaked up on him in the dark in this wide open alley, which is possible but highly doubtful. Or two, he was done by someone who knew him, more than likely somewhere else, and dumped here. I vote for number two," he concluded, his hand already back in his pocket, fondling the baggie containing Jeanette's watch.

"You get my vote," Burton nodded.

"Make sure they scrape his nails," O'Hare told the coroner's orderly.

"Always, Lieutenant."

"Come on, Burton. I think you and me should pay Tolby and Avon another visit," O'Hare announced.

Burton followed obediently, silently writing, as they headed for his car and Commonwealth Ave.

"I want every room on both sides of that alley gone over from top to bottom," O'Hare barked at one of the uniforms as they made the sidewalk. "If someone has a half-eaten jelly sandwich under their couch, I wanna know how it got there, who was eatin' it, and where they bought the fuckin' bread!"

"Gotcha," the cop replied obediently.

"He's an asshole!" Burton volunteered when they reached the car.

"Who?" The lieutenant asked.

"Antonucci," Burton offered. "he's gotta be such a hard ass all the time, you know?"

"Yeah, I *do* know," O'Hare smirked, "how do you think he got to be the boss?"

Burton hissed a laugh and hopped in behind the wheel. "I don't know, but someday I'd like to be boss. Do you think I got what it takes?" He asked.

"Definitely, Burton," O'Hare insisted. "I think you'd be perfect."

*****

"That's T-O-L-B-Y," Jeanette bristled, rolling her eyes at Duane. Much to their disappointment, the first two receptionists at the Child Welfare Offices had been less than helpful; a circumstance for which Duane felt at least partially responsible. The moment he'd mentioned his name they'd been ignored for a moment then passed on to the next secretary until he'd recognized the voice of the woman who he'd encountered yesterday on the phone. Unfortunately, the disapproval he read in her eyes made it quite clear she recognized his as well. Since then it had been straight down hill.

"I'm sorry," the woman said, as she stood back up and turned to face them once again. "I can't seem to find you anywhere, Ms. Toldy. Where did you say you were a resident?"

"That's Tolby!!" Jeanette spit "TOLBY! With a B, B, as in brain dead!"

Duane, seeing the frustration mounting to the point of no return and the tightness around Jeanette's mouth, put a calming hand on her shoulder and interrupted. "Ah, could you excuse us for a second?" He asked, ushering Jeanette across the office to the front windows.

"Sure, I gotta stay here all day," he heard the woman say through a mouthful of chewing gum.

"Duane, if that idiot doesn't start acting semi intelligent, or at least marginally lucid, I'm gonna hurdle that desk, and choke her ass!" Jeanette seethed under her breath.

"I know, I know, just let me have five minutes with her alone, ok?"

"Five minutes?" She asked incredulously. "Jesus, Duane, if idiots could fly this place would qualify as a God damned airport! What makes you think *you* can straighten it out in five minutes? We're talkin' government, here!"

"Just gimme a shot," he begged. "What harm could it possibly do?"

"Fine!" Jeanette agreed, "But don't say I didn't warn you." And turning away she exited the office into the hallway.

Walking back up to the counter, Duane pulled a pen out of his inside pocket, picked up a piece of paper, and began writing something down. As he wrote, he began to speak; short, and to the point. "Listen, let's you and me just cut through the garbage, here. I can't see any reason why you should make *her* life miserable just because you and I had words yesterday. After all, it's not me who wants the information, it's for her."

"I suppose you're right," the woman said, popping her gum "But that doesn't alter the fact that I can't find her name, does it?"

Duane felt a wave of anger begin to crawl up his spine, but taking a deep breath, he fought it back down and spoke slowly and calmly. "Here," he said, handing her the slip of paper on which he'd scribbled Jeanette's name. "The name is Tolby. With a B."

"Ok, I'll give it another shot," the receptionist gave in, "but I'm tellin' you, I really don't think it's there."

"Thanks," Duane volunteered. Then, forcing a flimsy smile, he headed for the hallway to retrieve Jeanette.

Within a matter of seconds Duane returned. With him, he brought a much less frustrated Jeanette, and a much more convincing smile. "Any luck?" He asked supportively.

The receptionist ignored his question and returned to the counter with a disappointed look on her face. Then, addressing only Jeanette, she smiled lukewarmly and offered some advice.

"Look, I can't find you anywhere," she apologized, "maybe if you just go on home and relax and I keep at it I'll be able to turn something up."

Duane saw a look of physical pain burn into Jeanette's weary features. He could almost feel the same stabbing sensation in his own heart that he knew she must be experiencing in hers.

Turning to face him, she silently pleaded with him to say something positive. Her eyes, barely damp with tears that could no longer come so easily, begged him to tell her everything was going to work out given time. He could not, so he opted for saying nothing. Perhaps sensing the same desperation Duane read on Jeanette's face, the receptionist volunteered what little optimism she could.

"Don't look so down, sometimes these things take time, and even if I can't find it here, there's always back at the home. A lot of the records are stored in the cellar there."

Duane watched as the look on Jeanette's face brightened slightly. He could see the wheels behind her eyes begin to turn, and he felt another sensation grip him. Only this time, the feeling originated lower than it had before, right in the pit of his stomach. Knowing Jeanette as he did, he dreaded to imagine the potentially troublesome possibilities posed by the otherwise harmless information the woman had just unwittingly offered up to her.

"So whaddaya say, kid? You want to get out of the lady's way and let her do her job?"

"Sure, ah, I guess so," Jeanette said with a disinterested glaze forming over her eyes. Suddenly she twitched her head ever so slightly in an awkward attempt to focus on the moment. She then tried to force a bit of a frown to conceal both her suddenly piqued sense of curiosity, and the plan that had already begun to formulate behind her feigned veil of indifference.

"You don't sound so sure," Duane said skeptically, his eyes flashing with what she recognized as seasoned suspicion.

"Well, frankly I'm a little disappointed," Jeanette breathed. But it was far too late for a masquerade. The mere look in his eyes was enough to tell her he was on to her ruse. "Ok, let's go, then," she smiled sheepishly. And as she nodded good morning to the receptionist, she handed her one of her business cards. "You can reach me at my home phone," she offered. "You know, just in case you come up with something."

"Sure, thanks, Ms. Tolby. We'll be in touch."

Jeanette bobbed her head in a condescending fashion, and heading for the door, she motioned with her hand for Duane to follow. They made their way down the hall and all the way to the sidewalk in silence, but the second Duane's feet hit the concrete, he put his hand on her shoulder and gently turned her to face him.

"What's runnin' around in that head of yours?" He asked warily. "Nothing, really," she lied. But when their eyes met, his knowing look forced her to be slightly more candid. "Let's just say I'm working on a 'plan B,'" she said. And as they climbed into his car, she felt a barely detectable, yet undeniable, sense of excitement churn in her stomach

*****

O'Hare sat, his eyes transfixed on Jeanette's brownstone waiting for Burton to return with the coffee he'd ordered; strong and black. It sounded like a stereotype, even to him. Like the "cop on a stake out" scene in every bad movie. But after riding that fine line somewhere between sleep and wakefulness for a scant three hours last night, the black coffee was a necessity he otherwise would do without. As he watched, he saw his partner's lumpy frame emerge from the coffee shop in the bottom floor of the building next door. Then, looking up, the detective stopped short, turned around, and re-entered the storefront. And just when he disappeared, Duane and Jeanette came into view as they hustled across Beacon St. toward her building.

The lieutenant waited patiently until he saw them close the door behind them. But the second they did, he hopped out of the car and crossed the green to meet Burton at the head of the stairs to the coffee shop.

"Here you go, Lieutenant," Burton said, handing O'Hare his coffee.

The Lieutenant took the piping hot coffee, downed half the cup, and winced as the sour ink like brew poached his esophagus.

"This coffee *sucks*, Burton!" He groused, tossing the half full cup into a nearby trashcan

"Yeah, I know," the detective admitted, "but it serves its purpose." The two walked slowly but deliberately toward Jeanette's building. And as they did O'Hare began to formulate what he was going to say to her, and more importantly, what he was going to make *her* say to *him*. He rang the doorbell three times before he heard the sound of feet padding down the stairs. Then, stepping back, he waited for the door to open with a tight smile on his face.

When she pulled the door open the Lieutenant met Jeanette's exasperated expression with a well-worn and friendly grin. "Good morning Ms. Tolby. Mind if we come in?" He asked, stepping over the threshold.

"I think you already are, Lieutenant," she frowned. And turning around she headed for the downstairs sitting room with the two cops right behind her. "Duane," she shouted up the stairs, "we have company."

"What is it, Lieutenant; can we make this quick?" Just then Duane entered the room, grimacing noticeably when he saw the officers.

"Got somewhere to go, do you, Ms. Tolby?" O'Hare asked pointedly.

"Yes, as a matter of fact I do," Jeanette said. "why do you ask?"

"Oh, we just wouldn't want to keep you. What time do you have to be there?"

"Ah...Ten, ten o'clock," she lied, trying desperately to remember what time the clock upstairs had said when she'd passed it to answer the door.

"Oh, we should have plenty of time." O'Hare smiled, "What time is it, now?"

Instinctively, Jeanette looked to the white spot on her wrist where her watch used to be. In that fraction of a second, the whole conversation they'd just had ran through her mind and jelled, as it became uncomfortably obvious what had just happened. She didn't want to look up to meet the Lieutenant's ice blue eyes. But the longer she stared at her empty wrist, the more foolish she looked. And when she finally looked up to address him, she saw in his hand a plastic bag; and in that bag a watch, her watch. This was worse than she ever could have imagined.

"Looking for this, Ma'am?" O'Hare asked, a smug grin riding his protruding, self-impressed chin. "It says here, its ten-to-four. That couldn't be right, could it, Burton?

"No, sir," the detective chimed, "I've got, nine-twenty-seven."

"Wh-where, the hell did you get my watch?" Jeanette stammered.

"I think you know *damn well* where I got this, Ms. Tolby. Why don't you tell me about it?"

"You're groping, Lieutenant. It's not becoming," Jeanette sneered.

O'Hare's eyes lit up like a pinball machine, his smile disintegrating as quickly as it had appeared. "I'll tell you what's not becoming, sweetheart! Orange jump-suits and numbers aren't becoming. Although there are a few ladies over at the Framingham State Prison who might disagree with me when they see *you*!" He growled. "Now think very carefully before you answer the next question. It could turn out to be in your best interest. Ever meet a dead guy named Skip Phillips?" He asked bluntly.

The picture of a two hundred and twenty pound cellmate winking and licking her pursed lips danced through Jeanette's head. It only took a second before she decided that the game was up. It was time to tell him everything. Well, almost everything. "I never really met him," Jeanette began. But before she could elaborate, Duane began to leave the room.

"You won't be needing me then, will you?" He asked, as he made the door.

"Oh, no, no, no. Not just yet, Mr. Avon. I've got a little something for everyone, today. Yep, I feel like, friggin' Kmart. If ya stick around you'll hear the name of the latest winner in the pine box derby," he said, pulling a piece of paper out of his inside pocket. "And the winner is....... Gary, God damned Stricktland. See, Duane. Everyone's a winner when you play for keeps. Have a seat, son."

"Now, just wait a minute," Duane protested.

"No! *You* wait a minute," O'Hare interrupted. "where were you between midnight and morning last night."

"I was right here, where *you* told me to be!"

"Oh, you mean with our other murder suspect as an alibi?" O'Hare wondered aloud. "Sorry, wrong answer, thanks for playin', have a seat."

Jeanette's head was spinning from listening to the exchange between the two. Everything had gotten so terribly out of hand.

But I haven't done anything wrong, she thought. I've been a victim in all of this. I've been a victim my whole life, this isn't right, I haven't done anything wrong. Her head spun faster and faster as she felt the contents of her stomach begin to make its way up her throat. But just as she became sure that she would be sick, she felt herself pitch forward, and saw the lights flicker once before she was engulfed in the black vacuum of unconsciousness.

CHAPTER FIFTEEN

As she slowly became aware that she was regaining consciousness, and not simply waking up, she realized that none of her surroundings looked the least bit familiar. Yet the gray-green cinderblock walls and the functional economy of the hardware used to outfit it reminded her of something. Everything from the simple hatbox light fixtures and the stainless steel switch plates, to the acoustic tile ceiling and the tightly drawn, two inch vertical blinds made it all seem cold and inhospitable. It was all so sterile, so nondescript. Still, something told her she'd been here before. It all seemed so, so institutional, she thought, and the word, although unspoken, stuck in the back of her throat. "The home..." she tried to whisper. But the dryness in her mouth and throat caused the words to be little more than a sickening hiss. She tried to sit up, but it was then that she realized she was strapped to the bed. She felt a scream begin to grow in the pit of her stomach, but much to her surprise it died as quickly as it had grown. Just then, as if on cue, the door swung in, and with it, it brought John O'Hare.

"Ah! So you're back among us, huh?" The lieutenant smiled.

In all the time she'd known him, and in all the times she'd seen his smiles, be they genuine or otherwise, she couldn't remember one that was as unattractive as this one. It was so smug and omnipotent, so ... victorious.

"What the hell is going on here, O'Hare? Get these damn straps off me," she heard herself drawl. It was only after she heard her own raspy voice drag reluctantly through the sentence that she realized how odd she felt. Her head felt as though it was stuffed with damp wool, and her ears were buzzing slightly from the substantial dosage of tranquilizer she been given to avoid any repeat of the other night's emotional explosion. Her eyes, meandering aimlessly about the room from one shiny object to another, finally found O'Hare once more.

"Hello, anyone in there?" She heard him say, as if from a distance. "Yeah, over here," he said, waving his hat. "I'd be happy to have the restraints removed," the cop offered, "they were only for your own safety as it was. After the way you fainted dead away earlier... Well, we couldn't take any chances, now could we?"

Walking to the edge of her bed, the lieutenant pulled a pair of handcuffs out of his pocket and snapped one end around her wrist, and the other around the side rail of the bed. "I'm gonna have to ask you to wear mine though," he said. "You have the right to remain silent. Anything you say can, and will be used against you in court. You have the right to legal counsel. If you can't afford counsel, the court will appoint counsel for you."

As she listened to the lieutenant recite her Miranda rights, she felt panic again begin to boil in her gut. But once again it was overwhelmed by the drugs she'd been given. Her mind began to wander and her eyelids grew heavy. And as O'Hare droned on, she silently slipped back into insensate oblivion.

The lieutenant, realizing his prisoner was being less than receptive of his required dissertation, shook his head, popped his hat on with a flick of the brim, and quietly left the room.

Once in the hallway he made his way down toward the administrative offices of the hospital. This time he would trust only Tunney himself to make sure she didn't just get up and walk out. Part of him was satisfied having finally made an arrest that could stick in these murders, but part of him couldn't shake the picture of Gary Stricktland, his head turned around backwards, his cold eyes staring blindly into the morning sun. Was Jeanette Tolby capable of the kind of brute force it took to do something like that? Physically, sure, he thought, any doctor would say that it could be done with twenty pounds of pressure; But by *her*? He doubted it. She barely looked strong enough to twist the top off a jelly jar. And as for overpowering a man of Gary's size, well, it just didn't ring true. And emotionally, she had all the raw nerve of a lost puppy. But at any rate, she was here, in custody, for as long as it took to find out one way or another. And besides, he'd been in this business long enough to know that under the right circumstances anyone is capable of murder.

When he reached the double doors at the end of the hallway, he pulled up short, checked the number on the room to his right, and entered Dr. Tunney's outer office.

"Excuse me ma'am, is the doctor in?" He asked, removing his hat.

"I'm sorry. He isn't to be disturbed, he's in conference," Tunney's secretary offered.

"I'll take that as a yes, then," O'Hare smiled, flashing his badge in her face.

"Sir, please!"

"This won't take a second," he said, slipping through the door and into the Doctor's office.

O'Hare was met immediately by a cold scowl from Dr. Tunney. "I beg your pardon, Lieutenant," Tunney growled, "can't you see I'm in a meeting?"

No sooner had the words left his mouth, than did the man seated facing the doctor turn around to look at O'Hare. The officer immediately recognized the second man as Senator Dean Tunney.

"Excuse me, gentlemen," O'Hare offered, a bit put off his game by the Senators presence, "Ah, this won't take a second." Then, regaining is poise, he smiled a bit wryly. "Evening, Senator. You know, I never quite made the connection, here. But-"

"You're interrupting!" Dean said angrily. "What *is it* that you want?"

"Well, for starters, you and your buddies up on Beacon Hill can come through with the funding you owe us so we can stop closing down precincts," O'Hare sniped sarcastically.

"Touché, Lieutenant," Dean smiled smugly.

"Actually I just wanted to make sure that your father knew that Jeanette Tolby was back in his hospital, and that I'd appreciate it if she wasn't allowed to just hop up and walk out again. This time she's a person of interest in a criminal investigation." As he spoke, O'Hare saw Dean do a slight double take, and his eyes widened ever so slightly

"If you're addressing *me*, Lieutenant," the elder Tunney barked, "then do so!" And as far as your prisoner is concerned, she'll be there when you need her. Now could you find someone else to bother, and leave us alone, please?"

"You can count on it, Dr. Tunney. I wouldn't have it any other way. You do your job, and I'll do mine," O'Hare grinned, dropping his hat on his head.

"Is that all?" Dean asked, then added, "Shouldn't you be out arresting somebody or something?"

"Possibly," O'Hare shot back, "shouldn't you be out closing down a police station or something?"

"You do your job, Lieutenant, and I'll do mine," Dean mocked.

"Touché, Senator," O'Hare offered. And turning, he tipped his hat and let himself out.

Once the lieutenant had left, Dean turned his attention back to his father and, he asked, "What do you suppose the cops want with Jeanette?" He asked, trying to seem impartial.

"Who knows, and who cares," his father said. "I told you before, find yourself another girl."

"One who's more befitting my social caste?" Dean asked sarcastically.

"Why not? What could it hurt?" Dr. Tunney said setting his jaw.

"Look, I've got things to do," Dean muttered, hoisting himself out of his seat. "I'll call you tonight, ok?"

"You do that. I'll be waiting. And so will your mother."

"Bye, Dad," Dean sighed. And with a half-hearted wave, he too disappeared out the door.

O'Hare sat silently staring out the window of Burton's Chevy as they weaved their way through the tangle of midday traffic that makes downtown Boston nearly impassable by car straight through the lunch hour. His thoughts were bouncing back and forth between Jeanette Tolby and Duane Avon. Duane, for all intents and purposes, had the motive, the strength, and possibly even the right to want to do Gary harm, but what about the others? He had neither motive nor opportunity. Jeanette on the other hand, had neither the strength, nor the motive. But she did have one thing that he didn't. That was damning evidence that put her at the scene of a crime that he could almost taste was connected in some odd and roundabout way to the others.

"Listen, Burton. I want you to drop me at the station and get over to Avon's place. Keep an eye on him and make sure he doesn't get out of your sight."

"What are ya thinkin', Lieutenant?"

"I'm thinking that maybe Mr. Avon got himself mixed up with a crazy broad that got him into something they both lost control of."

"Stricktland?" Burton asked.

"Stricktland," O'Hare nodded. "I'm not sayin' she had him take the guy out or anything. Just, you know, one thing led to another, Gary whacks Avon, Avon whacks back, and Gary turns up with his head on backwards. You know how it is, disproportionate escalation."

"Yeah, one guy hits another guy's car, the second guy yells, the first guy takes out a tire iron."

"Exactly, it happens in some form every night in this friggin' city," O'Hare said sarcastically, shaking his head in disgust.

The two fell silent as Burton pulled his car up to the curb in front of the station. As O'Hare exited the car, he leaned back in and gave Burton a wink. "Ya know, Sergeant, I think, just maybe, there's hope for you after all." That said he swung the door closed and headed up the stairs into the station.

When he entered the squad room, O'Hare could feel the eyes on him as he crossed the room. Quickly, he made his way to his desk. But just as soon as his butt hit the seat, he heard Captain Antonucci's voice resonating down the hallway from his office. "Where is he?" Antonucci was growling. "Well you tell him I want to see him. **AND NOW!**"

Instead of waiting to be summoned, the Lieutenant pushed himself out of his seat, and began a slow shamble for the Captain's office. All eyes were still on him when he made the hallway. And when he spied the young cop that had been sent to find him, he simply offered a pained grimace and a sentient nod. When he reached the door, O'Hare took a deep breath, and then knocked firmly three times on the opaque window to the office. "Come!" Was his only indication that he had been heard. But it was indication enough that the Captain was in a less than festive mood. At first he reached for the knob, but then let his hand fall back to his side. Something wasn't right here. Long ago, as a young uniform, he'd first had the feeling that overwhelmed him now. It was a feeling that he'd eventually grown used to and chalked up to instinct, but all the while he realized it was something else, something different than other cops seemed to have. He'd always had a very real, very keen sense of impending danger, a sense that had, up until now, never betrayed him. But this was ridiculous, that feeling was usually reserved for times when there was some hopped up junkie crouching in a dark corner of some abandoned building with a 44 and a reason to use it. He'd never experienced it at any time when he wasn't in real danger of physical harm. And he'd never ignored it. Not until now anyway.

"I said, come in!" Antonucci boomed.

Shaking his head, O'Hare grabbed the knob, pushed the door open, and entered the office.

"So nice to see you," the captain said sarcastically. "You know counselor Ferrel, I believe."

O'Hare reached out his hand to shake with the lawyer, but when he turned to face him, he recognized him as Gary's mouth-piece.

Dropping his hand back to his side, he sneered at the man. "Lookin' for more guilty scum to kick loose?" O'Hare grumbled.

"My *client* was never proven guilty of anything, Lieutenant. And, as we're both now painfully aware, he has become another casualty in a growing list of victims it's been your responsibility to protect," the lawyer said, ignoring O'Hare's barb.

The old cop sized up the attorney with as much contempt as he could muster under the circumstances. "So this is *my* fault?" He spit. "Now I'm expected to know which fool in this city is going to get themselves in over their heads and end up in a box?"

"In this case, **Yes!**" The captain interrupted, "you've been playing catch up since this whole mess got started, John. You're behind the curve, you're scrambling.

"Catch-up is the nature of the job, God damn it, you know that, Jerry. I've got a suspect in cust…"

"You're flailing, O'Hare, and it's not pretty! The bodies are piling up, and this department can't afford any more black eyes or bad press over this; *especially* in an election year!" Antonucci growled.

"It's no secret that you want to be commissioner, Captain," O'Hare shouted back, "and a lot of things have to go right for that to happen. I know that. I'm just asking you to let me do my job. And if everything works out you'll be right where you want to be."

"I can't take that chance!" Antonucci roared.

Embarrassed by his admission, the captain reached into his drawer, pulled out a file folder and slammed it on his desk.

The room fell uncomfortably silent, and seizing the opportunity counselor Ferrel pushed himself out of his chair, picked up his briefcase and started for the door. "This no longer concerns me, gentlemen," he offered, "I've got a court case in an hour and I need to prepare. I'll be in touch. Good day," he said as he pulled it closed behind him.

"Captain, I've got enough evidence to…"

"Go home, John. It's over. I'm putting together a task force as of tomorrow. You'll be expected to provide any information you have concerning this mess," Antonucci said, shuffling at the papers on his desk.

O'Hare was stunned, but it didn't affect his pride. He wasn't about to beg, and he wasn't about to let his boss know that he gave a damn. "Fine!" He said. And he too headed toward the door.

"Leave the shield, Lieutenant, **and** your weapon," The captain said softly.

Without turning around, O'Hare pulled out his wallet, dropped his badge, and then his firearm on the table next to the door and silently pulled it open.

"I'm sorry, John," Antonucci apologized.

"Yeah, me too," the cop said and pulled the door closed behind him.

PART THREE

THE TRUTH

CHAPTER SIXTEEN

Duane sat in his apartment staring into the dying embers of the fire he had lit in a feeble attempt to banish the chill he now knew was originating in his own gut.

"Jesus Christ!" He said aloud. "I tried to warn her, but would she listen? God damn it."

He had been mulling over their respective predicaments for four hours. So far he hadn't come up with anything he thought would help Jeanette, or *him*, for that matter. And with the ever present Burton still stationed directly outside his front door, his options seemed seriously limited.

As yet he hadn't been charged with anything. So technically he was free to go wherever he wanted, but with his shadow following him everywhere he went, he would have a difficult, if not impossible, time trying to dig up anything that could help them.

Suddenly the beginnings of an idea began to formulate somewhere in the deep recesses of his consciousness. Not really a plan, in the true sense of the word, but the idea that due to all that had happened, he unwittingly had not only hired himself his own personal bodyguard, but had gained a free pass to go anywhere and do practically anything he wanted.

Burton sat outside chomping on his second hot dog in as many minutes when his cell phone rang. "Burton." Was all he could manage.

"Yeah, Burton, O'Hare, here," the lieutenant barked.

"Hey, what's up? You want me to come and get you?"

"No, I'm home. I got canned."

"What?" The Sergeant choked.

"Yeah, *that's* right," O'Hare offered, "canned, suspended, taken off the case, whatever. It's all the same to me. Antonucci asked for my badge and weapon and told me it was over. You tell me what it means."

Burton just sat staring at his phone incredulously.

"You still there, Burton?" The lieutenant growled.

"Yeah, yeah, I'm here, but that's just not right. He gave us forty eight hours. Did you ask him why?"

There was a long pause, and then O'Hare, said angrily. "What God damned difference does it make? He just said, *it's over.* I don't know if he meant for *good,* or for *now,* or for *this case,* or what. Just, it's over. I just wanted you to hear it from me. You should be getting a call any time."

"Christ, Lieutenant, I- I don't know what to say" Burton stammered

"Nothin' *to* say, kid. Good luck," O'Hare finished. And the line went dead.

"Whoa," the sergeant whispered, kneading his forehead. "this *is* friggin' nuts."

Burton's radio crackled to life. "KC86865 Base to mobile 4, do you copy?"

Instinctively, he pulled it off his belt and replied. "Mobile 4, go on."

"Please return to the precinct, over."

"Can't do that right now. I'm on surveillance, and I'm out of the unit," he lied.

"Copy that, please advise when available."

"10-4. Mobile 4 out." With that he shut off his radio and started the car.

Duane watched out the window as Burton's green Chevy pulled away from the curb and raced off down Beacon Street. "What, the…" Then in a flood of revelation he realized this was the chance he'd been waiting for. Running to the front closet he grabbed his heavy coat, a pair of gloves, a hat and the emergency set of Jeanette's car keys. Then he picked up a track bag and hurried to the cellar to gather a collection of what he considered the only thing close to burglar's tools he owned and headed back upstairs and then for the door.

When he opened the front door a cold blast of fall air hit him square in the face. Cringing, he steeled himself against it and hustled down the stairs and across Beacon Street toward Commonwealth Ave.

Once he reached Jeanette's, and before he mounted the steps he looked up and down the street and then across to Beacon to be sure he hadn't been followed. Being relatively sure that Burton was otherwise engaged, he climbed the steps and slipped through Jeanette's front door unnoticed. Inside he stood silent for several minutes listening to his heart beat in his chest. When he was sure he was alone he made his way through the first floor hallway and out the back door to the stairs which led to the parking area behind the building. By the time he reached her car he was feeling confident, almost exhilarated about the plan that had so suddenly formulated in his mind. But he couldn't take full credit. It was the same plan that he was sure he had seen in Jeanette's eyes at the Child Welfare Offices.

*****

Burton pulled to a stop about a half of a block West of O'Hare's building in the heart of Southie, almost directly at the foot of Thomas Park Hill.

For all the bad press this much maligned community had received over the years it was still steeped in ethnic Irish culture, and a "we take care of our own" mentality. This was the land of Buddy Mclean, Howie Winter, Whitey Bulger and so many Irish gangsters before them. The citizenry always bold in their united support for the I.R.A and its martyrs. The scene of so much unrest and turbulence during the busing riots of the middle and late seventies. A world unto its own, tough and dangerous to outsiders and insiders alike, but for those who lived the life, it was home. A small pocket of humanity which, unrealized to the world around it, had at one point been the largest pocket of white people in the country living under the poverty level; few worked, many on government assistance, one of eight families with a male authority figure in the household and murder and suicide a regular visitor to the projects that crowded the streets and thoroughfares that made this community what it was, an island in the center of the world that, aware of but undaunted by its past, had stayed the course and pushed forward. It had changed much since then, but the more it had changed the more it remained the same. And still this bare knuckled tough community thrived, its cultural heritage intact and never stronger; its inhabitants proud in their Irish-American legacy and sworn to its traditions and blue collar values.

Although he himself was from British stock, still, Jack Burton always felt comfortable here. It was a real place with real people, people like John O'Hare.

As he climbed the steps to the lieutenant's third floor walk-up the Sergeant realized he didn't really know what he hoped to achieve by coming, but somehow he'd had to. O'Hare was a good and decent man, and a good cop, a cop who cared about his community and his job as well as the people whose lives it affected. He was a dying breed, and like the community from whence he came, he was as tough as a mason's tool bag and as proud a man as he'd ever met. He'd been his teacher and mentor. The only partner he'd had as a detective, and the only one he'd wanted.

Entering the foyer he walked the three flights up and balked at his partner's door. Then, raising his hand he knocked hard three times and waited for an answer.

"Hold on, hold on," he heard O'Hare say.

When the door swung open, the sergeant found himself speechless. The man who greeted him wasn't his partner. He didn't even look like a cop. He looked small. He was just some tired old guy, dressed in shabby slippers, a wrinkled Celtics T-shirt and ill- fitting jeans.

Thankfully O'Hare spoke and ended the awkward moment "Burton," he began, in his raspy authoritarian voice. "what the hell are *you* doin' here?" He growled.

"I came by to find out what the Christ happened," Burton said. "Can I come in?"

"Yeah, yeah sorry," his partner offered stepping aside.

The younger cop had been in this apartment several times in the past three years, but he had never noticed his surroundings to the extent that they jumped out at him now. It was a nice and homey five room place, four up and a five step walk-down to a cramped but bright kitchen that overlooked a tiny patch of grass and the alleyway that separated it from the identical building behind it. The place, as always, was neat as a pin. The American and Irish flags sharing a place of prominence on the mantel, the pictures of him and his late wife and those of their five children scattered about along with lord knows how many head shots of grandchildren. The overstuffed chair and couch, the ancient but pristine maple dining table, the obligatory picture of Jesus with the fronds from last Palm Sunday still tucked in behind the frame. Holy crap, Burton thought. Replace the Irish flag with a Union Jack and it was his late grandfather's place over in East Cambridge.

O'Hare led Burton down the five stairs into the kitchen, grabbed a glass out of the cabinet on the way, and took up his place behind his own, well-sipped, Jameson, neat.

"So, comin' over to check on the old man are ya, see how I'm holdin' up, as it were?" O'Hare said, sliding the other glass to Burton and pointing the bottle in the direction of it.

"No, no, that's not it at all." The younger cop lied covering his glass with his hand. "I'm just floored at how that son of a bitch could do this, and why?"

The twinkle in his partner's eye let him know in no uncertain terms that he wasn't fooling either of them. "When I got there, Strictland's shill was there. He didn't hang around too long, but I can only imagine that he was pulling a power play, asserting pressure. You know, threatening to go to the press or some such bullshit. At least that's how it sounded to me." The lieutenant finished, then took a long pull on his drink and drained the glass.

"So where do we go from here?" Burton asked.

Smiling widely, O'Hare said, "That's what I like about you, kid. You've got balls of granite and a head to match. You just don't know when to quit." That said he pulled open the drawer in the breakfast table and pulled out a plastic bag, tossing it to Burton. In the bag were Jeanette's watch and the spare key to his handcuffs.

"First off, you go over and get our little friend out of the hospital before someone finds out she's there,"

"Let her go?" The sergeant interrupted.

"She's not guilty of anything but stupidity," O'Hare growled. "we both know that, and I won't have her doing time because Antonucci wants this all wrapped up with a tidy bow! Then you best get back to the precinct. For all you know your ass is already fried. And if the opportunity presents itself see if you can't check on Avon, who I'm sure is by now off gallivanting through the countryside playin' private eye. And me, I'm gonna go get a haircut. And I might even get one of those damn cell phones," the lieutenant smiled widely. "Today's the first day of the rest of my life."

*****

"Damn!" Duane cursed. He'd been in the car and on the road for twenty five minutes and he was just barely into Brighton, about a third of the way to Waltham, and the traffic was crawling for as far as he could see. "I should've taken the highway. I knew it!" He said to no one. Tapping nervously on the steering wheel his eyes darted back and forth, then forward and to the mirror in anticipation of seeing Sergeant Burton's green Chevy. Then, mercifully, the traffic began to move and then speed up to an almost tolerable clip. At this rate the rest of the trip would only take him as long as the whole trip should have in the first place. His mood lightened considerably as the speed of the traffic steadily increased. "This is what *I'm* talkin' about," he said aloud and he reached down and cranked the stereo.

As he tooled toward St. Bridget's he tried to imagine what it was he was supposed to be looking for, and how it sure would help if Jeanette could be there so she could tell him when he found it. The thought of her being under arrest and held in the hospital caused him to pause and consider where he'd come from just a week ago. His life had been pretty simple then. He would gladly trade the maelstrom his life had turned into for all the day to day crap he'd put up with in the last year in a heartbeat. Just then his phone rang snapping him back to the moment. "Avon answering," he said.

"That's cute," Burton offered, "did you think that up all by yourself?"

"What is it, Burton?"

"Where are you right now?" The cop asked.

"That's none of your damn business! Why?" Duane countered, with a boldness that he hoped would take the detective by surprise.

"It doesn't matter. Can you meet me at Ms. Tolby's? I'm on my way to the hospital to bring her home and I'm not so sure she should be by herself for a while, since... well, you know."

It was several seconds before Duane realized he hadn't answered yet. "Yeah, yeah I can be there in about fifteen minutes or so," he said, baffled by the question.

"Ok, I'll be there as soon as I can," Burton said.

"You're just letting her go? Burton... Sergeant..." Realizing the connection had been broken, Duane dropped the phone in the seat next to him, his hand going directly to his forehead. "What the...? " He wondered aloud. Now he was sure that the only thing he was sure of was that he wasn't sure of anything at all. Quickly he turned left into a drive through parking lot and jumped back on the road headed back to Boston and Jeanette's brownstone.

Burton grabbed up the emergency light off of the seat, flipped it on and stuck it to the dashboard of his car, then turned on the siren and began to weave through the late afternoon traffic toward Boston City Hospital.

*****

Jeanette lay in her bed in her utilitarian room at the hospital intermittently choking down the fear she felt boiling in her stomach. Surprisingly her bouts of near panic were becoming less and less frequent. Could it be that her phobia toward hospitals and doctors was actually waning due to this forced total immersion therapy she'd been subjected to? Wouldn't that be an ironic by-product of her inexcusable incarceration? Or was it simply that the medication that she'd been given hadn't totally worn off yet? Well, she thought, whatever the case it was fine with her, although she hoped it was the former rather than the latter. The sound of keys diverted her attention to the door and she sat up, that familiar feeling of dread creeping back up her spine causing the hair on the back of her head to jump to attention. When the nurse entered Jeanette retreated to the other side of the bed in an attempt to escape whatever plans she had for her. Then Burton followed her into the room wearing what looked like an almost genuine smile.

"What the hell do *you* want?" Jeanette challenged, trying to look around him for O'Hare.

"Could you leave us alone, nurse?" The sergeant intoned in an uncharacteristically professional voice.

The nurse nodded her compliance and let herself out of the room.

"Where's your boss?" Jeanette questioned nervously.

"He's my partner," Burton said taking the plastic bag the Lieutenant had given him out of his pocket "He sent me here to cut you loose."

Jeanette looked at him skeptically. "What's your game, Burton?" She asked.

"Tell me something, sunshine," the sergeant said unlocking her handcuffs "did you kill anybody?"

"Of course not!" She said adamantly.

"Have you committed any other crimes we're unaware of?"

"No, nothing," she answered rubbing at her slightly chafed wrist.

"Then get your clothes on and I'll give you a ride home," Burton finished, and turning on his heels he walked out of the room.

Once Jeanette had located her clothes in the closet and gotten dressed she joined Burton in the hallway outside of her room.

"What's the deal, here? I mean *really*," she asked suspiciously.

"No deal," he said earnestly. "Do you want to go home or not?"

"Of course I do," she admitted.

"Then let's go before I change my mind," he insisted. And he turned and started down the hallway.

"Wait up," Jeanette implored. "I'm still not so steady, here."

Slowing down, Burton waited for her to catch up, took her by the elbow and continued toward the elevator and the admissions desk.

Before they reached the doors at the end of the hall the last door on the right opened and out walked Dr. Alistair Tunney.

"Excuse me," the doctor said pointedly "who are you and where do you think you're going with Lieutenant O'Hare's prisoner. "

"Jack Burton, Boston Police," the sergeant bristled, holding his badge in front of the doctor's face. "I'm the lieutenant's partner. And she's not a prisoner, she was being temporarily detained. I'm here on O'Hare's orders. We're moving her to the station for questioning."

"This is highly irregular. I'm not sure I like it. Not one bit," Tunney said sharply.

"It's not your place to like it or not, doctor. It is what it is," Burton countered, "and if you *don't* like it, take it up with Lieutenant O'Hare."

"Yes, yes I believe I will," Tunney threatened.

Burton took the challenge, whipped out his cell phone and speed dialed O'Hare's number. Come on. Be home, he thought, remembering that the lieutenant was going to get a haircut. The phone rang five, six, seven times. The sergeant could feel a sweat beginning to develop on his brow. If Tunney called the station this would surely blow up in his face, and probably cost him his job. Just as he was about to give up and break the connection he heard the phone on the other end pick up. "Yeah, O'Hare here," his partner panted.

"Yeah, Lieutenant, Burton here. Dr. Tunney doesn't want to release Ms. Tolby without your say so."

"Jesus Christ, Burton, what are you tryin' to kill me. I just ran up three flights of stairs to answer the damn phone."

"Sorry, Lieutenant he… Yeah he's right here… yeah. Ok."

He wants to talk to you. Burton said, thrusting the phone in the Doctor's face.

Tunney took the phone and put it to his ear. "Tunney, here," he said acidly.

"No... Yes, of course. I understand. This is highly irr... She's my patient, damn it! Yes I realize she's *your* suspect, but... Very well, but I *will* get to the bottom of this. Good day."

Tunney handed the phone back to Burton and stood bolt straight appraising the younger man contemptuously. "I *will* get to the bottom of this!" He growled.

"Yeah, so you said," the sergeant scoffed, forcing a smile.

"Get out of my hospital!" The older man barked.

"That was the plan, doctor," Burton offered and he took Jeanette by the elbow and pushed through the doors toward the elevator.

As they stood there waiting. The double doors opened behind them.

"So what is it," Tunney asked, "prisoner, suspect, or detainee?"

"Why don't you let *us* worry about that," Burton advised, and the two stepped onto the elevator and let the doors slide closed between them.

Dr. Tunney burst back into his office incensed at the exchange he'd had with the Sergeant. He didn't like to lose at anything, much less a power struggle with a second rate flat foot like Burton; especially in his own hospital.

"Are you alright, doctor?" His secretary asked.

"I'm fine!" Tunney fumed. "And why wouldn't I be?"

"No reason. You just seem…"

"Get my son on the phone," he ordered, disappearing into his office, and slamming the door behind him.

As Duane inched back toward Jeanette's building his blood pressure ticked up with every minute he spent in the traffic. He was still reeling from the phone call he'd gotten from Burton. Why, after all the bullshit, did they finally decide that she wasn't a worthy candidate as their suspect? Of course, he knew why, it was because she wasn't capable of anything that would warrant their suspicions, never mind their considerations as a murderer.

When he had barely crawled back into Kenmore Square he checked his watch. Twenty two minutes had passed since he'd told Burton he'd be there in fifteen to twenty. His pulse raised another notch as he reached the turn onto Brighton Ave. As he made the corner he looked to his left down Commonwealth. There he saw the Sergeant's green Chevy. "Shit!" he said aloud.

"Let me help you in," Burton offered.

"I'll be fine, Sergeant," Jeanette said, with no small amount of disapproval.

"You don't get it, do you?" Burton asked.

"Get what?" she said.

"Get that the lieutenant and I have been bustin' our asses to protect you and that boyfriend of yours from all the shit you've been tryin' to get yourselves involved in. Why do you think we're so far behind this whole thing? It's you. It's you and your buddy there. We've spent so much time tryin' to figure out your involvement in all of this, and keep you and him out of trouble we haven't hardly had any time to chase any other leads.

Jeanette sat looking at the detective for a long second before formulating a response. "Well, you just don't get it. This isn't about you and your boss. It's about what's happened to me. Me and the people I care about!" She tried to explain.

"Can I help you in Miss Tolby?" Burton offered again.

"Yes. Yes, I'd appreciate that," she admitted. " And thank you. Thank you for everything."

As Duane took the corner onto Brookline Ave. he noticed a black limousine cut off the car behind him and pull up snug to his bumper. "What the hell? Get off my ass!" He said aloud. Whipping the car to the left and pulling onto the street behind Jeanette's building. The limo followed as he pulled into the parking lot, and coasted to a stop behind him. The limousine cut off his way out and penned him in. His eyes widened as an uneasy feeling crept into his gut. What was this, he thought. Picking up his phone he speed dialed Jeanette's number.

"Hi, Duane," Jeanette answered. "Where are you?"

"Let me talk to Burton!" Duane ordered. "Quick!"

"He wants to talk to *you*," she said, holding out the phone.

"Yeah, this is Burton."

The detective listened for a second, and then took off out of the sitting room and down the hall to the back stairs.

Duane watched through his rear view mirror as an extremely large and seemingly very angry black man approached his car.

Just as the man approached his door Burton blasted through the back door of Jeanette's apartment. **"Freeze, *Asshole!*"** He shouted, drawing his weapon. Surprised, the man balked a second, then turned and headed back to his car.

"Stop, Boston Police," Burton shouted.

Ignoring the warning, the would-be assailant hopped into the limo and slammed it in reverse, tearing out of the parking lot and then down the street. Burton considered firing his weapon but quickly realized it would have been a poor choice given the circumstances. Dropping his bead on the limousine, he raced to meet Duane at the door to Jeanette's car. "You all right?" He asked.

"Yeah," Duane said. "Thanks. What the hell was that?"

"That was *me* savin' your ass," Burton replied" "There's somehing goin' on here that's bigger than anyone knows. No one who owns a car like *that* gets involved with a couple of simple murders unless it's something deeper than we can guess at."

Duane was confused. What was with this new development? This guy, who was previously considered an adversary, was all of a sudden their sentinel, their protector, their friend.

Jeannette stood at her back window watching everything that

had transpired between Duane, the man in the limo, and Burton. And considering what had occurred at the hospital, it had become exceedingly obvious to her that she'd had the two cops all wrong. O'Hare and Burton were good cops and good men who were just trying to do their jobs to the best of their ability; and all for the benefit of people who had no idea how lucky they were.

When the sergeant and Duane finally made their way back upstairs to rejoin Jeanette in her kitchen Duane was visibly shaken. Having not only witnessed, but been an unwilling participant in the few seconds of what could only be described as madness that had ensued in the parking lot and Burton's reaction to it had left him trembling, frazzled, and physically spent.

"Are you all right?" Jeanette asked, her voice quavering.

Duane just shook his head and raised his hand as he plopped down in the nearest available seat.

"I don't know how you people do this shit every day," he said to the detective.

"Sometimes I don't either," Burton admitted, "but I guess it's kind of like motorcycle jumping or skydiving, you know how crazy dangerous it is, but you also know you're really good at it, and the adrenalin rush is incomparable. And when you know you're doin' the right thing, protecting regular folks from the scum and bad guys, I'll tell ya, sometimes you feel like you could walk through a wall."

Duane just shook his head and tried to force a smile. "Thanks, again Sergeant," he offered weakly.

"Listen," Burton began, "you two just sit tight, and if anything happens, and I mean *anything* out of the ordinary, you call me as fast as you can, got it?" he finished, handing Duane his card.

"You got it," Duane said nodding.

"Believe me," Jeanette agreed, "I couldn't dial fast enough."

Burton had called in when he'd gotten back to the car and been told to return to the precinct immediately, and that Captain Antonucci wanted to see him as soon as he got in.

As he opened the door to the station the usual bustle, commotion and din associated with the room died out upon his entrance. When he began weaving his way through the desks all eyes were on him. A few of his fellow officers offered nods of encouragement, and one even volunteered a quick apology for the way O'Hare had been treated. The sergeant nodded his agreement and continued on to Antonucci's door. Knocking heartily, he awaited an answer.

"Come in," the captain said.

Burton opened the door and stuck his head around it. "You want to see me, Captain?"

"I do," Antonnucci replied, "come in. sit down," he added gesturing to the couch away from his desk. As Burton made his way across the room the Captain pushed himself out of his chair and joined him, sitting in the chair opposite his seat.

"How's it goin', Jack?" He asked surprisingly civilly. "Alright, I guess." Burton hedged. He wasn't sure what the game was yet but he understood one thing, this little pow wow had the potential to get really ugly, very quickly.

"You're a good cop," the captain began, "you're the kind of cop the department likes to pair with younger guys to show how the job *should* be done."

"I have a good teacher," Burton interrupted, being sure to use the present tense.

"Another good cop," Antonucci acknowledged. "But, let's just say we feel your talents could be better used..."

"Who's *we?*" Burton said cutting the captain off. Then, without really meaning to, he continued. "Can we cut through the bullshit, here, Captain? I know what's going on and I think it sucks."

"Ok," the captain said pushing himself out of his chair and walking to his window. "I have no doubt you've already discussed this with O'Hare. And it's obvious you disagree with my decision to suspend him. But now *you* listen," he continued, raising his voice slightly. "I had no choice. Strictland's shyster attorney was gonna go to the press with everything that's gone on in this case. That would be a bad situation for the department, and for *you!* In case you're unaware, this is an election year..."

"I know it's an election year, Captain," the sergeant interrupted again.

"I just don't get how that makes it acceptable to sideline the best detective we have in homicide when we're just starting to make some headway, for your own political gain!"

"Enough!" Antonucci roared, whipping around to face him, "The question is, Sergeant, do *you* like being a cop?"

"Yeah, I like being a cop!" Burton boomed back.

"Well then, you'll do it on the department's terms, or not at all!"

"On your terms, you mean!" Burton fired back.

"I am the department, Sergeant. And I've already assigned you a new partner. You either live with it, or I yank you off the case and you pack it in. What's it gonna be?"

"I'll live with it," Burton agreed halfheartedly.

"Good." Antonucci said, walking to his desk and pushing the button on his intercom. "Send Colzie in."

Two minutes later there was a barely audible knock at the door breaking the uncomfortable silence that had been hanging in the room since the end of their conversation.

"Come in, Detective," Antonucci said. And the door opened slowly.

CHAPTER SEVENTEEN

"Are you sure you're ok?" Jeanette asked. She had spent the last hour and a half apologizing profusely. Not only for what had happened to him this afternoon, but for what she had gotten him into in general.

"Yeah, for the last time, I'm fine," he insisted, "and I meant it when I said we're into it now, and way too deep to get out, so we might as well get after it and see what we can do about getting ourselves out of it. And if that includes going out to the home to find out what we can about what did or didn't happen out there, we might as well."

"Do you really think that's smart? I mean, after this afternoon and all, and what Burton said..."

"So now we're worried about what he thinks?" Duane asked.

"Well, kind of. I mean, this is starting to seem really dangerous," she answered meekly.

Duane's face turned up into the first real smile she'd seen on him for days and he let go one of those over the top laughs she'd usually found so annoying.

"You've got to be kidding me. *Now*? It's way too late for cold feet sweetheart, we're in up to our necks. It's sink or swim time, honey." Although his expression had appeared real enough at the outset, his tone seemed harsh, almost mocking. "I don't know about *you*. But I'm not gonna sit around and wait for that big old brother to come back and finish what he came here for. No sir! It's time we got proactive and took this dog by the collar and stopped waiting for stuff to happen to us."

"Ok," Jeanette agreed, less than convinced. But the whole time she was thinking that it had been just that same kind of poor judgment that had gotten them into this predicament in the first place.

*****

John O'Hare had been sidelined for approximately six and a half hours and this unfamiliar inactivity was already more than he could tolerate. For the last four decades he had been on the go from early morning, usually well into the evening, and more often than not, late into the night. He wouldn't have suggested that kind of lifestyle for everyone. But it had worked for him. But, he thought, if this was what he had to look forward to upon his retirement, he'd just as soon take a bullet on the job and end it nice and clean. Of course, he realized, that may no longer be an option. Nevertheless, this sitting around and waiting for nothing to happen had hours ago become excruciating. So he changed into his least wrinkled work shirt, threw on a tie, his coat and his wrinkled hat and headed for who knew where to do who knew what. However, he did know a couple of things. For one, this wasn't over for *him* yet, not by a long shot. And two, he wasn't going to let Burton swing in the breeze over this. That's not what partners do.

*****

Jack Burton couldn't believe his eyes when Brian Colzie ducked into Captain Antonucci's office and emerged from behind the door. The kid was six foot five if he was an inch, and he was as thin as a greyhound puppy. He had a shock of red hair atop his head, the rest cut high and tight, and his angular jaw and thin face made him look like something out of a comic book. Not to say he was gaunt or sickly looking, but he would have looked more at home playing guard for the Barnum and Bailey basketball team than doing covert surveillance in an unmarked police car.

"Sergeant Burton, this is Detective third grade Brian Colzie," Antonucci said.

Burton reached out his hand and bit his lip to prevent a chuckle. Colzie gripped the sergeant's hand like a pit bull and shook it hard, once.

"Sergeant, it's a pleasure." he offered in his best all business voice.

"Colzie transferred over from narcotics at the one-eight, special assignment," the Captain continued, "he graduated third in his class at the academy…"

"I've always wanted to work homicide," the younger cop interrupted, "narcotics was just a means to an end. I'm really excited to get going, and I can't wait to learn from a pro. I may be a little green, but…"

"Stand down, Detective," Antonucci ordered. "I'm sure the sergeant will fill you in on what he's working on momentarily. Now could you wait outside while I speak with him please?"

Colzie looked shocked, and maybe even a little hurt, but he obediently turned and walked out into the corridor.

Burton rolled his eyes and let his chin fall to his chest. "Captain, I…"

"Don't bother, Detective. He's yours and you better make the best of it."

"I'll do my best, Sir. But if he comes back in a bag…"

"It's *your* job to make sure that doesn't happen," the captain snapped. "That'll be all."

"I'm just sayin'…"

"That'll be all, Sergeant," Antonucci repeated.

Burton turned around and walked out into the hall where the younger cop stood, his shoulders slumped, head down. "Come on, kid," he said, "let's go catch us some bad guys."

The younger cop followed at the sergeant's heel as told.

"So, kid, ah, do you own a hat?" The older detective asked.

When they reached the car Burton instinctively hopped in behind the wheel and the younger detective squeezed himself into the passenger's seat, his knees practically under his chin. Reaching into his coat pocket he wrestled out a wrinkled golf hat and pulled it over his head. "Better?" He smiled.

"Somewhat," Burton allowed, realizing he looked more foolish now than he had ten minutes ago.

"Comfortable?" The sergeant asked.

"I'll make due," Colzie said, dryly.

"Don't take it personally, kid."

"Oh, no, don't get me wrong, I don't. I was talking to some of the guys before you got back. I heard what happened with the lieutenant, and *they* all think it sucks, too. Who am I to disagree? I hope I get to meet him some time. He sounds like a great guy."

"He's the best," Burton assured him. "and something tells me you'll get your chance."

*****

Duane pulled on his jacket and hollered up the stairs, "You ready to go?"

"I'll be right down!" Jeanette shouted back. Her pulse was pounding in her temples at the thought of what they were about to do. As she fumbled with the final lace of her hiking boot she had visions of any manner of unsavory characters confronting them in any number of irreversible circumstances. This was crazy, but it was just what she had been asking for since the beginning. It was a chance to bring this thing full circle. Maybe she *could* find out what had really happened to Billy and, with any luck, finally find out what had made her who she was and what she'd become.

As she made her way down the stairs she saw Duane at the bottom looking impatient. She wasn't sure she liked this new attitude he had assumed and she'd had enough of it. "Why don't you take a big pill?" she said.

"What?" He asked, his eyes flashing angrily.

"You heard me. Just, chill out. I mean, I appreciate everything you've done for me and I'm sorry for this whole mess, but I'm not some helpless damsel who needs you to tell me what to do and save me from myself. We're in this together, ok?"

Duane's face softened and he forced a strained smile. "Yeah, you're right," he admitted. "I guess I'm just on edge."

"Believe me, there's no need to explain," she said softly, "if anyone's been acting crazy it's been me. And I don't know what I'd do without you. Thanks. Thanks for everything. You're my hero," she finished and pecked him on the cheek.

"So, let's do this," he said with more confidence than he felt.

When they reached her car Jeanette threw him the keys and walked to the passengers' door. After letting her in he popped the key in the ignition, backed out and headed, once again, for

St. Bridget's home for Children.

As they turned left onto Beacon Street, they had no reason to detect the deep blue "89" L.T.D. that had inconspicuously pulled out five cars behind them and began following at a safe distance.

"You do realize we're probably gonna to have to break into this place, right?" Duane asked.

"Yeah, I know," Jeanette said, cringing slightly.

"I've got a couple of flashlights and some tools. I didn't really know what to pack, but it's all in the trunk," Duane said

"This is too weird," she admitted, "I've never done anything remotely approaching this before."

"Me either. What if we get caught?" Duane asked.

"Then I guess O'Hare and Burton will have a *real* reason to arrest us," she smirked," but I've got to admit, it's kind of exciting."

Most of the rest of their ride was spent in pensive silence.

*****

On the ride over, Burton explained, to the best of his ability, the case they were to be working on. For the most part he was entirely honest, although he left out a few selected facts, such as the incriminating evidence against Jeanette and the fact that he'd busted her out of the hospital earlier that day. When they approached her apartment the Sergeant noticed a black limousine parked a few spaces up from her door.

"Limo," he said, pointing at the car.

"Same one?" The kid asked.

"I don't know. I couldn't get the tags before," he said, pulling in a few spots behind it and killing the engine.

They sat and waited for the occupant to either exit or return to the vehicle and momentarily the door swung open.

As Dean Tunney made his way toward Jeanette's door the two cops watched intently.

"That guy looks familiar," Colzie remarked.

"He should, that's Dean Tunney, the Senator, and probably the next Governor of Massachusetts," Burton said. "What the hell is he doin' here?"

As they watched, Tunney strode to Jeanette's building and mounted her stairs.

"Why don't we ask him?" Colzie offered. When he looked at the sergeant he saw a glint of recognition in his eyes.

"Tunney." Burton repeated just above a whisper. "Yeah, you're right, kid. Let's ask him," he agreed, opening his door. When they approached Jeanette's building Dean Tunney was ringing the bell for the third time. Then he knocked once for good measure.

"Good evening, Senator," Burton said.

Startled, Tunney turned around and addressed the two men. "Good evening gentlemen," he answered suspiciously, "can I help you?"

"Maybe, sir," Burton began, "Jack Burton, Boston Police. Can we have a word?"

"If this is about precinct closings you can address any questions to my press secretary, Officer Burton," Tunney hedged, recognizing the name.

"No, it has nothing to do with that," the sergeant smiled.

The senator slowly made his way down the steps wearing a well-practiced smile. As he neared the bottom Burton noticed they were no longer alone. Tunney's driver had joined them.

"It's ok, Billings, they're just two of Boston's finest. I couldn't be safer, I'm sure. You can wait in the car," he said, returning his attention to the officers.

"Paying Ms. Tolby a little visit, Senator?" Burton asked.

"Well, I was, but she doesn't seem to be home right now," Tunney answered, looking up to her door and then down the street to his car.

"We're not keeping you, are we?" Burton asked feigning innocence.

"No, not at all," Dean dismissed "I've always got time for the local constabulary."

"So are you two *good* friends?" Burton said.

"I'm working on it," Tunney said, shifting nervously.

"The young lady seems to have hit a bit of a rough patch lately. I'm sure she'll be sad she missed you," the detective provoked.

"Are we just chatting, here, Burton?" Tunney asked, his voice beginning to show signs of annoyance. "I do have to meet my father for an early dinner. Do you know my father?" He added, going on the offensive.

"We've met," Burton said, sidestepping the question. "It's just that her friend Avon had a bit of a problem with someone driving a car just like yours, right out back of here," he said pointedly.

"Well that's your department, officer. Maybe you should be looking into *that* rather than spending time here with me?"

"That's what I'm doing, Senator," Burton asserted.

"Well good luck with that," Tunney said and turned to leave.

"Thanks for your help, Senator. And have a nice day," the sergeant needled.

Dean turned, smiled and waved, always the consummate politician.

After watching the senator drive off the sergeant climbed the steps to Jeanette's door and rang the bell and knocked hard on the window at the same time. When there was no answer he tried the door knob. It was locked as he'd expected it would be. Leaning in, he framed his face with his hands and tried to peer through the opaque glass of the door. "Shit!" He cursed under his breath.

"What's wrong, Boss?" Colzie asked.

"I told them to lay low," Burton said almost to himself. "Who knows what kind of crap they're out stirrin' up. They're gonna get themselves killed."

On the way back to the car the detective walked staring at the pavement. That son of a bitch Tunney knows something, he thought. He could tell by the narrowing of his eyes, the way his ears drew back ever so slightly and the way his jaw tightened while he listened. Those subconscious tells, along with his diverted glances and nervous shifting in place led the cop in him to believe he was hiding something, and quite possibly, something important.

"That *idiot!*" Tunney fumed.

"Who, sir, the officer?" Billings asked.

"I'm sorry, Billings, it's not your concern," Dean apologized. "I need to make a private call. Could you raise the sound shield, please?"

"As you wish, sir," the driver said, and he obediently pushed the button raising the window between them.

"Man, you were awesome back there," Colzie gushed. "You really got under his skin. And you didn't even have to say anything. You had him duckin' and weaving," he continued, all the time shadow boxing with the windshield. "You, my man, are one annoying S.O.B."

"Yeah," Burton replied, smiling thinly. "It's a gift."

*****

Jeanette's heart raced as they pulled into the driveway of Saint Bridget's. She wasn't sure if she was more afraid of what she might find, or what she might not. Or was it that they were about to break into a state owned building to rifle through sealed private records? Whatever the case, there was plenty to worry about. She could see the beads of sweat forming on Duane's forehead and assumed he was thinking the same thing.

"Pull around back," she said, "if I remember correctly there should be a cluster of trees there where we can hide the car."

"Gotcha," Duane breathed.

When they rounded the back corner of the building, just as she had remembered, there was a small horseshoe shaped stand of trees. It had been the spot that the older kids had claimed as their own. It was where they had congregated in a feeble attempt to avoid the constant harassment of the younger children who were summarily denied access. How cruel, she thought; those poor little kid's, who had wanted nothing more than to be part of something, anything really; and she had played a part in their exclusion. But she had once been one of those little kids. Admittance had been a rite of passage. She herself had been turned away until she'd turned thirteen. That had been the rule, and the rule had been adhered to.

The trees had grown considerably in the years that had passed, but that was to their advantage. The trunks were now large enough to almost completely obliterate the sightline into the small area in the center, while leaving plenty of room to pull the car well into the clearing. The only way anyone could see the car was from inside the building. And with any luck at all the building remained as empty today as it had been on their last visit.

Once out of the car, she stood for several minutes soaking up the very real and palpable aura of her surroundings. Equal parts of the joyfulness of youth, depression, melancholy and homesickness, it was a strange and pervading brew extracted from all the little lives that had been lived here in loneliness, desperation and despair.

"Are you ready to do this?" Duane asked quietly. "I'm freezing my butt off."

His voice snapped her back to the moment and she looked him in the eye.

"Yeah, yeah, I'm ready. Let's go," she said, beginning to head for the back door of the building.

As they approached the building in the quickly falling dusk, they never noticed the blue L.T.D. that sat under the tree at the crest of the hill that they had not long ago traversed.

Duane caught up with her at the bottom of the steps with the bag of tools in tow. They scaled the stairs slowly and both leaned in to try to look through the dirty window in the door. In the failing light the inside of the back hall was as black as a well. Duane reached into his bag and grabbed one of the flashlights and shined it at the window, but the years of filth accumulated there just caused the majority of the light to bounce off. It was useless.

"So what do we do?" Jeanette asked.

"Hell if I know. I've never done this before," he said.

Squatting down he began to fumble through the bag as though he knew what he was looking for. Extracting a claw hammer, a crowbar, a set of screwdrivers, some vise-grips and a two pound sledge hammer, he placed them in a neat line at his feet and stood to survey what he had hurriedly packed.

"Anything else in there?" She asked.

"Just my drill," he said, "but that won't work."

"Why not, can't we just drill out the tumblers like they do on T.V.?"

"No."

"Let's try it," she urged. And she reached into the bag and pulled out his drill; his electric drill. "Oh." Was all she could think to say when she saw the cord hanging beneath it. Then a smile crept across her face and she began to chuckle. The chuckle quickly turned into a laugh and the two of them dissolved into the moment.

"I told you it wouldn't work," Duane laughed.

"Sure it will, watch," she insisted, and walking to the door she grabbed the drill by the chuck and smashed the window with the handle.

The sound of the shattering glass ended the short lived humor of the moment and brought them both back to reality. Now they had actually broken the law, and whatever they decided to do next would certainly only exacerbate the situation.

While Duane gathered up the tools and tossed them back into the bag, Jeanette reached carefully through the broken window and felt around for the lock. "Damn it, I can't reach," she said angrily.

Duane took her place and began groping for the lock. Once he found it he could just barely reach it with his outstretched finger tips. Getting to his tiptoes, he leaned on the doorknob for leverage. When he did the knob turned and the door swung in.

"You got it," Jeanette chirped, "how'd you do it?"

"I turned the knob," he admitted awkwardly.

"Oh. Whoops," she said biting her bottom lip.

"Yeah, whoops," he agreed.

In the last twenty minutes the fall darkness had begun to devour the landscape, and when they stepped inside the building it was virtually impossible to make out anything. Clicking on the flashlight he just caught a glimpse of Jeanette's coattails as they slipped through the foyer door and deeper into the building.

"Hey, wait up," he whispered chasing after her.

"You don't have to whisper, Duane," she said in full voice. "There's no one left. They're all gone."

Jeanette pushed on through the darkness following an invisible path that was as familiar to her as the face she saw every morning in her bathroom mirror. Reaching the stairs she made a fluid left turn and began to climb them.

"Hold on," Duane said. "The lady said they kept the records in the basement.

"I'm going up first. There's something I have to see," she told him and continued on.

"Well you're not going to *see* anything unless you take *this*," he pointed out, handing her the other flashlight.

"Thanks," she offered flatly, adding. "The basement is through the doors on your left, third door on the left. Watch the last step; it's taller than the rest. And if they didn't fix the left banister it's loose."

"Thanks," he said, staring uncomfortably at her back. Shaking his head, he disappeared through the doors to find the cellar.

When she reached the top of the stairs, Jeanette hooked a right and headed to what had once served as the quarters for the older girls. It was a three room grouping with a common lavatory and small sitting room. Not much to speak of, but at least it had given them some privacy. At times it had housed as many as eight of them, at others as few as two. Upon entering the set of rooms it hit her. Through the musty odor of abandonment and neglect she could still detect the familiar scent that had been burned into her olfactory senses through years upon years of unintentional aroma therapy.

She was becoming more and more aware of the ghosts that resided here. She could feel their pain and loneliness; their feelings of aloneness, isolation and seclusion. Of course she could, she thought. Some of those feelings were hers. In fact she owned a piece of all of them, part and parcel. She felt a tear run down her cheek as she walked from room to room, the flood of memories washing over her, threatening to drown her in the sorrow and emptiness they carried with them. Feelings like these don't just go away with time, she thought. They need to be exorcized like demons sent to inhabit the psyches and souls of unsuspecting individuals and undeserving innocents.

As she turned to leave her light flashed back at her temporarily blinding her. And as the blue spots it left faded from her eyes she realized what had happened. She had shined the flashlight into the mirror on the wall. The same mirror she had brushed her hair in front of and used to apply the makeup she and her friends had innocently pilfered out of the purses and coat pockets of the nurses when they were otherwise occupied. The same mirror that she, and so many like her, had spent hours staring into as young teenagers wondering why it was that they were here and not somewhere else, anywhere else.

She crossed the room slowly, apprehensively, to gaze again into the inanimate object that had at times, so many times, felt like her only friend. As she approached it she realized that the same grit that had obscured their view into the back hall had accumulated in abundance on the glass.

Reaching out, she ran her gloved hand across the surface to remove the grime that had settled there. And when she did a face appeared, her face. But not the face she was used to, it was the face she had seen so many years ago in that very same place. The sad eyes looked back at her pleading her to take away the pain and loneliness they lived with every day. To dry the tears that no longer came so easily. To accept her for whom she was and tell her that all was forgiven. Then, in a mind numbing second the lips moved to speak. Before she could turn away the visage offered a small sad smile. "Welcome home," she thought it said.

She quickly whipped around and searched frantically for the door. She was feeling disoriented and dizzy. She could hear her heart pulsating in her head and feel it pounding at her ribcage. Her hands were beginning to shake uncontrollably. Words began to invade her thoughts in rapid succession, some she'd heard spoken, some she'd thought and some she'd just felt: Worthless, dirty, not good enough, contemptible, unworthy, pitiful, unfit.

"Nooooo!" She screamed, falling to her knees and covering her ears. "Stop! Stop! It's not true. I am good enough! I *can* be good enough! I'll be a good girl! Don't do it, Please! ***Don't take my baby!***"

CHAPTER EIGHTEEN

O'Hare focused his light inside the car then back at the broken window of the home.

"God damned kids," he mumbled under his breath. What did they hope to find here? And more importantly, what had led them here? Walking back to his cream white, vintage Impala, the Lieutenant pulled it around the far side of the stand of trees and doused the lights. He had followed them here only two cars behind them. But he'd been confident they would be unaware being unfamiliar with his car. As the traffic had thinned he'd followed at an increased distance, but follow he had. For a while he'd even thought *he* was being followed but when the car behind him disappeared as they approached the home he'd just chalked it up to an overactive sense of observation. He'd passed the home after they'd pulled in and made their way around the building, and then he'd circled back a few minutes later.

As he made his way toward the steps he heard an agonized scream come from somewhere inside the building. The words were muffled but the tone was unmistakable. Jeanette Tolby had found the trouble he'd been trying his damnedest to keep her out of.

The lieutenant rushed to his car, grabbed his old 38 caliber police special out of his glove box and took off in the direction of the screams and whatever it was that had caused them. Reaching to his belt he grabbed his new cell phone, flipped it open and dialed Burton's number.

*****

When he'd first opened the door to the basement Duane had been assaulted by the strong stench of mildew and disuse. But committed to the task at hand he'd soldiered on and descended down into the dark and damp recesses of the building. Once he'd successfully negotiated the final long step he'd found himself confronted with a labyrinth of rooms. His footsteps echoed eerily back to him off of the institutional green tiled walls. Most of the rooms were filled with old furniture and various household items but some were empty. One was filled mostly with old toys and other assorted children's belongings, but two were locked with heavy padlocks. He'd decided to concentrate on the two locked rooms which he deemed a more likely place to store important records.

A few minutes before he'd thought he'd heard voices, but after standing motionless for what seemed like several minutes he'd attributed it to being on edge and scared as hell.

Taking the crow bar out of the bag, he jammed it behind the hasp on the first door and gave it a good yank. The screws ripped easily out of the aged and dampened wood and he opened the door to find what looked to him like a medical treatment room. There was a cot against the back wall and there were several empty, glass-fronted cabinets with a large light fixture hanging over a stationary treatment table. "Wow, state of the art," he said sarcastically.

In the corner there were two, four drawer filing cabinets and a small desk accompanied by a rolling office chair. Walking to the files he yanked at the top drawer on one and it slid open with little effort. Inside there were dozens of G.I. green file holders, all with names. None of which were familiar. The last file was marked Curskin, Antonio. He began yanking open the drawers and checking the last file in each one. Hyatt, Marilyn. Lupold, Donald. Oswalt, Maria. Stutz, Imogene. Vrask, Petter. "This is the one," he said to himself. And thumbing back through the files, he found it.

Tolby, Jeanne Marie. "Jeanne Marie?" He said aloud. Checking the file after it he saw, Tolliver, Randall. And the one before it was inscribed, Tilander, Rachel. This had to be it. He was tempted to open it, but realized that the information contained in it was none of his business and he stuck it in his coat.

He turned to leave and realized that there was another file he should grab. So opening the second drawer in the first cabinet he quickly thumbed backwards through it until he found, Ford, William. Deciding he could do no harm to a dead man, he sat down at the desk and opened Billy Ford's file. In it was an in depth account of childhood maladies: fevers, measles, a broken wrist, various bumps and bruises, all run of the mill stuff. After several pages something at the bottom of the report caught his eye. The last line of the sheet was reserved for a signature, it read, *Attending physician*, and it was signed, *A. Tunney*. It was several seconds before Duane realized he wasn't breathing. Exhaling heavily he began peeling through the records. And the name A. Tunney appeared on every one, and as he continued on and neared the end of the file there was one sheet that caught his eye. Written in red ink were the words; Schedule for P.S.P. Pulling Jeanette's file out of his coat he opened it and looked at nothing but the name on the attending physicians line. About a third of the way through the file he found what he was looking for. After that point the name A. Tunney was there on every one. Flipping faster through the papers he found the other thing he was looking for. In red pen were the instructions, Schedule for P.S.P.

O'Hare had silently canvassed almost all of the first floor of the home looking for Duane and Jeanette. When he passed the stairs and headed for the other side of the building, he heard a faint noise coming from the second floor. At first it sounded like singing, but the words were garbled and muted. He slowly climbed the stairs and the closer he got to the second floor the clearer the sound got. By the time he'd reached the top step he realized that what he heard was Jeannette crying. He stole furtively toward the room and inched the door quietly opened. There, in the center of the room lay Jeanette. Speaking just below an audible whisper, whimpering pitifully, she was bathed in the soft glow of her own flashlight.

"Miss Tolby?" He said softly. There was no reply. "Jeanette?" he tried again, slightly louder. Searching his memory he remembered something he'd jotted down in his file. "Jeanne Marie," he said finally, in almost full voice and slightly more firmly. He watched as she slowly pushed herself to a sitting position and turned her head to face him.

"No. Not anymore," she answered.

"It's John O'Hare. Can I come in?"

"Ok," she said weakly as she wiped her nose and eyes with the back of her gloved hand.

He crossed the room slowly and crouched down beside her. "Are you alright? Can I help?"

"No...Yes... I don't know," she sobbed, throwing her arms around his neck and weeping bitterly. "Help me...Please."

The lieutenant felt his professional detachment melt in his heart and seep out through his pores like the breaking of a lingering forty year virus. Gingerly, he cradled her up in his arms and headed for the door.

*****

"Catchin' up on your reading, brother?"

The voice that had come from behind him hit him like a shovel to the back. It stunned him and sent an electric shock directly to his heart which emanated to all of his extremities only to culminate with a burning sensation in his hands and feet. For a fraction of a second he thought he was having a heart attack, but that didn't stop him from spinning in his chair and jumping to his feet grabbing his chest.

When he trained his light toward the sound of the voice he saw before him, the same very large and very angry man that had approached Jeanette's vehicle in the parking lot behind her building.

"Wha... what do you want?" He stammered.

"I think the question, here, is what do *you* want?"

"I just want to leave," Duane said, his voice trembling.

"Duane, Duane, Duane. It's too late for that, now, my man."

"Wait a minute. Can't we talk abou..."

"Talkin' time's done, my brother," the man interrupted. "This afternoon was talkin' time. Now's *doin'* time."

"Whoa, whoa! Slow down there, dude."

"Ah ha ha ha." The man boomed, "*Dude*? For *real*? *Dude*? Lord oh lord, blood. You whiter than you're little cupcake, there. Where is she?" He asked. His smile dissolved into a menacing sneer as he trained his weapon on Duane's forehead and took another step into the room.

"I-I don't know," Duane lied.

"Nope. Not good enough," he told him, pulling back the hammer on his 44 for effect.

"No, no, she's here. I just don't know where. She walked off into the building somewhere. I swear, I don't know where she went," he lied again.

Wiping the accumulating sweat out of his eyes, his mind raced. Was this *really* it.

"Well, I guess that's your ass, then."

Duane dove behind the examination table as the report of the weapon filled the tiny room with an ear ringing blast.

"**Drop the weapon,** *chief.* Nice, and slow," Duane heard the familiar voice shout.

The assailant whipped around and squeezed off three rounds into the darkened hallway, his target ducking behind the door jamb.

Taking the only opportunity he thought he'd get, Duane leapt to his feet and charged, hitting the man square in the lower back and driving him out the door across the hall and face first into the fieldstone foundation.

The thug's firearm bounced once and discharged again, then slid harmlessly into the darkness of the corridor.

Duane stepped back and the man collapsed under his own weight and crumpled to the ground, blood streaming from the deep gash on his forehead. Turning to look at O'Hare he saw him sitting, his back against the wall. He was grimacing, the victim of an unlucky ricochet. There was a black hole punched in the left shoulder of his wrinkled trench coat and his flashlight was sitting between his legs illuminating his searing blue eyes.

The first three shots caused Jeanette to scream and come out of her seat, banging her head on the roof of O'Hare's Impala. The fourth one sent her bounding out of the car and toward the back door of the home.

As she raced toward the steps, a car barreled around the corner of the building, causing her to turn her body and lose her footing. She slammed hard to the ground, bouncing and sliding to a stop still staring at the headlights that illuminated her.

"Jeanette!" A voice said.

"Dean? What are you doing here?" She asked.

"Jeanette, stay there, I'm coming to help you"

"Gun Shots, inside... Duane and the lieutenant are in there," she blurted.

"I know, It's alright," he said walking around to the front of his car.

"You *know*? How could you know?" she questioned, her confusion deepening.

"I know," he intoned, in the way of explanation.

Putting her hand up in an effort to try to shield her eyes from the headlights which were blinding her, she saw that he was carrying something. He was carrying a gun.

"This could have been so much easier, Jeanette," Dean said almost sympathetically. "If only you could have put all this behind you and tended to your own business."

"My own business? My own *business*? This is nothing but *my business*!" she shouted. "They took my baby out of my *body*, Dean! They *murdered* my baby!"

"It was for your own good, Jeanette. Can't you see that?" It was for your good and the good of your child."

She sat stunned by his words.

"It was a different time. Don't you understand? This place and places like it were seriously outdated. They were self-incestuous cesspools creating a need for themselves by bringing thousands upon thousands of unwanted children into the world every year and perpetuating the problem. My father and great minds like him were pioneers in chemical de-fertilization techniques. The preventive sterilization project was a stroke of genius. If the program hadn't been abandoned the world would be a better place. Uncountable sums of money would have been saved worldwide. Hunger and poverty could've been practically eradicated."

She sat, dumbfounded by his logic. "De-fertilization?" she said. "They stole my ability to *conceive*?"

"They saved you from yourself. You and tens of thousands like you."

"Like me and Billy," she said.

Dean didn't answer. He just took a step closer to her.

The back door of the home opened and Dean smiled as Clyde Tucker, his henchman, passed through it, but his relief was short lived as O'Hare and Duane followed him.

"Tucker, you God damned fool!"

When the trio made the head of the stairs Dean raised his gun and pointed it at Jeanette.

"That's far enough, Lieutenant," he advised.

Then another car slid around the corner. Burton and Colzie hopped out and aimed their weapons at Tunney. **"Drop the piece, *Governor*."** Burton shouted.

"I can't do that Sergeant," Tunney answered. "I'm not Governor yet, and I never will be if I do."

"I guess you'll just have to settle for mayor of your cellblock, then. Drop the fuckin' gun!" He repeated.

"No, Sarge," Colzie said, "you drop the fuckin' gun."

Burton turned his attention to Colzie only to see the barrel of the younger detective's Beretta trained on his face. No one breathed for what seemed like minutes.

Three shots tore the silence of the fall night. Burton ducked and Colzie stumbled backward falling in a heap on the light snow cover. Then Billings stood up from behind the open door to the limo where he'd been crouching when he'd fired. "No, sir," he said. "*You* drop the fuckin' gun."

"Billings, what are you doing?" Tunney shouted.

"Tendering my resignation, sir," Billings yelled back as he dropped his gun and raised his hands.

Dean dropped his gun and sprinted for the woods behind the home. He only made six steps before O'Hare fired three more shots, these into the air. That was enough to stop him in his tracks and cause him to thrust *his* hands in the air, as well.

Duane ran to Jeanette and O'Hare handed Dean's hired muscle over to Burton and proceeded to the senator. He grabbed him by the back of his collar, and began dragging him toward Burtons green Chevy. "You have no rights," he began, "and anything you say can, and probably will, get you clubbed over the head with my gun."

"What?" Tunney said.

"Strike one. Oh, by the way, I'm not a cop anymore," he growled.

"I want to talk to my lawyer."

"Steeerike two." O'Hare warned. "I've got just the guy."

*****

Captain Antonucci sat at his desk nervously drumming on his blotter. Pushing the button on his intercom, he barked, "Is Burton in yet!"

"He just got here Captain. And he's got someone with him."

"Send him in!"

"Ah, I don't think I could stop them, sir," came the reply.

Them? Antonucci thought, and he stood up behind his desk, his face already crimson with anger.

When the door swung open Burton walked in wearing a pressed suit and a sardonic smile.

"Burton!" The captain shouted. "What the hell went on out there last night!"

Following the sergeant into the room walked O'Hare. "Mornin' Jerry," he smiled.

"O'Hare? What the hell are you doing..."

Behind the lieutenant were the commissioner, two state troopers and finally, the Attorney General.

"Commissioner Freed, Mr. Attorney General, I wasn't expecting you..."

"No, we thought not," the Commissioner said coldly. "Why don't *you* tell us what went on out there last night, Captain."

Antonucci's legs turned to rubber and he dropped hard into his chair. "I, I wasn't there, Sir. But I plan on finding..."

"Be careful how you answer, Jerry," Freed interrupted. "There could be a lot riding on this."

CHAPTER NINETEEN

Jeanette sat bolt upright the second her eyes opened. The events of last night rushed into her head like a squad of storm troopers. Her mind did cartwheels as she remembered the scenes in disjointed fragments and in no particular order.

"Oh, my god!" She whispered, falling back against her pillows and covering her face with her hands. The things she remembered most profoundly were the voices. Not so much that they had occurred at all, or even the horrible content of what they had said. As disturbing as those things had been, the thing that made the biggest impression on her was that when she'd had the revelation of the abortion she'd been forced to endure at the hands of those monsters, the voices had stopped as suddenly as they'd begun. Still and all, the most disquieting part was that she had known all along and just refused to remember; except in her dreams.

Her eyes were moist with tears that wouldn't come. Her mind was numb with exhaustion, but sharp with remembrances that were incredibly painful and yet a godsend. This was going to take some time. This is where the hard work begins, she realized. It's one thing to know it and be conscious of it, but it was entirely another to accept it and live with the dull ache in her heart and the constant wondering of who her child would have been, given the chance.

There was a quiet knock on her door.

"Yes?"

"It's me, Jeannette," Duane said softly. "Can I come in?"

"Yeah, just give me a second," she said, trying her hardest to sound perky, or at least like herself. Hopping out of bed she made her way to the closet, threw on her bathrobe and took a seat at her vanity. "Come on in," she offered.

When he entered he saw her sitting at her mirror dragging a brush through her hair. "How are you feeling?" He asked for lack of a better ice breaker.

"Surprisingly well for someone who just last night found out who they are."

"You're you, sweetheart. The same you I always knew, anyway. You're just tougher and more resilient than I would've ever guessed."

"Well, you've only known me for about ten hours, but thanks. Thanks for everything," she said standing and walking toward him. Wrapping her arms around his chest she hugged him hard, then turned and headed for her bathroom. "Now get out and let a lady shower. I'll see you downstairs in fifteen."

"You bet, boss. And by the way, that guy from the Rock Pile called. Billy's tribute show is tomorrow night. You should probably call him back and give him your regrets."

"Regrets?" she said, surprised by his assumption. "I don't know about you, but *I'll* be there. How could I miss it?"

"Really?" He asked.

"Life trudges on," she said, pulling the door closed behind her.

******

Victoria Tunney knocked softly on her husband's study door. "Dear? Al? Alistair, there are two policemen here who'd like to speak with you." She tried the knob, but found the door to be locked. "That's odd," she volunteered. "I saw him go in there less than an hour ago."

"Could you stand back please, ma'am?" The trooper asked. Knocking less gingerly, he leaned in toward the door to listen closer. "Dr. Tunney, it's trooper Kelly of the Massachusetts State Police. Could you open the door please?"

When no answer was forthcoming, the officer stepped back and motioned for his partner to escort Mrs. Tunney out of the room.

"What is it? What's going on? What are you going to do?" She asked, her voice quavering with uncertainty.

"Ma'am, please," her escort asked softly. She hesitantly let him lead her out of the room, looking back over her shoulder every other step.

Once they had made their way out of the room, trooper Kelly drew his weapon, took one step forward and kicked the door just below the knob. Wood splintered and the door swung in.

Slowly, he entered the room and scanned every inch of it ceiling to floor. Thick smoke hung dense in the room and there was the smell of an obviously very expensive cigar present. There, in a high back reading chair facing away from the trooper and toward the large back window of his study sat Dr. Tunney, one hand hanging limply over the left arm of the chair.

"I'm going to have to see your other hand, Dr.,"

"Very well," Tunney said blandly and he showed his other hand which was holding his cigar.

Stepping closer, Kelly said,"Doctor, I'm going to have to ask you to come with me. Can you do that?"

"May I finish my smoke first?" the doctor asked.

"I'm coming around so we can see each other, Dr. Please keep your hands where I can see them.

"Certainly," Tunney agreed.

When he rounded the chair, he met the Doctor's tired and emotionless eyes .Aside from the red rims that encircled them, there was little in them as the stared blankly back at him.

"I was only trying to help, you know," he said.

"Excuse me, sir?"

"I was just trying to help. Help the poor, the disadvantaged and finally, to help my son. It all just got so terribly out of control in the end."

"Be that as it may, Doctor. I'm still going to have to ask you to come with me."

"Of course you are," Tunney conceded, and he reached over and stubbed out his cigar in the pedestal ashtray. " Could we forgo the handcuffs, officer, for my wife's sake?"

"I guess we could do that," Kelly permitted. "As long as you behave yourself."

"I'm 78 years old, son. Where am I going?"

"My guess would be to jail, sir," Kelly replied.

"Touche`, officer," the old man smiled weakly. "Well played."

*****

Duane and Jeanette sat quietly over a cup of coffee and toast. He was reluctant to press her for any more details of what went on at the home, and she was disinclined to elaborate on what she'd told him last night. But there was one question that he had to ask, so he called up what little courage he had left and blurted it out. "So why the name change?" He asked innocently.

Jeanette looked up from her coffee and her eyes bored into his with an intimacy he'd rarely felt in his life. "When you're trying to start a new life, sometimes you have to leave the other one behind," she said softly. I guess I was just in too much of a hurry to do that."

Duane nodded his acceptance and returned his attention to his toast.

When the doorbell rang they looked at each other uneasily.

Together they descended the stairs and Jeanette pulled the door open a crack against the chain.

"Sergeant Burton?" She said.

Pushing the door closed, she disengaged the chain and pulled it open fully. When she did she was happy to see O'Hare standing behind him.

"Can we come in, Ms. Tolby?" He asked.

"Yes. Yes, come in. Hey, nice suit, Burton. What did you get married or something?" She quipped.

"Never again," Burton shot back. "I only have to get hit in the head with a skunk once before I know I don't like it."

"How *are* you, Lieutenant?" She asked touching him softly on the shoulder.

"Well, I'm fully able to sit up and take nourishment," he replied, lifting his slinged arm as proof . "How are *you* doing?"

"Ok, I guess," she answered. "*Different*, but ok."

"Atta Girl," he winked and he proceeded past her headed for the sitting room.

"Hey, Lieutenant, look who's here. It's Lawrence Taylor," Burton said.

"Nice tackle last night L.T."

"You're one brave son of a bitch, kid," O'Hare said, and he patted Duane on the shoulder and continued on.

"More like scared out of my shorts," Duane confessed.

Once they were all seated O'Hare pushed his wrinkled hat back on his head. "We just thought we'd stop by and let you know what we've found out in the last ten hours," he began.

"Clyde Tucker was very helpful. At first he was hesitant to give us much of anything, but after a while we convinced him it was in his best interest."

"Yeah, he rolled over like a Golden Retriever," Burton interrupted.

"Can I continue, Sergeant?" O'Hare admonished. "It seems Billy Fairelane and Skip Phillips had some information that was less than conducive to Dean Tunney's election as Governor. It's only a guess at this point, but we assume it had a lot to do with the information in those files Duane found last night. Which, by the way, we never would have been allowed access to if you two hadn't broken in there. We can't really tie Phillips and Billy together, but we think, and it's just speculation at this point, that they may have had a bit of a dalliance. It seems Brian Foster was just unlucky enough to have been Billy's live-in and sounding board. All of which leads us to Strictland, the poor slob. It looks like his only mistake was drawing attention to you, which in turn drew attention to this whole mess. And as far as Tucker says, the woman in the Fens was just unfortunate enough to look too much like you."

Jeanette thought to tell O'Hare about her call from Skip, but at this point it all seemed moot.

"What about that other cop?" Duane asked.

"Can I tell them?" Burton practically begged.

O'Hare nodded his approval and the Sergeant Began. "Dr. Tunney contacted our boss several times to try to squash the investigation in order to save his son's bid to be governor. And when Stricktland got hit, and his lawyer caused a ruckus, it was the perfect opportunity to take the lieutenant off the case and replace him with that rat, Colzie. See, the captain wanted to be commissioner, but in order for that to happen, the commissioner would have to become District Attorney which would count on the District Attorney being elected to the Senate seat vacated by the Senator when he was elected Governor. And all of that counted on solving this case. That would have been a nice pile of chips in all of their corners."

"And what about you?" Jeanette asked

"Colzie," Burton said, "along with you, L.T., here, and the Lieutenant, if necessary. And they would have pinned it all on Tucker, nice and neat. It was brilliant, really."

"Too many moving parts," O'Hare declared, "there always are."

"We figure Tucker would have been next on the list and we told him so," the sergeant added. "We convinced him that one way or another he was going to take a fall. So he agreed to turn States evidence for a chance at parole someday."

"All of that seems like a hell of a long shot to bet your whole life and your career on," Duane observed.

"It always is, kid," O'Hare confirmed. "It always is."

Duane shook his head and looked at Jeanette, who in turn sat staring blankly out the window onto Commonwealth Ave. "You with us, sweetheart?" He asked cautiously.

"Oh, I'm sorry. Yeah, I'm here. I'm just wondering what happens next. I mean, where do I go from here? Who am I?"

The three men looked back and forth at each other uncomfortably; each of them hoping one of the others would have something brilliant to say.

Burton took the bait and cleared his throat. "Well, I don't know about you, but after my divorce my life changed in every way. I sat in my apartment for two weeks and didn't do anything except cry and moan and feel sorry for myself."

"That's your advice?" Duane asked, trying to suppress an incredulous smile.

"No, let me finish. So one day I had a breakthrough and I figured out just what I should do."

"And?" Jeanette prompted, the beginnings of a smile playing at the corners of her mouth.

"So I climbed into a bottle of whiskey, pulled the cap on over me, stayed there for a month and forgot it ever happened."

"Oh, Jesus Christ, Burton!" O'Hare boomed. "So your miracle cure is alcohol abuse, self-pity and denial?"

"Why not? It worked for me."

The three others looked at each other in disbelief and began to snicker in fits and starts until they all burst out laughing.

"What? What?" Burton said, his face turning crimson.

Taking the opportunity to make a clean getaway, O'Hare got to his feet still chuckling heartily.

"Come on, Doctor Burton we have to get out of here. We'll see ourselves out, kid."

Duane, who was bent over holding his stomach, snorted and offered a weak wave. Jeanette wiped at her eyes and simply waved them toward the door, giggling uncontrollably.

When they reached the hallway, O'Hare asked, "Are you out of your mind?" To which Burton answered "I find self-indulgence very soothing in times of need. It's like in that Tom Cruise movie, sometimes you just gotta say what the…"

Jeanette heard the door close behind them and watched them descend the steps, the Lieutenant gesticulating wildly and Burton following behind, his hands jammed in his pockets and shrugging his shoulders like a scolded schoolboy. Looking over at Duane who was just composing himself, she fell back in her seat and realized she was still smiling. Maybe, she thought to herself, maybe everything *is* going to be ok.

CHAPTER TWENTY

Jeanette sat at the table in the Rock Pile exhausted. She had loved the music up until now and the touching tributes to Billy had moved her to tears. All in all she was glad she'd come. It had been a much needed diversion and Duane seemed to be enjoying himself, as well.

She felt a soft hand on her shoulder which startled her and caused her to jump slightly. Turning, she saw O'Hare, dressed in a 1970's polyester shirt decorated with guitars and a pair of brown slacks from the same animal. He looked ridiculous, but she was glad to see him. Next to him, Burton was wearing a Jethro Tull tee shirt and acid washed jeans. Better, she thought, but not by much. She stood up and gave the Lieutenant a huge hug and touched Burton gently on the shoulder. "**I'm so glad you came,**" she shouted in an attempt to be heard over the music.

O'Hare raised his hands and shook his head to signify that he hadn't heard a word. Then, turning his head, he pointed to the earplugs he was wearing. She motioned them to sit down, and just as the two hit their seats, Duane returned to the table with a hot little number in tow.

"Hey, guys. When did you get here?" He shouted

The Lieutenant removed his earplugs and smiled broadly at Jeanette. "I don't know how you listen to this crap," he growled.

"Lighten up, John," Burton said, "This is good stuff."

"Yeah, lovely," he grimaced

"Aren't you gonna introduce us to your date?" Burton asked.

"Yeah, yeah. This is Stacy…" he hollered just as the music ended.

"It's **Jaycee**, asshole," she said giving him the finger and disappearing into the crowd.

The table exploded with laughter led by Duane and his over exaggerated howl.

"Listen," O'Hare began, "we can't stay, but I brought you something I thought you should have."

Reaching into his pocket, he pulled out a small box and handed it to her.

"What's this?" she said blushing slightly.

"Open it," Burton urged.

When she did she saw a watch; her watch, and it was ticking like a metronome. "Oh-my- God," she said, her eyes moistening as she fanned her hand in front of her face. "Thank you so much. But you didn't have to do this."

"It was the least I could do," the lieutenant volunteered.

"Besides, I couldn't use it, and Burton couldn't get it on over his fat little hands."

"Thank you. Thank you both," he said standing and pecking them both on the cheek.

Just then the M.C. began to announce the next act and, hopping up, the two cops said their goodbyes and quickly headed for the door.

She watched as they weaved their way through the crowd knowing that she probably wouldn't ever see them again. She was almost saddened by the thought and when she turned her attention back to Duane she saw him wading back onto the dance floor as the solo artist on the stage led into Bob Seger's, "Turn The Page." With a certain amount of melancholy in her heart she knew just what it was she had to do. Getting up, she put on her coat and headed for the door.

EPILOGUE

Had it really been over a year, she thought. Quickly checking her desktop calendar, she confirmed that indeed, it had been a full fourteen months since the horrific nightmare of recognition had invaded her life, her mind and every part of her being.

In the days, weeks and months that had followed Jeanette's life had changed irrevocably. Some things had changed for the better, some for the worse, but little to nothing remained of the life that she had led for the previous thirteen years.

Duane had moved out of the city and moved on to a new job in sales for a computer company in the suburbs. It was well beyond a reasonable commute on a daily basis so they saw less and less of each other. At first they had stayed in touch by phone regularly, but even those calls had become less and less frequent until they had dwindled into near nonexistence.

Billy Fairelane's demos and studio sessions had been worked into two posthumous albums that were, not only well received and critically acclaimed, but extremely lucrative. Of course, as Billy's manager, for signing off on the project, and for her input and work,

Jeanette had received a fairly large windfall as well as a cut of the royalties which continued to come quarterly.

Due partially to her work at the station, WHTS had been sold at a large profit and turned into a country music station. Jeanette received a substantial severance package and was immediately offered a position with the new station, an opportunity she graciously declined. Country music had never been her bag.

The memories she'd recovered that night at the orphanage had taken a toll during the first several months. But with the help of Dr. Bernhardt she had begun to put them in the past, where they belonged.

Still, occasionally, when she saw a mother laughing, playing or simply walking with her child, or heard the sound of children at play, the heaviness in her heart felt like more than she could bear. But it was usually at night that her heart ached most; when the quiet of solitude and her loneliness forced her thoughts to return to things that may have been.

She flashed back to the day she had stood in front of her Commonwealth Avenue brownstone for the last time. It was a sterling spring morning in May. Despite the feelings of loss and displacement that always accompany a change of address, the warm sun on her face and the excitement of future possibilities made her life seem open and fresh with opportunity. She was about to embark on that journey down Interstate 95 that she had put off for so many years. It was time to take her shot at the "Big Apple."

Her car was stuffed to the glove box with everything she owned that didn't go in the moving truck. Now the only thing left was for her to squeeze in among the knick knacks, the memories and the remaining stuff she probably should have left behind...

"Ms. Tolby, they need you on set. They want to run the close. Five minutes, please."

The interruption jerked her back from her reverie. "Wh-what? Excuse me?"

"The closing remarks; they want to run the close for the show in five minutes."

"Oh. Oh, of course. Sorry, Danny. I'll be right there."

Once the door to her dressing room closed she stood up and looked in the mirror. She straightened her hair and adjusted her skirt. Taking a deep breath she turned and followed the young man out the door. In five minutes she walked onto the soundstage, hit her mark and they counted her down to taping.

"The indictments came fast and furious. They stretched all the way from the department of mental health, to two of the major hospitals in Massachusetts; the great bastion of healthcare in the country. They continued on to the Boston Police force, the State House in Boston and even into the Senate in Washington. This was a story nobody wanted to tell, but everyone had to hear.

Be here next week, when this reporter takes you into the heart of a personal experience, when we delve, in depth, into this story of corruption, murder, and the abuse of power which led to the sterilization of hundreds of helpless children who were in the custody of the State of Massachusetts.

Until next week and from all of us here at Corruption Reports, This is Jeanne Marie Tolby saying thanks for watching. Good night, be well, and stay safe."

Special thanks and kudos are to my editor Jessica McClone. Without her support and guidance this work, in its final form, would not have been possible. Through her patience and hard work she made this story into a book and has earned my heartfelt gratitude.

About the author

Neil was brought up in a small New England town, in the land of Alcott, Emerson, Thoreau and Hawthorne; A heady place to say the least. It was a place that put a premium on the written word.

It wouldn't be until much later in life that he found his passion and his own voice. Neil currently lives in another small town just a stone's throw from the place of his birth with his wife of thirty years and surrounded by his children, grandchildren and countless close family and friends. Life is good.

Made in the USA
Columbia, SC
12 September 2021